Idol Love

Idol Love

Anuradha Marwah-Roy

RAVI DAYAL Publisher
Delhi

Published by

RAVI DAYAL Publisher
51 E Sujan Singh Park
New Delhi 110003

Distributed by

ORIENT LONGMAN LTD
Bangalore Bhubaneshwar Calcutta Chennai
Ernakulam Guwahati Hyderabad Jaipur
Lucknow Mumbai New Delhi Patna

ISBN 81 7530 029 9

Typeset by Rastrixi, New Delhi 110070
Printed at Rekha Printers Pvt. Ltd., New Delhi 110020.

This book is dedicated to
my mother who passed away without reading it,
and
Partho and Dubdub who I hope will read it some day

Contents

Part One

Rajni: A Love Story

Rajni means night. I associate darkness with her, and the desire for two interlocked bodies, and a sigh that contains the sound of breaking within it.

Rajni

Rajni came to me through an old friend, Anita.

A couple of years ago I had taken up the assign ment of compiling a volume called *Literature for Secularism.* The idea was to anthologize spontaneous expressions of outrage against the demolition of the Masjid. I was a member of the Movement for Secularism and the project was being funded by it.

Anita's husband Riaz Ratnakar is one of the founder members of MFS. Anita lives in the U.S., Riaz lives in Delhi.

Anita is one of my oldest friends although for the last fifteen years or so we have met only intermittently. She used to give me her 'nostalgic' time, thinking of me as Non-Resident Indians often think of the parent country: fixed and immobile in a mythical past. But that was before militant Hinduism attacked history and I, along with several other apolitical people, took up the cause of secularism and became a quasi-political protester.

The last time Anita and I met, I sensed a quickening of her interest in my life. She seemed to come closer. I was embarrassed at once. At thirty-five she was still soft and silky. I felt crude and broad beside her. I was sure she could smell on me the onions I had fried for the chicken curry that morning.

We were in a Udipi restaurant called Kovil.

'Papa was complaining that you didn't visit him the whole of last month', she said.

Anita thought of her father and me as different manifestations of the same indigenous spirit — and with reason. Her father would often wonder aloud why Anita couldn't be more like me: do a job of teaching *philo* (Philosophy) to undergraduates in a women's college, run the household, look after children, husband, in-laws, etc. For him I was the ideal modern Indian woman who hadn't let *work* intrude into *home*.

'I've been a bit tied up', I replied. 'My mother-in-law organized a string of pujas last month for my father-in-law's death anniversary and I was at her beck and call arranging for pundits and buying samagri.'

'My father will love you for this, but aren't you a secularist?' Anita asked with some surprise.

'I am. My mother-in-law isn't.'

'But how can you have pujas at home and talk about secularism outside?'

'These are obligations I have to fulfil', I replied, feeling trapped. 'I can't expect her to change her beliefs to suit mine.'

'Yet you want to change the world. I don't understand this about you people.'

It wasn't a question and I didn't reply. I could have said a million things: Hindu fanatics are not the world, personal faith has nothing to do with fanaticism, which is political, etc., etc. I decided to talk about her instead — show her that living in a middle-class Hindu family hadn't constricted my mind. I could accept other lives and life-styles.

'How's Fabian?' I asked.

'Fabian's very well, thank you', she replied.

She had written to me earlier from Atlanta where she now lived, programming computers, about her German lover. All I knew about him was that he wore spectacles and squinted in the sun as shown in the photograph she had sent me. And yes, he was twenty-eight, the post-script added.

I knew she would reveal him in precious monosyllables. He was her newly acquired wealth; she would disclose him very discreetly. Thanks to her experience of living with Riaz, Anita had now made discretion her hallmark.

At twenty-one she had boasted about love. Riaz was a star. He used to win everything — debates, accolades, hearts. She was the best looking girl in college. They came together while he was riding high on the offer of a fellowship from Chicago University. They were built up as romantic prototypes, the kind who would have passed into college history.

Anita's tongue had loosened during that period because of the violent opposition of her father. Anita's father, an industrialist and an erstwhile member of the RSS, was frankly incensed by his daughter's infatuation. Riaz Ratnakar was the only child of a Hindu bureaucrat and a Muslim doctor who separated immediately after giving him this oxymoron name. Riaz was brought up entirely by his upper-class Hindu relatives who called him Ratnakar. Inexplicably, he grew up to restore Riaz as his first name and chose Urdu as his area of research. He also proclaimed loudly that he would return to the 'motherland' once his research was done. To the Hindu patriarch, Riaz was a marked man in India because of his Muslim mother. This accident of birth could have been justified perhaps, but Riaz chose to wear his mother's identity like a caste-mark on his forehead and was set upon ruining his future prospects by studying a language that is politically identified with her community. Besides, the patriarch had heard that in the realm of academia the most successful earn as much as his chauffeur. Urdu, he knew, is the lowest in that lowly life, taught only to minority students in minority colleges.

So, anxious about his daughter's interests, he attacked Riaz like a wounded bull. Anita threw herself in between and fobbed off every charge with shining red idealism and a worthy disdain of the worldly, getting closer to the victim all the while.

At their wedding I found myself wondering what Anita would say to Riaz when she wasn't defending him.

They left for Chicago soon after. Her father spent eight years complaining about the endlessness of academic apprenticeship as Riaz flitted from one Western university to another, often with Anita staying back to complete her own projects. Since then, the patriarch had been floundering in the deeper perplexity of Anita's refusal to return and make a home even when the errant son-in-law's career as a Professor at Delhi University was assured.

'It's a bit nerve-wracking with Papa', Anita continued. 'The same old question: why don't I live here with Riaz now that Smriti has grown up?'

Parveen Smriti, Anita and Riaz's daughter, had recently turned ten. Anita began her dosa. She ate indifferently; cutting her food into such small pieces that she could hardly have savoured the taste.

'It must be difficult for you, Anita. It couldn't be easy being a single-parent in a foreign country.'

'It's difficult for Riaz too. But this is the life we have chosen.'

'Has Riaz met Fabian?'

'Yes. Riaz came to the States last month for a conference. He thinks Fabian's very nice — especially with Smriti.'

His wife's lover. But Anita had always been very particular about telling Riaz everything.

'Are you really happy living this way?' I asked Anita, slipping inadvertently from my carefully propped up broad-mindedness.

Anita raised her eyes. She had brown irises flecked with green. She once had a thick envelope in which she kept all the poems written to her by suffering lovers.

'I think so. Besides, there's no choice. Smriti definitely doesn't want to live here — either with her father or her grandfather. . . . I want to give you some material for your volume on secularism', Anita said.

'You're writing poetry and fiction?' I asked, taken aback further.

'Oh, no. These poems are by a woman called Rajni who died suddenly. That's rather sad. You remember, I told you about her the last time we met? She had been referred to Riaz from the History Department.'

'Yes, you complained that she called up at odd hours.'

'Morning and night. In fact,' — and this came in a rush — 'she had a crush on Riaz. She was pursuing him.'

'Oh!'

'She came to see him once when I was here for Anu's wedding last April. She had mascara on. She was married to an alcoholic, had small children — three girls. Her in-laws wanted her to have another child, try for a boy, and then she went to this little place in Rajasthan . . . '

'It sounds slightly unreal.'

'Riaz is very upset. Somebody sent him her notebook of poems. He doesn't know who could have done it. Couldn't have been her husband or in-laws. You know, in that kind of set up — by the way, she lived in one of those apartments near your place, in the Vaishali Group Housing Scheme. In that joint family set-up, she couldn't have spoken about her feelings to anybody.'

Anita could speak about Fabian to Riaz.

'Did Riaz reciprocate in any way?'

'He knew she cared for him. She showed him some of her poetry which he didn't like much. Farzana knew about her.'

Riaz could speak guiltlessly about Farzana with his wife.

Anita continued, 'He feels guilty — responsible in a kind of way. He brought her into MFS. He encouraged her to participate because he thought it would be good for her to involve herself in socially relevant activities. They used to go out together — lunch, etc. — at times.'

'Riaz breaks hearts, doesn't he?'

I knew it was a tasteless remark.

'Well, he didn't break this one on purpose', said Anita, reaching out for the bill. She would divide it scrupulously into half and pay her bit. This was a habit she had picked up from Riaz. I thought of Anita's father, a big, loud, florid man, flush with money and generous in an overbearing Punjabi way, who wouldn't think twice about paying even for complete strangers. But Riaz, all provincial influences expunged, compact and powerful like a racing car destined to win every race, would calculate the ideological repercussions of every gesture well before making it. Why did he go out with Rajni?

'Did the poems come by post?'

'Yes. There was no covering letter.'

'You said she died in Rajasthan?'

'Yes.'

'And it was suicide?'

Anita brought out a newspaper clipping from her bag and gave it to me. The waiter pointedly placed the change between us. I asked for two more cups of coffee.

The Collector Bereaved

> Ajmer. In a tragic incident last night, Rajni Gupta 32, sister of the Collector Rajat Govil, drowned in the well situated in the lawns of the Collector's residence. She is survived by her husband and three children.

'When did Riaz receive the parcel?'

'A month after the death. The newspaper clipping came with it.'

'How strange! It's almost an accusation.'

'Yes. This is how he sees it.'

Anita was silent after this. I realized this was no ordinary annual old-girls get-together for her. Our meeting had a much more complex purpose.

'Do the poems suggest any reason for suicide?'

'I don't know. I haven't read them.'

I looked at her with disbelief.

'There might not be anything relevant here for the secularism project', I said somewhat primly.

'There's bound to be. And even if it isn't directly, she was working for MFS. Surely that's more important?'

We came out of the restaurant and got into the car.

'When are you leaving, Anita?'

'Soon.'

'Does Riaz want her poetry to be published, too?'

'I haven't asked him. It isn't as if they are personal letters. If the poetry is published, perhaps he will feel less guilty. It might also be an answer — to whoever sent them.'

'But what have you told Riaz?'

'Nothing. I just made a photostat copy.'

I looked at Anita's slim arms as she steered her father's limousine. She had loved Riaz at one time. Was this love too?

'Anita, there might be all kinds of laws about poems that are published posthumously.'

'We can cross the bridge as and when. But if you don't even want to look at them . . .'

I hadn't wanted to. I didn't want to embarrass Riaz.

But I couldn't refuse either. I think I had already begun to feel responsible for Rajni because of the information Anita threw at me casually: 'By the way, she lived in one of those apartments near your place, in the Vaishali Group Housing Scheme.' I can see the Vaishali housing complex from where I live. It is a mirror-image of ours, down to the detail of the wrought-iron entrance gate.

Poetry

Anita had clipped the photostat sheets of poetry neatly into a file. The file was divided into two parts. In the first part the poems were short. Each stood ramrod straight in the centre with broad margins on both sides. There were thirty in all. Clearly, these were finished pieces. In the second part, there were hasty scrawls with wayward punctuation, and spelling mistakes, the lines slinking near the left margin. A single idea spilled over many pages. This was probably the working area. The working area also contained some Urdu couplets. I read them all several times, and for the life of me couldn't decide what to do.

The file lay on my desk for months as I negotiated the currents and cross-currents of daily existence. Mercifully, the volume had been shelved because of a shortage of funds and I was able to forget about it for a while. Then, summer came, with holidays for my children and me. The apartment we live in became an asylum where I took refuge and lost my sanity alternately as the children and the loo-winds of May drove me to delve deeper into my resources. During one such journey I came across Rajni's file again.

There was a shock of recognition this time — perhaps only because I was rereading.

The mirror-image of her writing stared at me frankly, giving away her life. The poems were so tightly tied to situations that they refused to soar away from literalness. In every word I saw her: naked, defenceless, and slightly ridiculous as most people are without clothes.

I was embarrassed. She could have put on the robes of a

martyr, a tragedienne, a princess in exile. Where was her imagination when she picked up the pen to write?

With a vague sense of discomfort, I went to the house where she had lived with her husband, children and in-laws, the libraries where she had worked. I wrote to her brother who didn't reply. I collected some inconsequential information about her, like two chapters of her Ph.D. thesis and the fact that she used a perfume called Anais. I spoke to Riaz. With all this information I pieced together the jig-saw of her existence in Delhi.

Our orbits overlapped so much that it seemed strange we had never met. I dimly recall seeing somebody who meets her description at the Central Library — although the photograph that was held out to me by her husband seemed that of an unknown woman.

But now I must tell her story.

Yeh na thi hamari kismat ki visale yaar hota,
Agar aur jeete rahte, yahi intezaar hota.

I was not fortunate enough to meet my love,
Had I lived longer I would only have waited longer.

Rajni was reading Ghalib's *Dastanbuy* as part of her research for a Ph.D. thesis.

Ghalib had lived in dying times. He had lived in the body of a sick civilization, perhaps as its last parasite. Rajni studies his prose — the chronicle of the events of 1857 — carefully, leaf by leaf. But it is the entangling vine of his poetry that beckons to her. It is the dying she has to catalogue but the vine quivers with life. She flits from bunch to bunch and perhaps even sings, *Kahate hain ki Ghalib ka hai andaaze bayaan aur*. 'It is said that Ghalib's style is beyond compare.'

It was difficult for her to understand the poet's political naïveté. After the fall of the Mughals and the establishment of British rule in 1857, didn't Ghalib realize that nobody could resurrect for him the graciousness of courtly patronage from which he had drawn sustenance for his poetry? Why did he continue to petition the British in a language they didn't understand for his dues as a court poet?

Rajni wonders about him: his craftiness in writing the *Dastanbuy* and the wheedling tone in which he addressed the British who were responsible for the collapse of his life. She contrasts it with the perspicacity of his personal letters and the insight of his poetry. How could he lead such a variable mental life?

The clock strikes two and she descends. She emerges from the Ghalib Academy in Nizamuddin to head for her home, now a wingless bird hopping towards shelter. She feels the sinking, the finality of her day though it is just afternoon.

She is engulfed in the crowd — her candy pink sari crumpled a bit. She flinches when a man whose mouth is puckered like an old wound — a zigzag line across his marked face — rubs his shoulder against hers. She covers her nose with her pallu when a truck loaded with rubbish parks right in front of her; she shudders when she crosses it. In her mind she sees herself drenched with the rubbish they are heaping on the truck: festered banana peels and used sanitary towels and slushy, mud-coloured slime one can't identify.

She hesitates at the crossing while the traffic blows like a storm around her. Gingerly, she puts one foot forward, testing the waters. Her white sandal is expensive, the encased pale foot dainty. The roar of vehicles makes her withdraw it in a hurry. She stands tentative and vague as minutes pass and then she clutches her brown leather purse and plunges, surfacing later, gratefully, on the opposite pavement.

While waiting for the bus she studies the sky for clouds, and salty perspiration drips from her forehead into her eyes and mouth. She dives into brown leather and emerges with a yellow tissue — crumpled and slightly dirty — and she mops her face with it.

She would have flown had I been bold enough to make

up such a story — pink sari hitched, gathered between slim legs like a Maharashtrian laang. I don't have the courage because I don't know where she will go from here. The song goes, 'If I had wings I would fly to you', *Pankh hote to ud aati re* . . . But *pankh hote to* . . . then there might not have been the need for a lover at all. Because isn't this what love is all about? Flight. And if she could have flown where would she have landed? In a stark, austere house where he lived? No, it isn't so easy. If she had flown, there would have been other options and I have always been intimidated by the idea of too many choices.

As I clip her wings, she dreams of him. His muscles bulge slightly. He is baked brown in the sun; he has no odour except that of sun baking the earth. His teeth are white and even; his mouth smells of nothing, not even the toothpaste he uses every day, twice. He can wear his socks as many times as he likes; his feet don't smell, neither do his armpits. He is a small and compact man. There is energy in his frame; there is suppleness where his limbs join the trunk.

His hair grows wild, untrammelled, slightly longer than convention permits, unreasonably curly and gloriously blue. Yes, filtering through her mind that is the colour his hair assumes.

She thinks of him as she scans the horizon for her bus. Where would he be? She didn't know, she never did. She imagined him reading: his voluptuous head of hair bent over a tome which he would master. He would never let it ride his comprehension. He would tame and classify, comment and criticize, move on. He wasn't in a hurry. He was a one-man Department of Urdu in the University. Of course there were other lecturers but he was the phenomenon: the boy from Chicago who had written the path-blazing book on Ghalib. He had made Urdu fashionable in the University. She felt she could sit at his feet, but would he let her?

Her feet ached. The bus was late. That meant it would be crowded. She would have to stand all the way home. Hard things would dig into her body — briefcases, umbrellas, penises. The bus would lurch and she would clutch at the overhead straps. There would be the inevitable odours all around her.

'*Saali, kutia, behen ka lauda*, the lights are all on and it's almost midnight. Will somebody's father rise from the grave to pay the electricity bill? Or that good for nothing hijda?'

The words poured like molten lead down her ears. Hijda. He meant her brother who had no children, just as all the abuses directed at the light were really meant for her. Rajni wrapped the sheet around her youngest daughter. She knew the eruptions would continue.

'Sleeping, aha maharani, nobody works except her, tired after fucking around the whole day. I should have cold food while the maharani sleeps.'

Rajni heard another voice, her mother-in-law's, the alcoholic's misunderstood, long-suffering, gentle mother.

'Why are you making such a noise, beta? Your father is not well. I will warm the food.'

'What happened to Daddy? What happened to him? And if he isn't well, why is this maharani sleeping?'

'She's tired, beta. Nothing's wrong with Daddy. Just a slight temperature. These children make such a racket the whole day, he can't rest at all.'

'Oh yes, orphans, they are orphans, poor things — the mother has no time. She's busy with her bloody seminars — bloody talk — just talk.'

His voice was slurring more and more, soon there would be release. Soon Rajni could forget, dream.

The barks were getting less sharp now. No, he was not a dog, he was a tiger: a maneater with blood dripping from his fangs. There wasn't much of her left for him to eat. Her three daughters — aged five, four and one — had seen to that.

Why had she done it? She was an educated woman, now researching for a Ph.D. She could find a job, perhaps. There was no need for her to stay married to an alcoholic. There was no real need to keep producing daughters until heaven favoured her with a son.

She wakes up at two in the morning. He is snoring. She puts on the bed-lamp; nothing would wake him up now, nothing. His face seems contorted. When had he last smiled at her? When had they last laughed together? The only communication between them now took place after he got drunk and abusive. Increasingly, she wanted to run away from the relationship. She could have taken a sharp kitchen knife and plunged it into his heart.

But she doesn't murder him. Hers is not the face of a killer. The eyes are tired but they still rise up eagerly to meet certain others. In fact, in the morning she will hide the vestiges of a troubled night. She will sit in front of the dressing table and apply some mascara. She will make her eyelashes stiff and uncompromising. She will redden her lips and put a blush on her cheeks. She will even wear a well-ironed sari and pin up her pallu. It might be much better to let tears show, but she is fighting a battle; she thinks she is falling in love.

At two in the morning she brings out a notebook and pen and writes. It is a poem. At three forty-five, her one-year-old sits up, bright eyed. She takes the baby to the bathroom and makes her pee in the wash basin; then she pats her to sleep and lies down herself. Now she will wake up with the alarm at six fifteen and pick up her eldest from her mother-in-law's bedroom. She will get the grumpy child ready for school. At seven the servants will come: the ayah and the part-time cook, wife and husband, both of whom live in the garage adjoining the flat. Later on in the day, the jhadupochawali will come, with whom she feels a strange kind of kinship. He often says that, because of her 'research' which gets them nothing, he has to employ an army of domestics who are eating them into poverty and destitution.

But she has played her cards well; her mother-in-law approves of the arrangement as it absolves her too from domestic drudgery and she can turn her attention to worthier activities like shopping.

Rajni exists because of the ayah-cook couple. She doesn't even complain when the ayah doesn't bother to disguise the indifference with which domestic help invariably treats poor relatives. At least she is allowed that time to get ready for the day: the day at the library.

If she's lucky her husband will get up today only after she leaves the house.

So she rushes to the bathroom after sending the child to school. Nobody in the house knows that she can legitimately spend this time at home. She has made it known that it is impossible to work in the house, without reference books. This is one of the threads in her web of lies, the precious web in which she catches moments of living. She is not an unattractive woman and currently she is obsessed with her appearance. These days she is a tapasvini-warrior. Her appearance is a part of her tapasya. So she drives away a nagging headache with two painkillers and a strong cup of coffee and applies a facepack of Fuller's earth, lime juice, sandalwood paste and milk while she sits on the pot. She comes out of the bathroom to collect her towel. Her youngest daughter begins to shriek at the sight of her muddy face. There is still time, so she clowns around with her while the ayah watches condescendingly. Everybody knows she can't stop her husband from drinking or abusing.

The ayah's husband, the cook-cum-peon, wants his wife to be less rude to Bhabhiji. But he is intimidated; he is conscious of having married above his station. After all, his wife's father owns a tea-shop. So he will cook the family's lunch and keep away a generous portion for her. Then, he will rush off to Bhaiyaji's office to act as the server of water, tea and cold drinks. He understands Bhabhiji's plight; he knows it's her fate in life; the same gods who decreed she should be an orphan, now decree that her husband should drink and abuse. He didn't beat her so it was all right, not too bad; after all, they had two cars, a house, a lot of money.

Bhaiyaji sleeps his drunken sleep and the sun of stubborn hope begins to rise on Bhabhiji's horizon as she rushes to dress up for the research library — a straw-coloured sari and silver jhumkas that along with the kajal in her eyes attempt a statement about her feelings.

Her mother-in-law watches her attempt a half-hearted breakfast. The mother-in-law watches her disparagingly: the producer of daughters, a failed wife who has not been able to harness her husband's weaknesses to her advantage. It has worked out well for the mother-in-law; she has passed from power to power. The men in her life have been protective, sympathetic, guilty as they ought to be, husband and son. They have laid the conscience money at her feet, year after year, which in her selfless way she has converted into strings of pearls, gold chains and bangles — for her son's daughters she has told everybody, because she herself is old. Now she has set her heart on a diamond-studded bracelet, the kind Marwari women wear; by the time the daughters are ready for marriage it will be priceless. And here the producer of those daughters sits nibbling at her toast, looking half starved in a sari that probably came from her dead mother's wardrobe — heaven knows her husband has not bought her any for ages — and ugly, blackish silver ear-rings that girls so love these days. She would have preferred a more normal daughter-in-law: somebody who cried less, somebody who was capable of extracting at least a gold chain from her husband. That would have proved more of a challenge for her. This girl was so distracted, always staring into space. The mother-in-law could do whatever she liked with this one, except keep her home. She was like a bird flapping her wings against cage bars in the mornings. Did she sleep with other men? So many seemed to ring up. She said she was going to the library and she came back with books and then actually read them; the mother-in-law had tiptoed into her room and seen for herself. The man she was talking to last night sounded so dull as she eavesdropped on her extension, a college lecturer, probably.

After breakfast Rajni dabs perfume on her inner wrist. Of course she has no business to apply Anais for the library, especially on the wrists. It is a research library. But her heart is thundering at the prospect of seeing his head of hair, gloriously blue and unrealistically bursting at the seams with true, grey matter.

Criticism

Stiff and eager, she sat in the reading-room. The straw-coloured sari, the jhumkas, the perfume, and the kajal — it was wrong, all wrong. This was a research library, the den of the hounds of knowledge. And it was not only the dress that was wrong, she was wrong. She invited criticism; she gave out odours. Even in the morning a faint smell of perspiration would emanate from her armpits in spite of the deodorant, the talc and the perfume she had used. I have often smelt this odour on women who have tried too hard to dress well.

One may well ask who I am in this story. Sometimes I'm the maker of her destiny, at times a powerless chronicler. But now she leans back on her chair, and at this red hot minute I feel the comfort of her fantasy and a languor steals over me. It is delicious; the vision of heaven unfolds before my eyes, an unashamedly sensual vision. His wonderful hair and his divine mouth! I can't be original with sex. My words and her thoughts are borrowed.

The poem she had written last night was called 'Waiting'. This was her first 'Waiting' poem and she called it just that, just 'Waiting' as though it transcended the particular and encapsulated in its three stanzas her life-long wait. It was a waiting that didn't dare to hope. She was superstitious. The poem was a sacrifice offered to propitiate the gods. Naked desire slit-throated on an altar!

She had reached the library holding the identity of a poet like a mask before her crumpling face, but now she was too distracted to hold it up. She was fantasizing about being irresistible. Even though she was painfully aware of the grey threads in her hair, the tiredness of her eyes; even though she knew she would look haggard by the afternoon.

Riaz was rubbing his nose, one of the gestures that characterize him. A moment earlier he had entered his cubicle in the library, jauntily like a schoolboy, slinging his bag carelessly across his shoulders, taking the steps two at a time.

He knew he was seeing Rajni later in the day. Riaz keeps a diary for his appointments.

They had met in her thesis-supervisor's house. The supervisor who prided himself on being an excellent host had introduced them to each other.

'Riaz, this is Rajni. She will be consulting you for her thesis.'

Rajni's husband had refused to accompany her for the dull academic evening. It wasn't often that she was by herself at a party. It wasn't often that she got slightly high on the wine that tasted so good.

Their conversation began with his questions about her ear-rings. It was a party. Enquiry about jewellery kept well within the area of research can sound like fairly normal weather-talk from a Professor — but only if he is old and rickety. Rajni bloomed like a flower after an unexpected summer shower under Riaz's scrutiny. She had never met a suave and attractive man who paid her this kind of attention. Riaz talked about the jewellery of the nineteenth century. Did she know about the mysterious power that was ascribed to sapphires? His eyes seemed to imply that a woman like her couldn't be unaware of the power her gems were exercising on him.

Again and again Rajni rewound and played their conversations in her mind. Fifteen days after the party she burst into his office in the University. She stated categorically that she had come only to meet him; no, not for anything academic. If he was surprised he didn't show it. It was lunch-time so he casually suggested lunch. She knew there was too much delight in her answer and that it was evident too soon.

The University has many levels of restaurants. It was not his politics to bother about his surroundings, so he took her to the closest. He did not apologize for leading her into the dilapidated coffee house. No doubt he thought he had reached a stature where modesty could never be mistaken for a lack of discernment. She noticed he ate efficiently and rather distractedly. She felt herself blush uncontrollably whenever he looked at her.

'So, you're a historian and you write poetry?'

'I don't know whether I'm a historian.'

'Not to know is liberating. Think how much knowledge can bind. But you know you write poetry?'

'What I write looks like poetry.'

'I'm interested in poetry.'

'I'd be frightened to show it to you.'

He seemed interested. 'Why?'

'What happens if you hate it?'

'Hate is a strong word.'

'What happens if you dislike it?'

'Look, students show me their work all the time.'

'This isn't a classroom situation', she interrupted, challenging him.

'It isn't,' he agreed thoughtfully, 'but tell me, what do you think my response to them is likely to be?'

'You may say throw them out.'

'Really, do I look like that kind of person?'

'Or you may say they have potential but . . . '

'I see you know critics fairly well. Tell me, who has read them?'

'Nobody.'

'What about your children, your husband?'

'My children are too young, I don't know whether my husband would be interested in reading my poetry.'

'Aha, that's worth discussing: do husbands read wives' poetry?'

'They would be scared to, I think. Do you have children?'

That seemed to surprise him.

'Yes, I have a daughter.'

Rajni wondered about his daughter. Did she look at all like him?

'You don't ask about my wife', he remarked suddenly.

'I didn't think of asking. To me children make all the difference.'

'Spouses don't, you mean?'

'No, not to the kind of person I am.'

'So, am I the man with the daughter?'

'I don't know yet.'

'Are you the woman with three daughters?'

'Yes, what else am I?'

'You are also a poet.'

'I think I write because of them.'

'That's interesting. You're an intriguing woman and I'm curious about your poetry.'

'No, it would be dangerous showing the poems to you.'

'Why d'you keep saying that? Poets are not the only ones who are vulnerable. We critics could be vulnerable too.'

He had to rush for a meeting. He gave her his phone number on a piece of paper.

'Ring up . . . soon. Let's meet and discuss your poetry.'

She had felt light and festive after that lunch. She was an intriguing woman. He could be vulnerable, too. She walked to the bus stop much faster than she usually did.

He had her poetry in front of him, and he was rubbing his nose. He had a meeting later in the day, but her phone-call last evening was rather frantic. In ten minutes he would have to emerge from his cubicle and go down to the lounge. He knew Rajni would have already arrived and awaited him. He would take her to the canteen for coffee. He had to make a decision.

Their Meeting

I

You said you don't like my poetry
because it says fuck
even to little babes.

I saw myself as a paan-chewing madam pimping verse.

But later in the day when you asked me
about ayahs who manage my children, how many?
I saw myself as a socialite with painted lips.

I blanched and ran to the loo
and scrubbed my lips.
In the mirror, they looked used.

But then I clicked open my purse
and took out a lipstick.
My verse may be screwed
but my lips will be adequately shielded.

II

Cold dosas between us, their guts out,
I indifferently spear mine, my dreams were different.

Your self-confessed gentleness keeps you bound
to your uncomfortable chair.

You talk poetry.
You have many words at your behest, it is easy.
In sinuous syllables I read your message,
as you talk on,
still bound gently.

I know I must unbind you
with skeletal prose.

I ask,
are you getting late?

Oh yes, I have to leave right away,
you say.

III

Which smell should I give you?
Toothpaste-mint or Aftershave-Aramis?

All I have of you is a back
and the sun streaking your hair
and your hands counting out the change
over the counter,
and the crumpled bill for our dosas,
ten rupees thirty paise.

It should not be thus,
so unremitting of emotion,
three ten-paise coins,
one, a little bent.

The Critic

In Rajni's file there are several versions of a poem called 'Woman-writer'.

I see her most clearly in this double-barrelled title. Contrary to expectations, she is not assuming an anti-man position, nor is she stating the obvious.

The woman in the title is more a choice of origins. Just as some writers, at a particular time in their careers, call themselves black. The title 'Woman-writer' affixed to a love-poem suggests that Rajni knew that her face had colour, but it was not the black of protest. It was the suffusion of a longing imperfectly blended with the fury of failure.

As the Professor spoke about her poetry, the woman began spilling into the writer and she became the woman scorned. Her heart that used to bubble at the thought of her poetry, began to feel like a wrung rag. The notebook that had expanded in her imagination to contain the awesome meaning of existence, contracted suddenly into imperfect syntax. She saw herself as a woman who wrote about unmentionables.

To be rejected by Riaz was unbearable. She squirmed with the injustice of his denial to her. He was being unfair, though she didn't quite know how.

She quarrelled with him incessantly in her mind. The worst of these fights was the deafening silence that followed her neurotic ranting.

How was she to negotiate the significance of this silence, the anatomy of his absence from her life? She who shut her eyes tight one night and said, no, I can't carry on like this, I will have to forget him? She made a valiant effort.

She tried not to think of him.

While returning home from the library she repeated the titles of the books, the bibliography that she had been given, like a rosary.

When they passed each other accidentally in the corridor, she acknowledged his smile with an equally casual hello.

She should have succeeded. After all, what was there to remember?

At two in the morning, she gets up and fumbles for her notebook. Her husband snorts in his sleep. She looks at him with exasperation. His stomach was giving him a lot of trouble these days. Everything tasted the same, he complained at mealtimes. The cook was cursed. Every day the mother-in-law pointed out that food cooked by servants can never really match the housewife's efforts and when she herself had been younger she had managed everything, hadn't she? But with girls nowadays working outside, home and children inevitably tend to get neglected.

Rajni sighs. She is defeated, so is he. Blame and guilt have gnawed into their marriage. She looks at the yellow tint in his cheeks. Perhaps it is his liver. Perhaps under repeated misuse it is giving way ultimately.

Then suddenly as she turns to the poem in hand, another image flashes in her mind. Then it comes in torrents: the pain of vacuity. When there is nothing to remember how can she honour the commitment of forgetting? How can she get rid of the incubus of fantasy? And she feels lips that she had never touched close to her mouth; as tears drench her cheeks she feels invisible repentant arms draw her into their security and she cries into the night, into sleep.

Waiting

You have closed the door.
I won't look in,
I won't knock,

I won't call,
I won't cry.
I am going to be
dead for a while.
I will sit here
unseeing,
unfeeling
on your doorstep.
I will wait
for you
to come and
open the door.

Riaz worried a little about Rajni. Of course, she had seemed too forward, too confident, too well-dressed. Privileged women — women who write in English in this country where it is the language of the elite — cannot be allowed to run away with the lion's share of women's pain. Real pain, like everything real, throbs in the lower classes in regional languages; anybody with any modicum of social responsibility would know this. Critics like Riaz make it their business to be as vigilant as the income-tax department about writers trying to make capital gains out of unearned pain.

But when he saw her walking past him in the corridor, looking crushed, he feared the snuffling out of her creativity. He felt responsible.

The next time they met he asked after her poetry — how is it going? She mumbled a reply he couldn't hear. Another time he waved to her from a distance.

Rajni had already started cheating; with this, fantasy became myth.

She decided to be Snow-white, to weave sweet-smelling mogra flowers in her hair, bite into an apple poisoned by a jealous, old woman and spread her tired body on the floor and cease: waiting for the prince's kiss. To wait like this is also to be in perfect control of the situation. To sleep like this is to believe there will be an awakening.

She waits and hours and days tick by. She has a trim waist

and firm, upright breasts and she is seized with a sense of waste. Her breasts haven't been caressed in years, as she would like them: slowly, finger-tips making circular motions around the aureole, palms gently cupping the globes, a tongue devoutly savouring the salt, a mouth hungrily sucking the honey. I am living her incomplete fantasy as she runs her fingers through her pubic hair, ripplingly, and parts her legs with a sigh. She shuts her eyes tightly, to keep out the image of the lover as it rises in embarrassing details before her; she can't make him do in her mind what she would in passion sell herself to get. She has decided to wait because she cannot climax screaming out his name, she cannot break free from hearth and home. So she climaxes without him, in the final burst of passion expurgating his name from her lips.

She called it waiting, but what is it if not a strategy of survival, getting through life without being dismayed at the sameness of one's own image in the mirror?

For many years she had waited for her husband.

Rajni thought she made a beautiful bride. She had done the make-up herself. Her kajal-lined eyes sparkled and her lips curved upwards. There had been her mother's jewellery, shared out between her and her brother's wife. She had particularly liked the long and elaborate ear-rings. They filled out her oval face, giving it completeness.

She was prepared for the wedding ceremony. As the pundit droned on, her brother and sister-in-law yawned and napped. Sunil's parents were carrying out the orders of the pundit with far more alacrity, she thought.

Sunil's mother had a strange kind of middle-aged sexiness about her. She looked like a woman who was being loved and spoilt. The sindoor in her parting was bright red. She wore almost as much make-up as the bride herself and as much jewellery. Yet she did not look overdone: her sari was tastefully chosen and her body bore the years well. How would she be as a mother-in-law? She had clasped the younger woman to her bosom when the wedding plans were finalized, but the gift accompanying the gesture was meagre: a slim gold ring.

There was something young about Sunil. She would love his rather thick eyebrows, his thick lips. She hadn't had much of a chance to talk to him but he seemed practical and reasonable; she would love him with a woman's love.

She would love his house too: a reasonable flat with practical furniture. But their room could still be draped with dreamy tapestries.

The first night after the wedding she sat alone on the bed on which some flower petals had been sprinkled hastily. They embarrassed her somewhat and she cleared them up, gathering them into a bowl.

There wasn't much time for preliminaries with Sunil. How silly to have expected a shared watching of the moon, lingering embraces and the slow and sensuous movement of the camera from the couple to the vase on the table, or outside the window to the voluptuousness of the waves in high tide! Here there was some fumbling and the shock of recognizing some gestures: the hidden penises rubbed on to the thigh in crowded buses, the violent grasping of the bosom, the heaving and pushing and then an indifference, a withdrawal. But sleep came anyway and the rupture of the hymen passed without much fuss.

Tears came much later, after months, when her body seemed divided into two parts: the upper remaining virginal, the lower fatigued by too much use.

'You don't love me any more.' She was much too aware of the fallacy inherent in the statement. She cried into her pillow, he looked on. 'I hate you, I hate you for fucking up my life . . .'

'Yes, yes, you would have been better off with that behenchod bureaucrat your brother had found for you.'

'At least he wouldn't have treated me like this.'

'Aha, he would have sat in your damned lap all day.'

'He wouldn't have kept me waiting half my life.'

'I have to work.'

'And you have to drink.'

'If one has a wife who complains all the time what's one to do?'

'Are you saying I have pushed you into drinking?'

'Well, yes, you have partly. Do I ever see you happy? You're always complaining.'

'You said we would see a play tonight.'

'Why don't you see these damned plays by yourself?'

'You know your mother objects to my going out with friends.'

'Well, why can't you make yourself useful at home? You moon around half the day, anyway.'

'I want to be with you sometimes. Don't married couples spend time together?'

'We can't keep sitting in each others' laps. Do I have to sit and look at you or something all day?'

'And what work don't I do?'

'With Mummy running the house, you feel you can exist in five-star comfort without moving a finger. My clothes are all over the place; do you have to wait for Mummy to settle them?'

'Why can't you settle your own clothes?'

'Oho, the maharani comes from a family where she did nothing but order servants around!'

'What d'you mean?'

'It's very clear. I think you should do much more in the house than you are doing.'

'I think you should do much more for me than you are doing.'

'Don't expect me to clean your shit.'

'Don't expect me to clean yours.'

She burst into tears. He would come to her, put his arms around her, tell her he loved her and really she shouldn't be so aggressive. And then they would play out their mating ritual which would put a stop to her tears and strangely enough stop the ache in her heart, at least for the rest of the night.

One day Rajni decided she had set too low a price on herself. The realization came suddenly, almost like an epiphany, after the birth of her third daughter. It came as she held the clean and soft new-born in her arms and as her insides churned because of the recent labour pains. She put the baby gently on her side and groped for the tray under the bed. As she vomited she saw herself ravaged and abandoned. She saw her swollen body, ugly and bleeding. Where was Sunil? Why wasn't he there to share the muck of childbirth? Why wasn't he there to hold her as her insides heaved? He had left half an hour before the baby arrived: his mother had said he wasn't required as he had already strained himself too much, staying up half the night with her in the hospital.

As her mother-in-law chatted with the nurse outside, she vomited in her room and withdrew from her marriage.

She closed her eyes tightly awaiting the onslaught. He had come into the room. His steps faltered though not too much; he would not fall off dead drunk. He was taking off his clothes: heavily, clumsily, fumbling for a long time as he usually did with buttons and zips. He got into the bed and shifted the baby. She shut her eyes tighter, willing her hands not to clench into fists.

Her body had stopped responding to his. He was not a rapist; he sensed her reluctance.

He fumbled with her night-gown; she sat up and took it off. He stroked her breasts, she flinched. Her face was blank. She reached out her hand and put off the bed switch. In the dark he felt her face crumple. Like a circus animal she slithered down and took his penis in her mouth. He was ready in a few minutes. She parted her legs and took him in.

It was over, she could sleep. She put the baby between them and turned away.

'Give me your hand.'

'Go to sleep, Sunil.'

'I like to hold your hand.'

'That will wake up the baby.'

'Can't the baby sleep on the side?'

'No, she will fall. Sunil. I have to get up at six thirty.'

'Let's go to Anil's house tonight.'

'What for?'

'Why do people go to each other's houses.'

'To sit and drink, of course.'

'Come on, let's go. His wife was saying the other day that Rajni never comes for any of the parties.'

'I think you more or less make up for me, Sunil.'

'That's a silly thing to say.'

'Anyway, what do we do with the children. They need their sleep.'

'We can leave them with Ma and the ayah.'

'So that both of them complain for the next three days. No thanks.'

'But you leave them at times when you go out on your own.'

'I have done it precisely once, when I went for my friend's wedding and I will do it for the second time on Thursday as Dr Kapoor is hosting a dinner for Ph.D. students.'

'Yes, yes, go on your own to your stupid dinners or go with one of your boyfriends.'

'I know what a bore these parties are for you, not a drop to drink.'

'Rajni, come and sit here.'

'I will send Ma. I have to make your khichdi.'

'Isn't there anybody else in the house who can make khichdi?'

'Well, the cook is unwell too. And the ayah has taken the children out.'

'Doesn't matter! I don't want it.'

'What will you eat then?'

'I can eat later.'

'No, you will be tempted to eat heavier food and then your stomach problems will begin again. Let me call Ma. She can take your temperature, too.'

'Why can't you take my temperature?'

Rajni pretended not to have heard as she disappeared very quickly behind the curtain with the paisley pattern — now faded and frayed — that she had bought to cordon off their private space from the rest of the family, ten years ago.

Politics

As Rajni waited for a mythical future with Riaz, a momentous event almost cleaved the country apart. Hordes of Hindu fanatics gathered in Ayodhya and one dark day brought down a Masjid. This is the birthplace of Ram and we take a vow to construct a temple here, they chanted, wielding implements of destruction to bring down old masonry. The government looked on as faith challenged history and won. Anita's father called me up the next morning, proclaiming in a voice quivering with emotion that now at last after centuries this country would become what it used to be in the age of Ram — an ideal abode of the Hindus. 'We will at last usher in Ramrajya', he said.

'What about the Muslims?' I said trying to jog his conscience. 'Surely they don't deserve this insult to their faith? Some of them fought for the independence of the country.'

'Arrey, they are all traitors. Their sympathies are always with Pakistan. Don't you see that whenever there is a cricket match between India and Pakistan, these Drohis cheer for Pakistan?'

I shut up. I don't know very much about cricket. Besides, what I really wanted to say to him might have punched holes in the close-knit fabric of my family that was draped around the television in the same room.

Riaz had family near Ayodhya. His mother's aunt's descendants lived near by in Faizabad. A week after the demolition, Riaz wrote a touching account of his parents' courtship and marriage against the backdrop of the fight for Independence when the aunt, imbued with Congress-nationalism, had taken on her own community to provide refuge to the Hindu-Muslim couple. We are Indians, she had said. Later, in 1948 she refused to move to Pakistan asserting firmly that this was the land where she would die. The aunt's house was pillaged and burnt during the riots that followed the demolition. Riaz described the debris of her family's meagre possessions. In this personal account published in the largest selling English-language newspaper in the country, he did not theorize about nationalism or communalism. He didn't need to. I cried when I read the article; I attended all the meetings of the Movement for Secularism.

Riaz was born under the secular star. The fact of his parentage — Hindu-Muslim — alone would have been enough to elevate him above ordinary mortals. Moreover, he was articulate. So, those days not only did he become a secular prophet, but even the book in which he had critically evaluated Ghalib's poetry, pointing out among other things the poet's irreverence towards the die-hard clergy, began to be quoted as a revelation on the eclectic spirit of Islam.

As Riaz became the reference point for so much secular legend-making, he metamorphosed into a holy image for Rajni and she felt she could legitimately sit at his feet once again.

'Had anybody in the country even imagined that the communal volcano, so grassed over by our secular platitudes, would burst forth in this manner, spewing hatred and violence? Now, we as a nation will wear the broken Masjid like an albatross round our necks for years and years of severe penance. I feel shaken. It is as though the familiar ground is slipping from under my feet. This attempt to distort history is also an attempt to handicap identity. If we lop off years of Muslim rule as foreign encroachment, we are left with a very incomplete image of ourselves. I shudder at this incapacitation of the self. As a movement we need to avoid the language of "us and them" and focus on the commonality of experience.'

The police was herding the processionists gently into a van that would take them to jail, but those who didn't want to court arrest were being allowed to leave. The arrest was tokenism. Public meetings were banned and the ban had to be enforced even though everybody knew that those who attended such things were just a bunch of harmless ideologues. Rajni couldn't afford the luxury of a prison with the secularists. There would be too much explaining to do at home otherwise.

'In spite of our repeated efforts we have not been able to get permission for all our volunteers to go into the curfew-bound areas of Old Delhi. However, as a large amount of perishable foodstuff has already been collected, we have persuaded the police to get it distributed in these areas. We have also been able to procure two curfew passes with the help of some journalists.'

There was work to be done, but Rajni stood at the edges, frightened that her politics would not stand scrutiny.

'Mandir masjid gurudwara have divided up Divinity,
They have divided up the earth, the sky,
Let's not divide up humanity.'

The chorus sang full-throatedly. The procession moved in a file of four, a python, down Mandir Marg. The mood was sombre and silent. The 'intelligentsia' was marching to protest against the wave of communalism that had engulfed the country after the demolition. University people formed most of the crowd. Rajni had tried desperately to ignore the leap of hope in her heart when she dressed for the procession, seemingly casual but with too much care.

It was getting darker. The distinctive head of hair was visible just a little ahead. He was handing over the placard he had been carrying. Rajni tried to quell the upsurge in her.

He was bending down to tie his shoelace. People filed past him, soon she would be at his side. She turned her face away resolutely.

'Hi!'

'Hello.'

'Don't run away, Rajni', he said, straightening up.

'The world isn't big enough, it seems.'

'Aha, so my suspicion is confirmed.'

'What is your suspicion?'

'You've been avoiding me?'

'So, you noticed . . . ' She could have bitten her tongue off. Avoiding him had been hard work. She was having to attend all the events organized by MFS.

'I must say it has been rather pointed.'

'It was meant to be.'

'What makes poets so nasty?'

'You mean bad poets?'

He lifted his hands in a gesture of supplication. 'Didn't you say you wanted an honest response and didn't I say I don't read much poetry in English?'

'H'm.'

'It's a fault of my ear. You see, it is attuned to the sonorous syllables of Urdu. And one compares everything to the best one has read. Of course, poets don't like comparison. As Ghalib said,

Hain aur bhi duniya mein sukhanvar bahut achche
Kahate hain ki Ghalib ka hai, andaaze bayaan aur

There are many good poets in the world
but it is said that Ghalib is incomparable.

This is a rough translation.'

'Quite inappropriate', Rajni shot back. 'I too will quote Ghalib to you,

Har ek baat pe kahate ho tum ke tu kya hai
Tumhi batao ki yeh andaaze guftagu kya hai.

And my rough translation is:

With every statement you say why the hell do you write,
You tell me whether this is what the criticism of
poetry ought to be?'

'Yes, one of my favourites, also. By the way, it is *kaho* not *batao* and the translation of *guftagu* as criticism of poetry seems to me a remarkable sleight of hand. But what does the couplet and its transposition have to do with what we are discussing?'

'I felt you disapproved of *me* more than you disliked my poetry.'

'And how did you reach this amazing conclusion?'

'Why did you want to know how many ayahs I had to look after my children?'

'Did I say that?'

'Yes.'

'I apologize. I had no business to do that. But why did you mind so much?'

Rajni did not answer for a while.

'The question seemed to suggest that I have more leisure than is good for me', she said at last.

'But it can also be seen as a sympathetic question. It could suggest concern for your household responsibilities.'

Rajni did not reply.

'But I suppose my "intentionality" is of no consequence with you. I'll say sorry again.'

Rajni walked on quietly. A man came up and started talking to Riaz.

The upsurge in her become a storm. Dammit, did she have no self respect? Riaz just had to smile for her legs to turn to water. Why had she come for this demonstration? He surely would know why. He was one of the major academics in the Movement for Secularism. And then to tearfully bleat Ghalib to him and that, too, incorrectly!

They had almost reached the Gandhi Smriti. It was quite dark.

'Had chhahiye saza mein, ukoobat ke vaaste,
Aakhir gunahgaar hoon, kafir nahin hoon mein'

he said softly, just behind her. She turned to look at him.

'It means "punishment should be proportionate to the crime, I may be a criminal but I am not an apostate"', he continued.

A torchlight procession had just joined theirs. They were singing Gandhi's favourite bhajans.

His hair shone blue-black in the light thrown by the torches.

'Maafi', he said folding his hands as if to join in with the bhajan singers.

Rajni felt the storm abate; the breeze lifted her pallu and she let it flutter behind her.

There was a guest-speaker from Bombay.

'Thousands mutilated, looted and raped; hundreds murdered. Pathetic crowds at the VT station waiting to get tickets to some place, any place where a trident will not be stuck in their guts because of the religion they profess. The scenes are reminiscent of the bloodshed during Partition.

'But while mourning the death of our secular ideals, let us not forget to do some soul-searching. The Bombay riots have taken place because all of us subscribe to the conspiracy of silence. We did not protest against the goonda elements when they started chalking their agenda in public places. We gave them legitimacy by talking to their dons as if they were national leaders. They said what they liked in their newspapers and we did not take them on. The press, the journalists, the intelligentsia — all are to blame. We are paying the price for our pusillanimity. Today when they enter our houses to plunder and pillage, why are we taken aback?'

Riaz was sharing the stage with the speaker. People looked at him for a response. Would he allow himself some anger at last?

Riaz spoke slowly and emphatically.

'The Bombay experience as narrated to us by T. Rajnath will strike a chill in all hearts. We in Delhi must learn from it. We must definitely speak out against communal politics while there is still time. But we have to devise ways of protest that are peaceful and effective. It is important to remember Gandhi's satyagraha at this point. Gandhi taught us to protest against carnage with love . . . '

His name has a mellifluous sound to it — Riaz Ratnakar — if one says it fast enough, that is. Only such a name could lend itself to deification in secular times. How did Riaz feel about the greatness that was suddenly being thrust upon him? It would have been impossible to ignore it. To reject it would have been irresponsible. So Riaz began to fulfil the need of the hour by being great. When people persuaded him to don the mantle of leadership he stepped back, self-effacingly telling them to focus on issues rather than on personalities, to forgive rather than mount the offensive. Did he choose such a stance because it was the safest in this era of shifting certainties? Or did greatness come to him as leaves come to a tree when rain enriches the soil? Whatever the answer, it does not make a difference to Rajni's story.

Rajni knew very little about Riaz. She cherished that lack of knowledge. She felt that his blue hair was the ultimate reality. For a while she didn't try finding out anything more about him. All that she did was to dial his number often, listen to his voice or that of his slightly deaf maidservant, once or twice to ask for him, once or twice even to gather enough courage to talk to him. Those were magical days.

> I believe in love
> just as I believed in fairies.
> Long back, in short frocks,
> I grazed my knees
> looking for them under hedges.

On a more mundane plane, however, Rajni's supervisor felt that she had been dragging her feet too long. 'Social Reorganization of Delhi after 1857' — Chapter 1 of her thesis was as far as she had got.

In April, eight months before her death, already drunk on the secular spirit, Rajni went back to the Ghalib Academy at Nizamuddin, to catalogue the death and destruction that had changed the face of the city after the uprising of 1857.

The British were systematically setting out to destroy the spirit of the Muslims. Especially under suspicion were those who had something to do with the Mughal court. Ghalib, the poet laureate of the Emperor, had reason enough to feel that an age of glory had passed away. When Rajni read about Delhi in his letters it was with the excitement of rediscovering the present. In response to the following line by Mir Mahdi,'My friend, this is the language Delhi people speak', Ghalib wrote,

> 'Oh, Mir Mahdi, aren't you ashamed of yourself? My good sir, "Delhi people" now means Hindus or artisans, or soldiers, or Punjabis or Englishmen. Which of these speak the language which you praise?' . . .

And

> Bountiful master, do you think that Delhi still prospers, and that the Fort thrives and that the Empire continues, that you ask about the writings of Hazrat Sheikh (Kalimullah Jahanabadi) and for news of Sahibzada Shah Qutub ud din, son of Maulana Fakhr ud Din (God's mercy be upon him)? 'The cow ate up all this and the butcher killed the cow and the butcher died on the road'(i.e. all this is gone beyond recall.) All these things lasted only so long as the King reigned. Even the house of Kale Khan (whom God has pardoned) has been razed as though a great broom swept it away; not a scrap of paper, not a thread of gold, not a wisp of wool remains.' . . .

And

> Let me tell you the Delhi news . . . The gate to Bara Dariba has been demolished. The rest of Qabil Attar Lane has been destroyed. The mosque in Kashmiri Katra has

> been levelled to the ground. The width of the street has been doubled. God, God! The domes of the mosques are being demolished, while on the thresholds of the Hindus' temples, the flags and banners flutter in the wind. A great monkey, strong as a lion and huge as an elephant has been born. He roves the city, demolishing buildings as he goes. He has seized the little domes on Faizullah Khan Bangash's mansion and shaken them one by one until he destroyed them to their foundations and brick rang against brick. Monkey, the deeds you do! And in the city too.'

Rajni emerges from the Ghalib Academy and walks towards Lodi Estate. Too many temple pennants in the Lodi Institutional Area confront her. Surely the area didn't look like that last year? She wonders about the aggressiveness of Hindu worship after the Demolition — the maha-aartis in Bombay, the deafening bhajans on loudspeakers in Delhi. In the bus, the chapter begins to formulate in her mind, oscillating between the present and the 1860s. Why did Ghalib, who at one time jokingly declared that he was but half a Muslim because he drank wine, sound like a bigot in these letters? His newly assumed religious identity was like repartee: vengeful and stinging, and sometimes embittered and defeated.

Did secularism have space for protest and hatred? Or was it only a conglomerate of acceptance and love, always about offering the other cheek?

How would Riaz answer these questions? Why did his answers matter so much to her? She took out a catalogue card and noted down a question — to ask him, when they met. It was number six on the list — a bit squiggly, as the bus was lurching.

The Leader

You are cigaretted lips, blue hair,
You are coarse fibre:
an idea behind high-powered glasses.

I am soft silk, styled hair.
But not really.
I play at being lovely.

I could play other games.

Rajni reached the house. Academics are usually short of money and his house was in a rather shabby locality of the city. She pulled herself short — but the shabbiness also had a snobbery that took for granted a virtual who's who of the city on a first-name basis, she reminded herself.

The bell clanged somewhere inside. Almost immediately the door swung open. She wore smart black trousers and a loose blue shirt. She had long hair that reached her waist, framing a Madonna-face. Rajni had expected a maidservant though she had wildly hoped he would open the door himself. She had imagined him in a crisp, white kurta-pyjama, his blue hair a little tousled perhaps.

'Is Professor Riaz in?'

'No, but he's expected back any minute. Would you like to wait for him?'

'No . . . yes, I think so . . . '

'Come in.'

She followed the woman into a sparsely furnished room.

Who was she — wife or friend? She too had been waiting for him, her hair loosened. She was now impatiently gathering it into a bun, gesturing vaguely to her to sit. Rajni looked around. There was an old upholstered sofa: large and cumbersome, which had probably seen better days — larger, more gracious drawing-rooms. Then there were a couple of rather elegant cane chairs, newer; perhaps bought at a sale from one of the mushrooming boutiques; or made especially for him, perhaps even designed for him by some man dressed in flowing arty clothes — exclusively for Riaz, embodying an old-boys' network peculiar to elite institutions. Her thoughts oscillated between awe and condescension.

The woman disappeared indoors. What did she contribute to this room? Was she the wife who lived in the U.S.: the mysterious lady hardly anybody had seen, to whom he dedicated his books? Did she have a daughter by him called Parveen Smriti whom he also invoked lovingly in dedications? How could she bear to be away from all this: the sepia photographs on a little table, and fresh flowers in a beer mug — which was incongruously shiny and blue with a crest of some American university on it?

'He hasn't come yet', she said, stating the obvious.

'I think I should leave', Rajni said, getting up.

'Do sit for a little while more. You have waited for so long. He should be back any minute. Can I get you something to drink?'

'No, thanks. Do you also teach?'

'No, no, I do something far less interesting. My field is computers.'

'What exactly do you do?'

'Programming. I don't live here. I work in Atlanta. You must be his colleague.'

'No, not exactly. I'm doing history.'

'Did he know you were coming?'

'No, I thought I would take a chance. I'll go now.'

'Oh, I'll tell him you came. Would you like to write down a message?'

'No, I'll call later. Thanks.'

As she shut the door, Rajni noticed that the woman had loosened her hair again. Was she going to stay on? Why did she live so far away programming computers? Why did she travel such a distance to wait for him?

Rajni felt her back stiffen with eagerness. Her heart thundered. He must have settled easily on the ground, behind her; his supple body assuming the contours of stylish carelessness. He touched her lightly on the shoulder, his fingertips brushing against the neckline of her blouse. She felt her skin tingle.

'Hi, you came to see me?'

The seminar room was crowded. All the chairs were taken. The younger people were moving to the floor to make room for late-comers.

'Yes, I waited for a while.'

'Anita told me. I meant to come back quickly, but then this man from Jadavpur wanted to discuss his work urgently. He was going back that very day. Do you have something to show me?'

'I'm struggling with Ghalib's letters.'

'I wonder whether I'm the best person for the letters. Anyway, has your supervisor given you a bibliography?'

'Yes. I have a rough draft of the chapter with me. I need to discuss a few more points with you.'

She couldn't tell him that she had almost burst into tears when she hadn't seen him that day. She was thirty-two and a mother of three. There were stretch marks on her abdomen, below her slightly rounded belly. The stretch marks on her thighs were like clawed out flesh.

'Let's meet after this', he gestured towards the chairperson and the speaker. It reminded her of Anita — the sweep of the hand, the slight superiority, the Westernness of the gesture. She wanted to mimic them. 'These people' — Rajni always said 'these people'. How was she different? She smelt different. She leaned back towards the Professor, hoping for a whiff. How would he react if she placed her palms on his chest and sniffed?

She pondered over her humiliating self-image. Why? She had heard the word so often, hurled so often, so near her: *kutia*, bitch.

She took down the words of the speaker in her neat rounded handwriting. Her own words were elsewhere, in a little diary. These seemed alien. These were their words, his words. She felt a sense of reverence for them.

There were ripples she couldn't understand in the audience. The speaker was powerful; she felt his speech drizzle a bit on her mind, like a passing shower.

A girl in jeans signalled wildly to her from across the room. It was the question hour. The girl wanted Riaz. Rajni turned to convey the message. He had already caught the girl's eye.

He made his way across the room, inclining his head towards the speaker — an apology, a congratulation? Rajni felt tears rise in her eyes. But he was supposed to see me, she thought ruefully.

She walked out from the seminar room and stood unsure of herself.

'Rajni, I'm sorry but I'll have to go. You see, the MFS is planning a music function at Banaras. Some people have come from Bombay and I'll have to go. Can we meet some other time?'

'Yes . . . but . . . '

'If you have some reading to do, perhaps you could wait in the library. I don't know how long this will take.'

'I think I'll take the chance', said Rajni, colour suffusing her cheeks. Did she have to sound so desperate?

'Okay, but I warn you I don't know how long this will take.'

Why had she deliberately got into this situation? She took out a journal from the magazine section. She had a lot of reading to do. Words teased her and dipped into images:

I thought today would melt
into just another day.
It didn't; it congealed
and I saw your face.

Yet another poem. Rajni was suddenly tired of the theatricality of the situation. Here she was writing poetry for a man who was busy drafting memoranda for secularism. She got up impatiently. The chair squealed, heads lifted from books and then bent again.

She met him at the door.

'Rajni, come and join us. I wonder why I didn't think of this before. We need more people with History. You've been attending all the meetings of MFS, haven't you?'

Rajni did not join the core-group of MFS because of Riaz; for her MFS was Riaz.

The blood-sport had started for her at last: the Movement for Secularism on the one side and Hindu fundamentalism on the other. It's saffron was like a red rag to her secular bull — with the ringside audience cheering the matador.

'If you want to live in Hindustan, loudly utter Vande Mataram', screeched the walls to her.

'We have shown these Mussaltas', said Rajni's husband. 'They will have to exist in India as Indians.'

Rajni's mother-in-law lit the diya before the idol every day and loudly asked her eldest grand-daughter to wash her hair. Did she think she was a Mussalman to go around with unwashed hair till ten in the morning?

'These Mussalmans breed like vermin', said the jhadu-pochawali who had five children herself.

'You people are no less', replied Rajni's mother-in-law looking accusingly at Rajni. 'In this country very soon there will only be Muslims and low-caste people left. It's we, the foolish caste Hindus alone who follow family planning — whether we have boys or girls. Soon, our race will be extinct.'

Caste Hindus? Race?

Rajni felt a wave of hysteria rising in her. What did her mother-in-law think the jhadupochawali was? A nineteenth-century Dasi, born to serve the caste Hindus, but never allowed to be one of them? It was all falling into a pattern.

> TOI, Delhi. THE POLITICS OF 'RAMINISING' HINDUISM AND THE RESISTANT PLURAL TRADITIONS, Riaz Ratnakar.

In this essay Riaz argued that the claim of Hindu fanatics of representing the majority in India was hollow. What they were projecting as Hinduism was actually Brahminism. The majority among Hindus comprised the lower-castes who were often not even allowed into temples. Riaz called the privileged upper-classes 'Ramins'.

Ramins. It was a clever term — derived at once from Brahmins who are at the top of the heap in the hierarchy of castes, and Ram who is the icon representing upper-caste values. Riaz went on to say that there are many strains in the Indian tradition that go against 'Raminism'.

MFS planned many cultural events that year and produced a brochure that Riaz wrote.

> More than anything *Mukta Naad*, the concert MFS is planning at Banaras on the fifteenth of August, is an attempt to break out of the marginal position culture occupies in the political arena. Why should politicians be allowed to become the spokespersons for our heritage? Why should they be allowed the narrowest interpretation of our plural traditions? To hear some of them talk about Indian tradition, one would conclude that the great Bhakti and Sufi movements are fictions, that the fine urban civilization that flourished under the Mughals is a figment of the historians' imagination.
>
> Doesn't the name *Mukta Naad* sound wonderful — full throated, deep and reverberating? Through Hindustani and Carnatic music we hope to present the most

> compassionate form of the deity Ram. It is our belief that the masses are still steeped in the mythology of the family-man Ram. The attempt to convert him into a prickly warrior icon is bound to lose out. Perhaps the scheming politicians will have to invent a new deity to fulfil their evil designs.
>
> Some doubts have been voiced about the tactical correctness of the function. How can classical music counteract the propaganda of hatred unleashed by the fundamentalists? The schism between the arts and life that we often agonize about is, I think, a bit of an elitist dilemma. I sincerely believe that when we doubt the reach of classical music we are underestimating the intelligence and sensitivity of the common people. At the concert held last month in Old Delhi, for instance, we had maestros — many of whom belong to Muslim families — sing songs that spring from Hindu mythology. People who had never heard classical music were stirred to the extent that they went up to the singers with observations like, 'You are the true devotees of Ram; the politicians(those who misuse religion) are all self-servers.'

Rajni went up to Riaz; 'I don't think I'll be able to go to Banaras.'

'I understand your constraints.'

'I wish I could. I want to, Riaz.'

'If you want to so much, perhaps you should, Rajni. What are the practical difficulties?'

'None. There are two domestic helps who can, with a little assistance from my mother-in-law, manage the children.'

'Well, if it's only her obduracy, then perhaps you can deal with it.'

'You credit me with many more resources than I actually have. If she comes to know that it's for the cause of secularism, she will use every trick to stop me from going.'

'All of us have both these — constraints and resources. Try and reason with her. You're a strong woman, you seem to have a lot of energy, the capability of putting in a lot of socially productive work.'

'Thanks.'

He touched her lightly on the cheek before hurrying away, 'What are these tears doing here?'

> But I am exasperated by your lips,
> that softly form
> these thousand endearments
> inaudibly —
> cobwebs,
> brushing in darkness
> against my cheek.

The Declaration

She tried rehearsing her declaration many times. She was obsessed with it; she was obsessed with words like 'heart' which she strung into sentences. They looked like cheap bead-necklaces that are sold at the Sheetla Mata Mela in the small town where she was born. Sheetla Mata, the goddess of the pox, to appease whose heat many cooling things are used: cooled food and beverages, and then a mela, loud, festive, garish.

Her love was garish: shiny red, parrot-green and a magenta that embarrassingly loses colour.

Most of us can't take such cheapness and spend a lifetime burnishing, sublimating, repressing. And some of us, made reckless by the crudity of the rural mela want to get on to the clumsy dolna: a vertically placed merry-go-round made of wood; creaking, as it is propelled by sweaty men who also have to collect fifty paisa each from the women and children getting on to the dolna. No, no, not more than six in each. You, bai, have not paid for the child. No, no, even a three-year-old has to pay, get down mataji.

Rajni feels the heady fear of being thrown into space in a risky contraption. Long back, burrowing her head in her maidservant's lap and holding on to the wooden bar of the dolna, she had been too cautious; she had gripped too tightly. The men had been maddened by their power. They pulled and pushed and grunted with the satisfaction of flexing their muscles, and the women squealed in terror and delight; but she clenched her fists and refused to let go. Afterwards, looking at the flushed face of her maidservant, she held out her hand for sympathy. Across the wrist was a reddish blue weal where the bar of the dolna had rubbed into her skin. Ooi, why did you grip so tightly? Why were you so scared? The blood drained from the maidservant's face.

She wouldn't hold on this time. Reckless, she reached his house one morning. He was ill, she had heard. He had been ill a long time. Actually, he had the viral fever. She didn't know what she was going to say to him. But she was propelled by a mysterious force.

Riaz's hair was tousled. He had lost weight. It had been rather a bore to be in bed for ten days. The deaf maid had done the morning cooking and left, the house was silent.

Riaz opened the door. Rajni stood at the doorstep. Her face above the yellow roses was suffused with colour.

'Oh, hi!' He was not expecting callers so early in the day.

She handed him the roses, wordlessly.

'Thank you so much.'

She followed him into the drawing room.

'How are you feeling now?'

'Much better! But ill enough to deserve roses.'

He looked around for an appropriate vase. There was nothing that would hold the long-stemmed blooms.

'Where should I put these? Let's see how bright you are.'

'You can keep holding them, you look kind of decorative with the flowers in your hand.'

He burst out laughing, tilting his head backward a little. Rajni noticed the evenness of his teeth perhaps for the hundredth time.

'Tell me how to stand.'

'You could stand in the tribhanga position, like this.'

'Did you learn dance?'

'Yes, I learnt Bharatnatyam for a while.'

'What else did you learn?'

'I can't tell you everything I know in one morning.'

'So how's the family? How are the children? How's the poetry?'

'Now you have asked all there is to ask.'

'Yes, so that one can settle down and relax.'

'You don't look ill. I mean, you have lost weight but . . . '

'I know I look fairly wholesome. That's because I've shaved this morning.'

'Aren't you going to ask why I'm here?'

'No, of course not. But first tell me what you'll drink. There's whisky.'

'At eleven in the morning?'

'Well, there's coffee. You must remember that the first time we met you were stashed.'

Rajni looked up at him. He was smiling. How could she tell him that drinking for her didn't have the pleasant flirtatious connotations that he had assumed. Nevertheless, she played along, 'What nonsense! I just sniffed at some wine.'

'That story's good enough for the spouse. How does he take your drinking?'

'Very kindly. He's seldom sober himself.'

'This must be fun for the children.'

'I don't know. I haven't dared ask them.'

'Well, coffee then?'

'Yes, but with lots of milk.'

'Come and make it yourself.'

Rajni followed him into the kitchen. It seemed the natural thing to do. He was swift and competent in the kitchen, except at times when he couldn't see what was right under his nose.

Then, he suddenly said, 'You mind if I lie down? I'm ill, by the way.'

He lay down on the divan. After a while he closed his eyes. Rajni sat opposite, sipping her coffee. Without his glasses his eyes looked like slits. His skin glowed, brown and, yes, wholesome. That was how he had described himself. Like brown bread, good and grainy between the teeth.

'Why are you smiling?'

'Oh, was I smiling?'

'Yes, rather naughtily.'

'I was thinking how edible you look.'

'What! A cannibal-poet?'

'No, just a man-eater', she retorted, slightly astonished by herself.

'Are you comfortable on the chair?'

'Yes.'

'You can sit here, otherwise.' He pulled a floor-cushion on to the divan, propping it against the wall. 'This will provide a back-rest.'

With her heart thundering, Rajni settled down on the divan. He was just inches away from her. He looked quite untroubled by the proximity.

'You didn't show me your chapter.'

'I still have some work left.'

He closed his eyes again. Rajni's throat was dry.

'It's a rather unfinished draft. I needed more help with the theoretical aspect', she said.

'Yes, after Banaras I have been rather tied up, and then I fell ill. But that's the usual story of my life.'

'I met you precisely twice for a quarter of an hour in all.' Her voice sounded tearful even to her own ears.

'Sorry, was it this bad?'

Rajni felt tears well up in her eyes. She made no effort to hide them. 'I wanted to see you so much.'

'What is it, Rajni? Give me your hand. That's a nice, soft hand.'

Rajni found herself with her head on his chest. She closed her eyes and deep within her a parched landscape drank in the early showers.

Seconds ticked by. It seemed hours before Riaz's hand reached her back and began to stroke it gently.

'Riaz, I had to come today.'

'Yes.'

'I couldn't take it any more.'

He was silent. Rajni couldn't see his face, she didn't want to.

'Don't make me go back, please.'

'In a little while you will want to, won't you, Rajni?'

'Yes, but I will want to come back. Kiss me please, Riaz.'

As their tongues interlocked, Rajni realized with a shock how seldom she had been kissed. She didn't want to let go. Her lips demanded more, every time he made to withdraw.

'Young lady, this is not such a good idea.'

She didn't want to speak.

'Do you know anything at all about me?' he asked.

'I know you are married.'

'Look, Rajni . . . '

He was quiet, and then after a while he drew her into his arms and began kissing her. His hands entered the front of her blouse and cupped her breasts. Rajni clung to him, desperate for him not to leave. Then, suddenly he seemed to go away again.

'No, no. This won't do!'

'No, Riaz? But why?' The cry was laden with pain.

'No, Rajni . . . ' He got up abruptly and disappeared inside.

Rajni wanted to beat her head against the wall. She wanted to shriek. He had gone away. He would not come back.

When he returned after ten minutes, she was sitting on the chair. She had run a comb through her hair and repaired her kajal.

'I must leave now.'

'It's getting late. You have a long way to go.'

'Yes. Hope you get well soon.'

'Thanks. Thanks for coming to see me.'

A Journey

Riaz told me reluctantly that Rajni left Delhi for a vacation, soon after surprising him with her declaration of love. I think she wanted to leave her husband, he added.

She went to what was called her maika by her in-laws. This time it was located in the Collector's residence in Ajmer. She died there.

It was almost the end of the summer vacation when I got a letter signed by Mayank Govil, inviting me to Ajmer. I had written to Rajat Govil — Rajni's brother, much earlier, telling him briefly about the volume and how I had chanced upon his sister's poetry. There had been no reply.

I decided to make the same journey too. At that point death seemed an inexplicable adjunct to Rajni's story and I wanted a conclusion.

Her brother spoke about their childhood together, her Bhabhi told me about Rajni's children. Blood relationships traverse a treacherous terrain: the past and the future. The area is misty as memory plays bo-peep with desire and guilt. This is where points get lost or stretch like question marks unto eternity. I didn't find a conclusion but I found other stories in Ajmer. Some added up, others cast their shadow backward, making everything that has been told, darker.

The train drew up at the Ajmer station at eight thirty. Coming out with my luggage I was startled by a line of horse-drawn tongas. I decided on taking the more familiar autorickshaw. Nevertheless, by the time I reached the tourist bungalow, I was quite shaken up by the way it had veered through the streets, narrowly missing cycles, scooters, cars, buses, tongas, tempos, cows, sheep and even a herd of buffaloes. From the driveway the building looked like sugar-icing: chocolate brown and candy pink. It was called Khadim.

The rickshaw braked at the entrance and a bearer resplendent in slightly soiled livery saluted me smartly and made off with my suitcase and handbag before I could stop him. I ran after him to recover my bag. It seemed a town of black comedy rather than a site for tragedy.

There was more. I had neglected to check the meter or settle the fare with the autorickshaw driver before starting from the station.

'Fifty rupees', he demanded.

As I was protesting, a grey car drew up alongside and a man jumped out.

'Shrimati Roy?' he asked.

'Yes.'

'Sorry Madam, I must have just missed you at the station.'

'Who sent you?'

'Collector sahib, Madam.'

'Oh, this is very kind of him. Will you tell him I am very grateful?'

'Madam is expecting you at the residence.'

'All right. I will be ready in half an hour.'

It left me no time to get my bearings. In Khadim, however, my stock had gone up further. Not only had I arrived out of 'tourist season', I was also known to the Collector. I was shown into a large room by four stewards. I hurriedly made for the bathroom. There was no water in the taps. I washed up with half a bucket of water that stood in the corner. With the stickiness of train travel still on me, I sat in the car prepared for a comfortable drive. The car swung into the gates of a huge mansion in about four minutes.

Rajat, Rajni's brother, has a striking resemblance to her, I was told. He too, was tall and delicate-looking. I found other closenesses, but that is the substance of this story.

During Rajni's last visit to Ajmer, Rajat was functioning under strict instructions from the Central Government that the post-Masjid communal situation should not be allowed to trigger off a riot in the town.

Roses! There were millions of them, pink and heavy-odoured on the blue *shanil*. Rajat was thinking of Minka's red lips and dark eyes. His wife Minka would have been the toast of the town, but in Ajmer they didn't toast appearance, they worshipped the reality of Rajat's exalted position. Had he married a monkey, people would have worshipped her as the female incarnation of Hanuman.

'The Dargah of Khwaja Gharib Nawaz of Ajmer, the founder of a Sufi silsila in India', Rajni had intoned far too passionately, Rajat thought. For him it was only a monument, perversely still in use, situated in one of the most congested and lawless areas of the town.

The incense was overpowering in the mehfil-khana where the Qawwali was going to be held. Minka's perfumes were like that; her perfume called Poison would make his head reel. It was quite dirty outside the sanctorum. Even though this was a special occasion — the Urs was going to begin and the whole place had been spruced up — the outer portions continued to look unwashed. Men moved around in white kurta-pyjamas, with woven caps covering their heads. Rajat adjusted the handkerchief on his head. He should have come prepared for this. He had been told to carry some headgear to the Dargah. Really, he needed that handkerchief to block out the smells; an odour was filtering through the heavy incense, probably the odour of open drains that surround the Dargah.

The Qawwals had been especially invited from Delhi for the programme today. The mehfil-khana was full. There were hardly any women. Rajat looked with distaste at the S.P.'s wife. Why had he brought her along? Didn't he know that this was a breach of propriety? Since medieval times, women and young boys have been excluded from Islamic gatherings and Muslims till today haven't progressed very far in their thinking; everybody knows this. The bureaucrats were here to woo the populace and not alienate it by flouting tradition. Anyway, to get one's wife along to a gathering of paan-chewing, lecherous Muslim men was a solecism that only the S.P. was capable of. Rajat would never even think of bringing Mayank to such a place.

Mayank, Minka, moon. Her parents had given her a boy's name to protect her from the evil eye. He had fallen in love with her the moment she appeared in the dilapidated room wearing a canary yellow chiffon sari, bearing a tray of sweets for the young I.A.S. probationer who had come to 'see' her. He had planned to 'see' at least ten girls before he would decide on which one. After meeting Minka, he was wildly impatient, in spite of injunctions from friends about not selling himself too cheaply. After all, her father is just a petty official in the P.W.D. That impatience to possess her had not left him even after ten years. Where would she be now?

The Qawwals took their place after seeking the Dewan's blessings. Rajat stole a look at the Dewan. He sat facing the Qawwals. His silver beard and white apparel gave him an aura of peace and dignity. The Qawwali mehfil is the Sufi way of attaining the state of haal or ecstasy, the union with God who is seen as the beloved, Rajni had said. He had not replied because he was impatient with Rajni's shrill championing of a cause that she hardly understood. To hear her, it would seem that the culture of this country was vested in the smelly by-lanes of the Muslim ghetto. He had not asked her to accompany him. The Qawwali would probably be in chaste Urdu and what would she understand of it?

The Qawwali started with the vigorous clapping of hands.

The hands of the Qawwals seemed to be percussion

instruments in their own right, so loud and reverberating was the sound.

Tori surat ke balhari (Nijam). Beholding your countenance I offer myself in sacrifice.

There was a ripple of excitement in the mehfil. Cries of wah wah almost drowned the voice of the Qawwal. Some even repeated the words after him. It appeared to be a well known piece. Rajat wondered how it qualified as Islamic. He understood the words perfectly and except for this bit about the Nijam, it could have been sung in a temple without any ado. The lines were repeated many times.

Where would Mayank be now? Where in the acres of land dedicated to the Collector's residence? What would she be doing? She loved the gardens. She loved the house. She kept the house beautiful, even though it was large and unwieldy and his pay cheque quite small. He didn't quite know how she managed. Most of the time he didn't know what she felt. She seemed to sail through life with very few entanglements. Immediately after their marriage, she had readily agreed to stay back in his hometown for six months to chaperon Rajni who was in the final year of her M.A.; far too readily he had thought. She had been with Rajni for six long months. She was with Rajni today. He felt the horrifyingly familiar tightening of muscles.

Really, the odour of the drains was too much. He had casually mentioned that Muslims are dirty by habit. How angry Rajni had been! Rajni's reactions were rather predictable. Delhi's academia these days was shouting itself hoarse in support of the downtrodden Muslims; they didn't have to deal with the Khadim Mohalla goonda element nor sit here subjected to an intermingling of smells. Minka had said yes, of course, it is poverty that makes them so.

> *Sab sakhian chundar mori maili dekh hansin narnari*
> *Ab ke bahar chundari mori rang do rakh le laj hamari (Nijam piya)*
>
> All the other girls saw my soiled veil and together they laughed

This springtime dye my veil for me, O protect my honour (Nijam beloved).

People were making offerings of money to the Dewan. This stanza brought an avalanche of currency notes. The Qawwal seemed delighted and sang the same lines in various ways. A lackey from the Qawwal side went up to the Dewan and brought back the loot. Rajat wondered whether he should make an offering too. The S.P., he saw, had ambled right up to the Qawwals and was placing a five-rupee note on the harmonium. Couldn't the man see that everybody else was going through the Dewan? The Chief Qawwal greeted him with a broad smile and Rajat was relieved that no one had taken offence.

'Muqarar, muqarar' said the S.P.'s wife. Rajat looked at her in surprise. Her sari had slipped from her head and even from her bosom. The neckline of the blouse showed the comfortable rise of sizeable mounds. He gestured to her to cover her head. She leaned towards him, exposing more flesh.

'Wah, Bhai sahib. You should have brought Bhabhiji along. This is a very special treat. They sing this only at Nizamuddin for the Auliya. It was composed for him by his lover Amir Khusrau', she hissed and mercifully adjusted her clothes.

Should she be talking about homosexual lovers to her husband's superior? Rajat wondered. And if the Qawwali was really about perverted sex should these people be singing it in a religious place? Their ways were truly incorrigible.

A man in threadbare clothes was dancing. The clapping had reached a crescendo. Rajat felt it throbbing in his head. People were swaying in time with the music. Was this what Rajni had been talking about: the union with the beloved?

Suddenly everything went blank, the villainous face of the S.P., the yellow and pink chunderi sari that his wife was wearing, the voice of the Qawwal.

'He needs air, give him air', said a well wisher. 'Collector sahib, Collector sahib', he wailed histrionically. 'This is a faint.'

'No, no, I'm fine. It's the heat. I'll be all right.'

'What happened Bhai?' asked the S.P. twirling his moustache. 'Instead of Bhabhiji, are you going to deliver the good news?' he guffawed. The S.P. was getting on. He was due for retirement six months hence. He was of local origin, related to half a dozen local politicians. He took liberties that Rajat was loathe to condone.

'I'm all right', Rajat said asserting his position. 'Let the programme continue.'

Minka and he had no children. It was difficult to associate Minka's trim figure with motherhood. She had never expressed any wish to have children and he was reluctant to see her swell and lose her shape. But hadn't things been changing imperceptibly all these years? Minka too was changing: a hardening, a shrivelling, a withdrawal? But she looked the same: the same baby-doll eyes, large and astonished, the wavy hair that she now wore cropped close to the face, the same slightly pale complexion that she heightened with blush-on and lipstick. Minka had filled his life, and still filled his life. Sometimes she became an obsession, now more so since Rajni had come visiting.

How thin Rajni had become recently. Rajat hated the way she lived, constantly under pressure from her three bawling daughters and her drunkard husband. Rajni was the same age as Minka, but so worn. Why did she keep having children? He couldn't confront her with the question. He felt they were his own eyes that rose to accuse him. Accuse him of what?

He had been a considerate brother, hadn't he?

The Qawwal's voice sounded reedy. *Tori surat ke balihari*.

He didn't want to think too much. He didn't want to think about the odour and stench that were affecting only him in this huge gathering.

Rajat leaned out of the car and asked the guard at the gate, 'Is the green car in?'

'No, sahib, it went out fifteen minutes ago.'

No wife. It was almost as if Minka had timed her departure

to coincide with his coming home. She must have gone out with Rajni. What did they talk about — these two — Rajni's slightly haggard face lighting up at Minka's loveliness? It was almost sexual. Was Rajni in love with Minka too — god, was he going mad? His own sister and wife! But they spent so many hours together. Right from the beginning Rajni had appropriated Minka. She is so lovely, Bhai, she is so beautiful — Rajni had always been gushy. She had surrounded Minka. She wouldn't let Minka enter the kitchen: no Minky, you don't belong here. She would do her hair, even tie her sari for her: like this Minky, let the curves show.

Their parents had died in an accident when he was twelve, Rajni merely five. Both the children had been brought up at the mercy of an aged, slightly deaf aunt who left the world with a sigh of relief the day Rajni turned sixteen. He had always had to take care of Rajni — right from the beginning: getting her a fringe hair cut, buying her the first bra, telling her about menstruation. He had, hadn't he? Right from the beginning. Was it his fault that she married that drunkard? Arranged marriages are always a bit of a gamble, and then Rajni had put forward such impossible conditions. It has to be Delhi, Bhai, my work is there. That wasn't a Rajni he had recognized. After finishing his training, when he came back to the house to take away his bride, Rajni had already moved to Delhi to start her M.Phil. in Modern History. When he met her again she had seemed mulish about not wanting to give up her course, which hadn't appeared anything outstanding to him. He could have otherwise arranged a match for her with somebody from the services, if not from the I.A.S. at least the Police or Income Tax.

Sunil's qualifications had not been bad; he had seemed all right. He was a civil lawyer who would in time inherit his father's practice. It was a joint family — nice people — and it seemed Rajni would be able to 'adjust' to their ways. The house they lived in was rather small though, but one couldn't expect mansions in a big city — Minka kept saying poor thing, poor thing, as though he was responsible.

Rajat entered the house with a sense of weariness. What was he to do? The huge rooms seemed almost menacing in their stillness. The sitting room was large enough to contain a modern-day flat. In fact, it was the size of Rajni's house. This was Rajat's favourite room in the house. It overlooked the gardens. Even in summer, when there was a breeze one could sit here without a fan. Ramsingh entered to open the windows. Rajat sank into the sofa.

'Some tea, sahib?'

'Yes, Ramsingh.'

'Jiji sahib hasn't had hers yet. Should I get hers too?'

'Oh, is she home? I don't hear the children.'

'Memsahib has taken them with her.'

That was unusual. Minka usually did not enjoy venturing out with her nieces.

Rajni entered the room, looking more drawn than usual.

'Your Bhabhi has been very brave today.'

'Yes Bhai. What made you come home so early?'

'I'm not well. The Dargah programme tired me out totally.'

'What's wrong Bhai?' There was a catch in her voice as though she were pitying him. He was irritated. From where did she get that compassion — surrounded as she was by chaos?

'Nothing much, just slight giddiness. What about you Rajni?'

'It's not worse than usual', Rajni didn't hedge, didn't pretend to misunderstand. 'My mother-in-law says things will improve once we have a son.'

'You're crazy,' Rajat expostulated, 'look at yourself, you will die and then Sunil is not even . . .'

'I won't die in childbirth, Bhai. Statistics will bear me out, so will history. Women have been known to survive fourteen, fifteen.'

'Well, it's your life.'

'My life — it never was. Tell me about alternatives.'

'The alternative is a gynaecologist, an operation or just pills.'

'And after that — Bhai, what happens after that?'

'Rajni, tell them you can't. Surely they can't force you in this day and age?'

'Don't you ever read the papers, Bhai? Do you know how many women are burnt because they refuse to beg for coloured televisions for their husbands' families?'

'You mean they can — Rajni we don't belong to that stratum. We are educated, we are . . . '

'I don't know — at times I feel envious of my jhadu-pochawali. When her husband beats her, she yells, screams, hits him back, her mother-in-law joins in then. The other day, she beat both of them: the husband was drunk, her mother-in-law is old, anyway. She was triumphant. I gave her tea and breakfast, they had locked her out of the house. She says they will come and beg at her feet — they will have to — they can't run the house on nothing. She earns eight hundred rupees doing the sweeping and swabbing in five houses, you know. She knows her worth.'

'And you envy her?' Rajat asked sipping his tea. It tasted bitter.

'H'm. Tell me about alternatives, Bhai.'

'I don't know what you mean', Rajat felt tired and sick. What was she talking about? Could she leave Sunil with her three daughters? Where would she go? What would she live on?

'Does he beat you?'

'No, of course not, Bhai.'

'Are you sure you want to leave him?'

'I think so.'

'What about the children?'

'I want my children.'

Did Rajni mean it? Probably not. The area around her eyes was dark and moist. She must have been crying. How often did she cry? She once laughed so much. It used to get on his nerves, especially after he married Minka. It was as though she was playing the little sister shown in commercial Hindi cinema: pigtails and giggles galore. Minka had seemed so dignified beside her. At times he had been ashamed of

Rajni. Now, she sat still and silent, as though playing another part. He felt brutal.

'Well, a lot of women suffer in their marital families, Rajni.'

She raised her eyes to meet his. 'I'm not claiming any uniqueness.'

Rajat wanted to touch the dark patches under her eyes, kiss the swollen eyelids. He went and sat near her and put an arm around her shoulder.

He could feel her tremble. She had started greying, he noticed with a shock. She was thirty-two, only thirty-two. Tears welled up in his eyes. He touched her cheeks lightly; how bony her face was! They resembled each other, the same oval face with soft, heavy-lidded eyes. He wanted to cry, get inside her skin, he wanted to be her. He wanted to feel her thinness, her bones; he wanted to feel her tiredness in himself.

He heard the car approach and, unknown to himself, sighed with relief. Rajni looked at him quizzically. He caught that look and flushed. Really! Why couldn't he wait for his wife without being made to feel unnatural? Why did Rajni make him feel that way? And why was he obsessed with Minka? They had been married long enough.

'Bhai, why did you go to the Dargah without me? Why didn't you take me? You know, in Delhi I often go to Nizamuddin Auliya's Dargah.' Rajni sounded young and peevish.

'What do you have to do with Dargahs?'

'They were the great Sufis, Bhai, the teachers of love through music and poetry.'

'I'll ask someone to take you. You academics romanticize everything, don't you? I see only filth, squalor and goondaism in Khadim Mohalla — very little poetry.'

Minka was glad that the evening was over. Three children! The oldest child — five and a bit, or was it six — did not seem to be a child at all. She was all Rajni: the same heavy-lidded eyes, the oval face — but what a difference there was in their expressions. Rajni used to smile so much — this child sat prim, aloof and deadpan: the arched lips showing no inclination to curve further, not even while watching the clown at the circus. The other two were not good looking, taking after Sunil. The four-year-old had guffawed loudly and demanded popcorn; the baby, of course, had slept through it all, on Minka's lap, crumpling her chiffon sari. The baby had a smell about her, just like a puppy. She felt like a puppy too — warm and a bit wet on the face with spittle — nuzzling into Minka's midriff. Minka wondered at herself: she didn't like children and here she was out with three. But Rajni needed this break; she had sobbed all afternoon.

Minka looked at her oldest niece again, 'Did you enjoy the circus, beta?'

'No, Mami.'

'Why not?'

'I want to go back.'

'You will, beta, very soon! Are you missing Daddy?'

'There's nobody to give him his sweet lime juice.'

'Why, there's your grandmother and your ayah.'

'Grandmother can't manage everything. She's old.'

'But see, Mummy wants to stay here for the holidays with her brother and her Bhabhi.'

'Who is Bhabhi?'

'I'm her Bhabhi.'

'Mummy's selfish', she said clearly and turned away from Minka. Minka felt a wave of anger engulf her. She wanted to hit the child. And here was Rajni crying her eyes out for these demons. Who had taught the six-year-old all this? Why did people have children in the first place, especially couples like Rajni and Sunil who had never got along?

'Mami, can you get my reservation done?'

What an adult question. Did the child think she could travel alone in the overnight train? Minka wanted to laugh.

'But Mummy will miss you then.'

'Grandmother and Daddy are missing me now and they are not even well.'

'What's the matter with Daddy?'

'Daddy drinks because he's not happy.'

'Why isn't he happy, beta?'

'He is not happy.'

How do you communicate the father's drinking problem to a child? Daddy isn't happy and is to be given fruit juice. Rajni had been such an effervescent creature. Now she was like a house with its windows shut. Rajni's effervescence had been difficult to stomach. She had been all over her, inundating her with compliments, choking her with affection, not letting her breathe. Minka had felt punished with love. And then those six long months — when Rajat was away in Mussoorie for his training — with Rajni in that crumbling house. Rajni had been so restless. Opening and closing windows, climbing up and down the stairs. She knew Rajni was involved in a love affair then. The boy in question had been awful; Minka shuddered at the memory. He was a motor mechanic or something: tall and vacuous and very good-looking. When he came home he hardly spoke, just thrust his broad chest in the conversation. The small town had buzzed with rumours. They were seen together everywhere and well-meaning matrons would call up Minka to say that her sister-in-law was getting involved with a most undesirable character — a mere motor mechanic — and that as she now occupied the place of her mother, it was her duty to check the affair.

It wasn't her nature to interfere, it wasn't her nature to run other people's lives.

Rajni had alternated between emotions: weeping one minute, laughing hysterically the next. Minka had tried to extend support; she had let Rajni cry on her shoulder, let her giggle uncontrollably. It had wearied her, and made her very tired.

Now, after years this new avatar: a snuffed out Rajni, a Rajni with dark circles under her eyes, a strangely beautiful and thin Rajni.

Minka relaxed slightly as the car swung into the familiar gates of the Collector's residence.

First Love

Why didn't the open spaces around the Collector's residence open up new vistas of hope for Rajni? She burrowed indoors. She spent most of the last day of her life in a room that Minka euphemistically called the store but which was actually a dump for all the old and ugly things that had earlier cluttered up the family house. The family house had been sold, Rajat told me. We got a pittance for it — it hardly covered the cost of Rajni's wedding, he added.

The store fascinated Rajni. The numerous attendants in the Collector's residence played with the children and she spent all those precious hours in the huge but airless room, a duster in hand, absent-mindedly flicking dust off chipped Moradabadi lamps, broken chairs and tables with three legs. Surrounded by the relics of her past, with the dust settling like fine powder on her hair, she mumbled to herself thinking of childhood.

Where was Bhai? She had looked under the bed, behind the green almirah, in the box-room. He had promised he would be in this room. Bhai, don't hide in the other rooms, I get scared looking for you.

The garden was sunny. She liked the guava tree the best. It's lower branches were like steps.

She put one foot gingerly on the trunk of the tree. She held on to a branch and heaved herself up. She got clumsier as she ascended. Midway up the tree, the branches joined to make a kind of frame. She put one leg through it, then half sitting she tried to put in the other. Her blue frock got caught in a twig in the process. She tried to loosen it with one hand and lost balance. The twig grazed her thigh and she landed with a thud on the thick, round branch. She felt like crying; she was bruised between the legs.

She could look into the neighbour's house from there. There were three children playing outside. She had never seen them before; they must be house-guests. They were playing solemnly, quietly. She could see bright blocks: red, green, blue, magenta. What were they?

The girl wore a pink frock. Her hair was tied with a little pink bow. She had pretty pink socks on also. Rajni looked at her own frock; why didn't it fluff out around her the way the little girl's did? And she didn't have any matching socks either. She only had school socks, white, and most of them laddered. The shop where they bought their socks didn't have the kind the girl was wearing.

A woman came out with what looked like buns. She was wearing a printed gown. She was handing the buns to the children.

Rajni felt hungry. Chachi couldn't have cooked lunch; she must be doing her puja.

Where was Bhai? And why didn't the woman call her to play with the children? She could see her quite clearly on her perch on the tree.

The children had started playing again.

The house must be neat and tidy inside — like Mala's house in the cantonment area. Mala's house had little statuettes arranged on the mantelpiece. There were little dogs and birds and little houses like those in picture books. There was no dust anywhere.

Her own house looked so poor — were they poor? She must ask Bhai. She knew they were orphans. She had heard the word used often. Chachi said it too. She couldn't bear to invite her friends to her house; the chairs were so dirty, the cushion covers were encrusted with grime and the day Kanu didn't come to clean up things became messier than usual.

She suddenly saw Bhai cycling furiously up the street. He must have gone to Arvind's house. She would complain to Chachi. But then that would annoy him. Bhai loved Arvind more than he loved her. Nobody loved her, nobody. Not like those children in the opposite house who were given buns when they were hungry.

Tears ran down her cheeks.

'Rajni, why are you crying?'

'Where did you go, Bhai?'

'I'm bigger than you are, Rajni. I went to play with big boys.'

'Why can't you take me with you?'

'Nobody brings sisters with them.'

'I have no one to play with.'

'Why don't you go to Archana's?'

'She's gone out for the holidays.'

'Okay, I'll play with you now.'

She came down gingerly, Rajat helped her down.

'Rajni, you're a good girl, Rajni.'

She screamed in the dark. There was a big, black thing. It was slithering past her. She screamed again. What happened Rajni? She cocooned herself in the sheet, shivering. What happened Rajni, bolo re? Her throat was parched. She desperately wanted a glass of water. Water, Chachi. Oho, a creak of more than the bed, of old bones. Here, water.

It didn't go away. It sat in the dark. She was afraid to breathe. Kanu had told her not to breathe loudly. Ghosts like children who breathe thick and fast huff-huff-huff. It was crouching behind the door. Chachi would not have her in her bed because she often wet it. Dirty. Then Bhai would say kuttee and not talk to her.

Om bhoorbhuva swaha, tatt savitur vareeniyam. The Gayatri Mantra a hundred times. How much was a hundred? Many, many times, so many times that sleep would descend in sheer fatigue. At such times she could see sleep like a tent around her, but taut and unyielding. She would pray for it to fall and envelop her.

Chachi. Sleep *na* Rajni *re*, what is the matter? I am scared. No *re* nothing — sleep — droned Chachi, half asleep, tired, too old.

Chachi, Chachi. Go to sleep, Rajni, hush — quiet, don't scream.

The toilet was too far from the house. She could pee in the drain, in the bathroom; though Chachi said she shouldn't now, as she wasn't a child anymore. But she wanted to pee so many times in the night — again and again — especially when she couldn't sleep.

'I want to sleep with you, Bhai.'

'No, Rajni, you're a big girl now. You must sleep by yourself.'

'Bhai, a ghost comes at night.'

'You know there's no such thing.'

'There is, there is . . . I've seen it . . . '

'What does it do, Rajni?'

'Nothing.'

'Then why are you scared of it?'

'It's very dark at night and Chachi puts off all the lights. She doesn't wake up when I want to pee. Let me sleep with you, Bhai please. It won't come if I sleep with you.'

'Rajni, you silly girl, how can I sleep like this?'

'What d'you mean?'

'Why are you clinging on like this.'

'I can only sleep like this.'

'Okay, let go of my collar — okay, you can hold my arm — Rajni, don't dig your nails into my arm. Rajni — *Rajni* — girls are not supposed to sleep like this with boys.'

'No, Kanu told me it's all right to sleep like this with brothers.'

'Rajni, you are so soft — like a kitten — Ach, you're stinking. When did you last wash your hair?'

'On Sunday.'

'It's Friday today — dirty girl!'

'Bhai, tell Chachi to get some shampoo for me.'

'Why?'

'Then I'll have long, lovely hair. Egg shampoo!'

'Who told you about egg shampoo?'

'Archana's mother has an imported shampoo.'

'I'll get you an imported shampoo when I become a cardiologist.'

'What's a cardilogist?'

'Cardiologist — a doctor who treats diseases of the heart.'

'Is Ram uncle a cardi?'

'No, silly. Cardiologists practice only in big cities. There isn't a cardiologist in this sinkhole.'

'Then — will you live in Delhi or Bombay?'

'Yes, I'll work in a big hospital. Then I'll go abroad, very often. Why are you snivelling, Rajni?'

'I'll have to stay here all alone. I don't want to stay only with Chachi.'

'Okay, you can stay with me in Bombay.'

'Kanu was saying I will have to get married and live with my husband.'

'Yes, girls have to get married.'

'What about boys?'

'Boys can do what they like.'

'No, I won't get married. I'll stay with you, Bhai.'

'Okay, now go to sleep, Rajni.'

'Bhai, you also smell like me — of sweat.'

'If you talk again, you'll have to sleep by yourself.'

'Rajni, is this the time to come home?'

'Why, it's just six o' clock.'

'College gets over at three.'

'All of us went to a reataurant.'

'Who?'

'Archana, Poorva, I. And two or three boys.'

'Which boys — Shyam and Rajeev?'

'Well, yes!'

'I think we've spoken about this before.'

'Yes, we have. And I don't see why we have to be so narrow-minded.'

'Rajni, we are part of a small-town community. Surely you recognize the fact?'

'Bhai, we needn't have double standards, like a lot of people do in this city.'

'We have to accept things for what they are. Do you know what these boys say about you ?'

'There's nothing to say.'

'In the evening a lot of them get together for a beer. They often boast about the number of girls they can get.'

'Get for what?'

'For a movie or a picnic.'

'So?'

'Do you want your name to be mentioned like this? Do you want to keep your dignity or not? Girls from good families don't behave in this manner.'

'And what about boys from good families?'

'Rajni, will you stop being unreasonable?'

'If you go out with girls, I'll go out with boys.'

'That's like cutting off your nose to spite your face.'

'It's my nose.'

'Let's keep it where it belongs, for the time.'

'Okay, then we'll go for a picnic to the magic graves tomorrow. Just the two of us. No girls.'

'And no boys.'

The picnic was fun in the beginning, cucumber sandwiches and warm coffee, till they started counting the graves. The first time Rajat counted them he said sixty-eight triumphantly, but when she counted them there were sixty-nine, then again seventy, sixty-six. The evening was chilly and windy on the hill and they descended silently, fatigued.

She wanted to tell Bhai about Shyam, now that everything was over between them. She thought of him with mounting embarrassment. How could she have let him do the things he had done with her? Shyam had wept and threatened to commit suicide when he heard of her plans to shift to Delhi — *'Chandi ki deevar na todi, pyaar bhara dil tod diya'*. 'A silver wall hasn't been broken, but a heart full of love has', he proclaimed in filmy style. His world was the shrill music of cinema, its cloying emotions, its sentimentality. He was beautiful like those lies, his chin had the tilt, his hair had a puff. She had loved him for it, but the aftertaste was bitter. Minka had pointed out the cheapness of his attire, the meanness of his conversation. But where was Bhai? Where was he? Bhai had gone away to Mussoorie, to Minka, to the mountains. She would go away too. To Delhi, and to do an M.Phil.

Death

The fourth summons from Delhi. My husband's impatient voice on the phone, early in the morning at half-rate trunk call billing, 'Have you gone mad? You said three days, it's already a week. What about the children? The younger one has a cold.'

I made pacifying noises, promising to take the train that evening. I had not slept all night; my head was hammering with pain, but finally, it was all over, even for me.

I had been unable to leave Ajmer until then. I felt there was something that Mayank and Rajat wanted to say to me. Finally, last evening they told me their conclusion to Rajni's story.

I was sitting by the well in which Rajni had drowned, staring a long while at the dark waters which refused to yield a recognizable reflection. Suddenly Minka darted out from the thickets and caught hold of my hands.

'Oh, it's not safe. You are too close to the edge.' She let go of me, embarrassed.

We walked back to the house uneasily. Minka had been unforthcoming to the point of rudeness in the beginning. No, she couldn't see why anybody should work on a collection of Rajni's poetry. No, she wasn't ready to talk about it yet. Nevertheless, at every lull in the conversation she would reach out desperately to me. If I was that keen, could we talk about it after lunch? Perhaps Rajat would know better.

We had been through Minka's varying moods. Rudeness would be followed by an extremely repentant gentleness.

That evening for the first time she voiced the name we had deliberately avoided the whole week.

'How do you know Riaz Ratnakar?' she asked after we returned from the garden.

Rajat raised a drawn face from the newspaper he was reading and looked directly at me for the first time.

'He's married to a very good friend of mine', I replied.

'I didn't know he was married', he said.

'It's a bit of a non-marriage. Anita lives in Atlanta.'

'You know about them?' Minka asked.

She meant Riaz and Rajni. 'I know Rajni and he were friends. He is very upset.'

Rajat closed his eyes in pain. 'Damn these guys.' He got up and went out of the room.

'I want her poems to be published', Minka said suddenly. 'I also want that man to cry, to suffer all his life.'

Which man did she mean? Brother, husband or the desired lover?

'Who?'

'Riaz, of course.'

She was trembling. 'I sent him that notebook, so that he should be upset, I want him to be further upset. Tell him, tell him Rajni was pregnant when she died.'

Minka didn't look at me. Still sobbing, she said, 'The autopsy showed the foetus to be fifteen days. Sunil had been in America for a month. Luckily, we realized what was wrong before showing the report to her in-laws. Rajat got it changed.'

Rajni gift-wrapped herself for Riaz many times. Of course he was honest enough to warn her off. He told her he did not see the man-woman relationship in conventional terms. She knew he meant Farzana and Anita; she knew he meant he did not see relationships as personal property. But she could not believe that she was not being possessed when every molecule of her being was crying out for his ownership;

she could not believe that something similar was not happening to him. She lived many lifetimes in the precious minutes they spent together. She couldn't let go. He kept telling her that there was no future in the relationship. He was being scrupulously honest when he decided to show instead of tell.

'There is a party next week at a friend's place. Would you like to come?'

She would have gone to the end of the world if he had asked her.

'Yes', she replied.

'Let me warn you, these parties tend to get a bit wild. Sarosh the host is well meaning but he is young.'

'Who's coming? Do I know any of them?'

'I don't suppose so. You might have heard of Jasvinder, the artist, and Farzana.'

'I've heard of Farzana . . . ' she said angrily.

'No doubt you've attended her concerts and listened spellbound to her.'

'Yes.'

He laughed a little before dipping his kebab in sauce.

'M'm. I taste green mint here.'

She went to the party after an elaborate construction of deceit. She was going to Kalpana's birthday party and would spend the night there if it got late. Luckily Kalpana was not on the phone and lived too far away, in the university campus, for anybody to call her bluff.

Riaz's car was old and battered. But she felt like a princess being charioted to a ball. As they approached the long driveway she extended her hand slowly towards him, he pressed it lightly before turning back to grapple with the gears.

The house seemed huge. The room they were shown into had several levels of flooring, all in gleaming marble the like of which she had never seen before. An onyx fountain in one corner spewed droplets of water. In another corner stood a marble nymph-like figure with wings.

'Obscene, isn't it?' said Riaz in her ear. 'Sarosh unfortunately has rather garish taste.'

Sarosh turned out to be a very young man — to her fevered imagination he seemed to be in his teens. His hair, tied in a pigtail, was plastered to his scalp with a lot of jell. He put his arms around Riaz and kissed him on both cheeks. She braced herself for a similar greeting but he just said a casual hi and moved on.

There were already a lot of people moving around in the room. Riaz introduced her to some, but the faces seemed to merge into each other. His world, that's the only name she could put to it. She had met a few of them before, at rallies and meetings.

'So, you decided to put in an appearance, after all', she heard him say. She turned around and saw a porcelain-perfect face looking at her.

'Rajni meet Farzana.'

Farzana was small. She wore an embroidered salwar kameez. Her shoulder-length hair was tied loosely into a bun. She had kajal in her large eyes and wore a kumkum bindi. Rajni in a green tussar sari and pearls at once began to feel overdressed.

'Hi, so you are the famous Rajni.'

'I'm Rajni. I'm not so sure about the adjective.'

'She's famous for her yet unpublished magnum opus', put in Riaz. 'What will you two drink?'

He handed them their glasses and was suddenly besieged by three young men who had problems, they said, about the next venture of MFS.

Rajni was distracted by a venerable-looking man whispering in her ear.

'Who are you, beautiful?' He had a white beard and a shock of silver hair. He wore a shocking-pink kurta.

'I am green mint chutney on sizzling toast', she heard herself say.

He laughed. 'And I am Candy-floss and Ice Cream. Why aren't you drinking?'

She emptied her glass in a gulp. She was stone sober.

'I need liquidifying.'

'What are you saying? Do you need to pee?' he asked, guffawing at his own joke.

'No', she pointed to her glass.

'Okay, Chutney.'

Riaz was rid of the three doubters now. He was with Farzana. He was sitting on the stepped floor, on a higher level than her. They seemed to be arguing. She suddenly raised her face up to his and he lightly traced a line on her cheek with his finger. He was laughing.

'Your drink', said Candy-floss. Rajni took it from him hoping he would move away. It was getting late.

'When is dinner? I'm starved.'

'Oh, there isn't any, honey. There is that, though.'

He pointed towards a group of gaudily dressed women who had just entered.

'Who are they?'

'Who do you think — baijis from the bazaar, of course.'

'My god. Have they been invited — were they asked to come?'

'Yes, paid heavily, I suppose.'

The women were in their Sunday best. Cheap nylon saris with imitation zari, large artificial jewellery, red and pink lipsticks. Their breasts thrust out from their bodies, painfully pointed. They settled down in the middle of the hall and began tuning their harmonium and tablas.

People were settling down wherever they were to watch the performance. Farzana was sitting next to Riaz with an arm on his shoulder, looking on frowningly.

The nylon of the women glinted in the half-light. Their teeth between their painted lips looked ugly and yellow.

The guttural voices began. *'Choli ke peechey kya hai, choli ke peechey'*, a film song that was weathering obscenity charges those days.

Candy-floss was looking tolerantly at them, 'The idiosyncrasy of the elite. What will we stoop to next?'

'I hate it', Rajni said vehemently, almost in tears.

He put his arm around her, 'Ch-Ch Chutney. Don't react so violently, one can see it as fun.'

'These women are being made to look so cheap.'

'It is their business to be cheap. Look, we are only providing them clean business.'

The audience was getting raunchy. Quite a few were singing along with the women. A couple of men were dancing. She couldn't see Riaz and Farzana anywhere.

Candy-floss's hand was stroking her arm. She saw Riaz flitting by, balancing a couple of drinks.

'Hi, enjoying yourself?'

'Yes', she said, her spirits rising at the sight of his face. It seemed to be all right, good fun. She gulped down her drink.

'Have you seen Sarosh's collection of miniatures?' asked Candy-floss.

'No', she said distractedly. Riaz was with Farzana again. It was a party. Why was she behaving like a jealous wife?

'Come, let me show you. That will calm you down.' Candy-floss's hand, dangerously near her breast, was pushing her towards the staircase. From the steps she saw Riaz bending towards Farzana. Perhaps he was kissing her. She felt a thousand explosions in her head.

The women were singing a resilient film song, *'Ja re ja o harjai'*.

'You are very attractive, Chutney. Won't you tell me your name?'

She knew what was happening. Would you like to see my etchings paintings miniatures? Candy-floss's hand was on her bare back hurrying her.

'No, my name has nothing to do with it.'

The room they walked into was not lit. They did not try to find the light. Candy-floss's breath smelt of stinking drains. His hands roughly parted her thighs even before her sari could come off totally.

His finger felt broad and callous within her. He squeezed her breasts relentlessly. 'You sexy bitch.'

She felt the rough pile of the carpet like sandpaper on her back. She panicked and tried to push him off. He pinned her arms to the floor and bit her hard on the neck, making her scream. 'Come on, don't tease.' All at once, he was inside her, with his weight squarely on her. She turned her face to the side and breathed in dust. Her mouth opened again to scream louder but his hand covered it.

'You're a hot number, aren't you?'

When she thought it was over, he made her turn. Waves of pain shot through her as he attacked her behind. She whimpered into the carpet, too tired to cry out.

Was it rape by an unknown man that killed her?

She died fifteen days after the party.

And it was death by drowning.

The desert-sun was parching Rajni and the water of the well beckoned. Why not? She could never escape. She jumped in almost as a challenge.

But women like her have no right to be profligate. Only the prudence of desiring the occasional oasis is permitted them. When the water invaded her inner spaces she thrashed around and screamed. She clawed at the slippery walls of the well. Nobody heard her cries for help. Time slipped out from her agonized hands.

Part Two

The Writer in the Future

The construction of the temple at Nizamuddin used a technique which is centuries old — dating back to the Vaastu shastras, which in turn are about the science of magic in architecture — we had been told. Somewhere in these shastras it is said that certain combinations of metal, being cleansing or purifying in nature, bring about prosperity. As prosperity is an obsession in Raminland, the pre-existing Dargah and mosque were 'wrapped' in an auspicious eight-metal alloy with the help of the most expensive foreign technology to cleanse them of their history. This modern 'temple' was then dedicated to Poornaramin — the God of good living — who is responsible for all this anyway.

Another Rajni

I turned a hundred and one years old yesterday. Once again I am sitting in front of a pure screen trying to find words to start my fifteenth novel. Gross wastage of technology! What I have is a state-of-the-art multi-screen that at the touch of a button can become a window to the world. It is a videophone cum television cum computer. But I use it stubbornly only as a mirror, inscribing in it images from the self.

There are images still waiting to quicken in my womb.

Once there was Rajni. That was long back: when the world was without God, without Poornaramin, without Sadhoos. There was Rajni when this sweet-smelling city was a whore called Delhi with a malodorous breath and lungs choked with soot.

Rajni means night: I have her in a book.

But a Rajni persists in this saffron age, in this holy city of Rajdhani that was saved for some of us — the Ramins — by Poornaramin. Rajni came to me on my birthday last year. This story that holds a mirror to the hundredth year of my life is about her.

Last year when I turned a hundred, in accordance with the law — Ardhangini-law that applies to married women — the state revoked my widowhood. I was given charge once again of my wardrobe which had been entrusted to my sons after the demise of my husband. My jewellery, now worth several crores, was also restored to me. The ceremony is called 'the gift of the past'.

Rajni came that very morning. It seemed like a divine visitation although she must have been around for some months, living just a few yards away from me. But that day birds burst into song and my flat was suffused with a pale green light.

That was my call-bell, a simple affair compared to the contraptions that other Ramins have in their homes. One of my grandsons has a robot that goes from room to room saying, 'Somebody to see you', in English, German and Japanese. Of course, most Ramins speak only English. Officially everybody is supposed to know Raminlingo as well, but the younger generation — the one thrice removed from me I mean — speaks only a kind of English when it uses words at all.

Jagdamba, my dasi, came in. 'Madam, the parivar is here.' My entire extended family had come visiting as though there was a death. I hadn't received them together like this in my flat for years. Had the past been this eventful I would surely have ceased earlier. I at once began to suspect that my grandsons had come to find out what I was planning to do with my jewellery and clothes. I thought with dread of my sons. Had they come too? I hated to see them old: with grafted artificial skin and hair; faces shining like those of plastic dolls.

I asked Jagdamba where she had seated them.

'The men in the drawing-room, women and children in the guest-room, Madam', she replied, sounding uncharacteristically subservient.

I entered the drawing room with my head bowed. All the men clasped their hands in greeting. My eldest son was looking incredibly pink. Memories began to flow: did he remember anything of his childhood? He was eight and the process of cleansing the country was going on. His school was declared anti-Ramin and attacked. I thought of his coming home that day and vomiting in the washbasin, again and again. He had high fever after that for almost a month. He had babbled and been in a coma. Torn blood . . . no, ma'am, only English . . .

'Ma,' he said, formal and distant, 'the parivar pays its homage to you. The gift of the past.'

He came closer and draped a red stole embroidered with gold around my shoulders. His fingers barely brushed against me. My eldest, who I had nursed for three years.

I bowed further, wondering why the ceremony needed to be performed with such fanfare.

'You have made us what we are', said my grandson, the one who goes to the U.S. every week with his wife to watch blue films publicly in a theatre.

I felt tears rise in my eyes. I wish they wouldn't talk about my life. I didn't want their review, their reading. I had existed, fulfilled a promise I had made to myself years ago, hadn't I? Yes, I would grit my teeth and write on. I hadn't done anything else besides that. It wasn't my doing — all this.

'We want your blessings', said a grandson who works in a liaison firm and spends every single evening attending parties hosted for or by Business. Most of my family is professional: middlemen, chartered accountants and company secretaries — professions that are respected — careers that have been planned and executed with care. The eldest son pulled off a coup by getting his son into the Sadhoo Math — the training school for politicians. With this connection in the government the fortunes of the family rose further and placement in the choicest sectors for all its members became fairly simple. That boy is now Controller of the South Rajdhani Temples. He is the only one who does not live in the family-colony. His kutir is in one of the temple compounds. He wasn't there that day. Had he been, I would have had to get up and curve my spine like a bow to seek his blessings.

There are others in the family who are also upwardly mobile. I hear that my second son's grandson is engaged to a girl in whose family a sati was performed five years ago. People say the sati, the girl's aunt, was mentally deranged, so thought nothing of signing the Satibond: this is to certify that Mahasat has descended on me and I undertake to ascend to heaven with my husband. Nobody is to be held accountable . . . etc.,

etc. Sati leads to instant wealth for the family concerned because they can immediately build a temple after her. It is still considered a nouveau riche device, a solid Sadhoo is much better.

'My blessings are always with you', I said. 'Where are my Ginis?' Gini, the abbreviation for Ardhangini, is a word that still sticks in my throat a bit.

One of my grandsons led me into the guest room. My spirits lifted in spite of me. How beautiful the Ardhanginis were! Shapely necks and arms emerged out of the pinks, blues, reds, yellows. Had married women always been like this? I knew there is a process called Fair and Lovely Transformation in vogue. It is, however, expensive and has to start pretty early in life. When the girl is eight she is given a series of injections and then there is a fairly complicated skin-grafting involved. It takes ten years. But it seems Ramins are going in for it fairly widely. I suppose it is cheaper than maintaining unmarried women at home or training them for a profession.

'Oh, Ma', said a young woman in a yellow dress flecked with gold dust, suddenly. She was wearing a big diamond-bindi on her forehead, 'Ma, we are so proud of you. They announced your gift of the past at the grooming school also.'

I wondered why this Gini was still at school as the self-grooming degree is usually attained before marriage. If she needed further education, she should have moved up to one of the Ardhangini courses in training colleges for married women by now. As if reading my thoughts an incredibly beautiful woman — obviously her mother-in-law — said, 'The parivar was not satisfied with the grooming course she had done in Kanpur, so we enrolled her again, here in Rajdhani. Can you imagine, the degree there had only one Diet and Slimming course!'

The mother-in-law was wearing a blue sleeveless choli. Her arms looked like those of a twenty-year-old. She must be at least forty if she has a daughter-in-law. But I knew she could be younger, as girls are being married off very young, these days. She could also be under one of those 'Young

Forever' or 'Apsara at Fifty' treatments. I wondered how these women manage to look so happy despite the constant threat of needles that they live with. The courageous sex.

'Ma,' said another woman, 'we will look forward to having you over for the KC ceremony.'

I realized that, as I had been released from the solitude of widowhood, I would be expected to move my old bones again for fasts and ceremonies. I would probably have to take part in engagement rituals and even the process of selecting girls for my numerous male descendents. This doesn't sound like work, but one is lucky if a single marriage proposal is finalized in two years. It is the job of the Ardhanginis to do it all: right from getting the horoscopes matched to computing the dowry and the jewellery, and scanning the calendar for auspicious days. Even with the most advanced software, it takes months. So much has to be fed in: name, age, preferences, habits, date of attaining puberty; so much data has to be obtained: compatibility, profile of progeny, post-menopausal adjustments; and every suitable boy receives at least a hundred proposals.

I began to think of the section on Ardhangini-law in the manifesto of the Sadhoos that had created so much controversy earlier in the century. It began with 'Where women are honoured there the Gods rejoice, but where they are not honoured, there all rites are fruitless.' Tradition had been the war-cry of the Sadhoos. The ideal religious state that they proposed would set itself the task of restoring the dignity that women had lost 'due to the mindless process of westernization and secularization unleashed in the preceding era'. Women are the bedrock of family and religion, they had asserted. Those who chose to marry and propagate the race should be compensated for it. On the other hand, women who want to work outside the home should be released from household responsibilities; our tradition has place for both Ardhanginis and Sadhvis.

The logic was impeccable — many women's improvement groups hailed it — yet I had felt incapacitated when I relinquished my teaching job to balance home and children.

The women were chattering among themselves. So many seemed to have shrill voices, though most must have been trained in music. While training for a future as an Ardhangini every girl receives some education in the arts: music, dance and painting in the grooming schools. The Sadhoos have been very vigilant about preserving our golden heritage.

The mother-in-law of the 'unfinished' Gini had moved closer to me. I felt a wave of perfume besiege my senses; I couldn't think any more.

'Can you believe it Ma,' she whispered, 'Rajni has hardly had any training in flower-arrangement.'

Rajni, the name caught fire and began to burn between us. My past was catching up with me. Rajni ! 'Gini', I admonished her, as was probably expected of me. I was shaken by the coincidence. It was as though I was living in a badly crafted thriller. Nevertheless, I droned on, 'Shouldn't you have checked all this before the marriage?'

'Oh, Ma,' she said, tears filling her eyes, 'my husband — your grandson — is to blame.'

'Child, this is the responsibility of Ardhanginis.'

'I know that, Ma. I told him I didn't want a girl who is accomplished enough to take my son away entirely from me. So he found this one who is so un . . . '

'You mean he spared the time to go and see a prospective bride for his son?'

'And Ma, he insisted. Rajni's mother died when she was four or something. She was brought up mainly by men, her father and her brother. Her father and your grandson are very good friends.'

'Was the dowry adequate?'

'That was about the only thing that was adequate, Ma. The alliance has been such a shock to me. The family barely meets our social standards and then this girl — she's almost wild.'

'Gini, with you in charge of her education, I at least have no fears for the future. Just take her under your wing. You have done right to enrol her in the self-grooming course.'

'Ma, my son is spending a fortune on her. He has even appointed a fashion designer to supervise her wardrobe. You should have seen the kinds of things she used to wear when there was merely a vastra-dasi to help her. And Ma, she actually talks to the servants — long conversations.'

'This is worrying, but nothing that cannot be remedied. But tell me, what has she done for eighteen years? She must know something.'

'Ma, I blush to tell you. The child was allowed to fritter away all her energy on music. Your grandson was captivated by her singing. In vain did I tell him that if he wants to listen to music, he can go to a show. I jokingly even said that I would employ a music-dasa or dasi to sing to him all day and night. He needn't make a girl his daughter-in-law just because she's been allowed to neglect all her essential education in order to learn singing.'

Laughter began to bubble inside me. This obsession with music must have been a calamity! Didn't my grandson know that a suitable wife is as important as a foreign degree in the corporate world? Interpersonal relations are the business of Ardhanginis, and one of the reasons why Ramin boys are successful internationally is that their entire households are dedicated to furthering their professional lives.

I looked at Rajni who had moved away. She was watching us. Her expression was weary, too weary for the face it sat on. The face was young like all the others around me, not exceptionally pretty; but it seemed tired of trying to look good. Her mascara too had smudged a bit. She saw me staring at her and moved away further.

The Gift of the Past

That night a spectre called Rajni watched over me as I tossed and turned in bed. I got up and began pacing up and down the flat.

The Dasas sent by my eldest son had already arranged the six steel almirahs containing my Ardhangini possessions in a row in the spare room.

The green almirah had a mirror, chipped and yellowing with age, on its door. I looked into it without interest. The image that looked back with equal lack of interest seemed to have sepia tints in it, like an old, forgotten photograph. I saw an upright figure, so thin that it was a white fissure in its surroundings. The face with its white, papery skin and eyes of indeterminate colour seemed to be an equal absence.

The almirah opened with a loud creak. I fitted the key in the locker and turned it with some difficulty. It was full of little boxes and velvet pouches. There seemed to be hundreds of them, tightly packed. I loosened out a little box. The red velvet lining held a ring, a large dark-blue sapphire set against tiny, glittering diamonds. My engagement ring.

The second box contained another ring — tiny rubies. Too tiny; they looked rather cheap. The third pouch held a black-and-gold bead necklace.

And then I was turning another key expertly, with a little pressure towards the left. I knew exactly what I was looking for. The locker had a secret compartment which slid open without a creak. I took out the plastic file from it. No moisture had got in. What was this? Having found what I was looking for I was at a loss. Papers. Why had I kept them here? And why had I, zombie-like, gone through the motions of unlocking a skeleton from my cupboard?

I turned on the reading light and leafed through the papers. A citation from the Department of Culture for the best instructive fiction of the year and some reviews! They were all concerning Rajni. Some papers fell out. As I put them together again I saw a little square of ivory against the newsprint. It was a short hand-written note:

> Dear Shrimati Roy,
>
> Congratulations. Thanks for sending me your award-winning book *Rajni: The True Story of the Secularists.* It is very different from the MS I had seen, which if I remember right was called *Rajni: A Love Story.*
>
> I don't think the aftermath of the present events is going to be easy for any of us. If Rajni is your way of survival, good luck with it and other similar writing.
>
> I am afraid I no longer have any place to keep books. So I am sending yours back to you.
>
> Goodbye.
>
> Omar

Omar — yes Omar Onkar — on a beautiful winter night when the moon rose suddenly in the sky, his hair was shining blue.

Almost involuntarily, I began to mumble some Urdu poetry, '*Yeh na thi hamari kismat ki visale yaar hota.*' I felt something unfamiliar rustling within myself: a desire to reach out to a figure with blue hair.

Suddenly, a pain arose as though from the heart: blue hair — people don't have blue hair unless they dye it that colour. Blue hair — that was in the novella he had referred to in that note. I was thinking of Riaz in *Rajni.*

A scab fell off and revealed the scar — still red and tender after fifty-seven years. The publication of *Rajni* in the midst of political turbulence had dealt me many blows. It was because of the way the book was read at the time.

It was quickly established that Riaz was Omar, and as no woman associated with him had died of love, Rajni was me, and the love-affair ours. It was Omar, the Secularist rebel, that the press was interested in, so I was absolved of a role in the matter; but then I was divested of my own personality as well. It became a game. It was as though I was tied across a rotating board at which they aimed their arrows. The board rotated till I was phased out and only my outline remained as a testimonial to the blindfolded marksmen's skill.

I flipped through the reviews of *Rajni*: 'Politics of Writing', 'Truth and Fiction', 'In the Name of Fiction'.

> I need to state my belief at the beginning, especially as the review I am writing is that of a novella that teeters on the brink of kiss-n'-tell; in which a much respected academic Omar Onkar transparently called Riaz Ratnakar, has been portrayed as a playboy. For some of us Omar Onkar is synonymous with a modern day David who is struggling with the U.S. fattened Sadhoo regime of Raminland. It is an impertinent struggle, even a foolish struggle but my metaphor is . . .
>
> The ascribing of libertine sexual mores to a real life activist in the secular movement is a master stroke of libellous writing. The fortuitous connection established in *Rajni* between secularism and libertinism, is making use of the popular conception of secularists as being 'totally westernized' and by that definition out of touch with 'the real India'.

And

> In my view *Rajni* comes across as a strong political statement only because it is written like a personal allegory. The fictional Rajni is cast as the mirror image of the writer's own self.

My mirror image: Rajni? She was a mother of three daughters and fell in love disastrously with the blue-haired Professor.

I walked to the mirror and stared at it.

I reached out to touch myself and encountered cold glass.

I almost wept again. Rajni had become me, even for myself.

It had started with the miracle many years ago. The coming of Poornaramin jolted my world of fiction to life.

I kept protesting about the difference between fiction and reality, but in a world overcome by miraculous images who would listen? I could only watch as images — my own and others — strode over my life.

The Miracle

Lulled by the even pace of time after the Masjid event, nobody was paying much attention to the forebodings of the Secularists. The little beliefs in quaint images, the story-telling by politicians, had always been a part of the charm of this age-old country. There are other weightier issues to grapple with — like corruption in public life, everybody said. But that was before the fifteenth general elections.

The party that claimed to represent the 'majority' community in the country was returned to Parliament as the single largest one. However, a coalition government had to be formed as a clear majority eluded it. General unease followed. It's saffron P.M. was besieged by too many shades of grey.

Another bomb-blast at Lajpat Nagar. Delhi trembled with indignation. What is happening to law and order? Do we have a government? screeched the headlines in the largest-selling English-language newspaper of the country. The photograph below showed charred remains of what was once a car and a child once studying in class 5 D of a public school in Delhi. Fifth bomb-blast of the month, twentieth of the year. The authorities knew that the list of names claiming responsibility for the incident would grow as the days passed. Past experience had shown that the gorier the incident, the longer the list of claimants.

He threw the newspaper across the room. It didn't matter!

'We have traced the bomb, sir.'

'Yes?'

'To the Nizamuddin basti, sir.'

It was what they had expected. The little by-lanes of the basti harboured a network of criminals. He studied the smiling face of his deputy carefully: it mirrored the expectations of his party. As the leader of the political party that represented the 'majority' Hindu community, he was expected to welcome conclusive proof of 'minority' Muslim terrorism. This incident would provide further reason to chastise earlier governments with the charge of pampering the 'minorities' and making Frankensteins out of them. The deputy smiled because he was confident that this government wouldn't behave like the earlier governments. The earlier governments had sold themselves to the 'minorities' for electoral gain. For example, even though a fully flourishing sex-racket, including the making and distribution of blue-films, had been unearthed at the Khadim Mohalla around the Ajmer Dargah, previous governments had not moved to punish the culprits. The case was scuttled lest it assume communal overtones: the victims of the lust — tender young girls blackmailed into prostitution — were all Hindus, the culprits all Muslims. Their party was 'fearless' in such matters. His deputy expected him to send the armed forces into Nizamuddin and cleanse it of anti-social elements. He wanted him to act as the defender of the masses.

'Bury the report.'

'What?'

'Bury the report, I said.'

'I don't understand, sir.'

'The government is going to be silent. The press release should say that we are making all efforts to trace the criminals.'

'It would be impossible to prevent a leak to the press.'

'We are not responsible for what the newspapers choose to say and it is their duty to report their findings. I am talking about the official press release.'

'The elections are round the corner.'

'Exactly!'

'People expect us to act.'

'Tell me, once this report is made officially public what course will be left open to us?'

'Armed forces.'

'Armed forces in a religious place? Killing of priests? Alienation of a whole community?'

'It has happened before.'

'Yes, and we must learn from the past.'

'It's a no-win situation, sir. We are already being blamed for the collapse of law and order.'

'You've forgotten the Gita, haven't you?'

'The Gita?'

'Yes. Didn't Krishna say to Arjun before the battle, 'O Son of Kunti, whatever you do, whatever you eat, whatever you offer as oblation to the sacred fire, whatever you bestow as a gift, whatever you do by way of sacrifice, offer it all to Me?'

'Does that mean you are going to leave everything to God?'

'Of course! The press release should also say that the Prime Minister is going to pray for the country. I want the puja at the Ramappa temple covered by every scribe and camera in the world.'

The deputy emerged from the room convinced that the octogenarian had at last lost his mind.

It was a miracle. Millions witnessed it! Thousands recorded it for posterity. Foreign newsmagazines would put it on the cover.

At eleven minutes past eleven in the morning the Prime Minister prayed at the ancient Ramappa temple at Warangal. The twelfth-century Nandi bull carved out of black granite accepted milk from the ageing politician's hands. As the stone statue sucked milk drop by drop the world quaked with India as its epicentre.

Trunk lines jammed with messages about similar phenomenon being experienced by Indians all over the world. All over the world — in Minnesota, Helsinki and Melbourne — the devout made offerings of milk to idols.

The queues got longer and longer at temples and milk-booths all over the country. Will the god accept baby-food? Will the god accept dairy-whitener?

Banks, post-offices, schools and colleges closed down in the middle of the day. Nobody remained at the counters, nobody in classrooms.

Milkmen in remote towns had a field day adding cups of milk to buckets of water and selling them at double the normal price of milk.

The gods were indulgent. They drank up everything that was white and full of faith.

For seven days and seven nights there was a virtual holiday in the country. The 'masses' spoke about it in hushed whispers. The liberal intelligentsia spoke about the need for faith.

When a scientist challenged this orgy of milk drinking, he was assaulted by his lab assistants. When a lecturer spoke in a derogatory way about the gullible illiterate, her students walked out of the classroom.

The country was gearing up for something momentous. If stone is imbued with life in broad daylight, it can only be for something spectacular.

After seven days and seven nights, the miracle ceased abruptly.

It is said that they went there because they heard a voice from the sky asking them to do so. Three priests from three temples of Delhi witnessed the rebirth of Poornaramin in the Nizamuddin Dargah, at eleven minutes past eleven at night. 'I am Poornaramin. You who believe will henceforth be called Ramins. The time has come to assert yourselves by assuming my name. The time has come to drive away the traitors who have eaten of this land and betrayed it. You will see me everywhere in this new country, which is also thousands of years old. For Ramins, this country was mine then as it is now', said the voice, and the rest is the history of Raminland.

In the mid-term elections that followed the party of the 'majority' under the new leadership of the saffron-clad Sadhoos swept the polls with an unprecedented majority.

Unravelling the past is difficult for me. Memories begin to flow like pus and blood from an open wound. But that's how Rajni became me and started to live again.

I won't try to staunch this flow. I won't try to get back to my routine of breathing-eating-shitting-writing that I have ritualistically followed in my little flat for so many years.

Why does it pain so? Has my past putrefied in this purified city?

She is a whore who has been used by conquerors through the ages. On her body are the festering sores of disease. Her breath is malodorous, her lungs choked with soot. She will have to undergo purification by fire. Our Rajdhani will be born out of the ashes of this fallen woman called Delhi.

The first Chief Sadhoo's eyes pierced through to our very souls as he addressed the nation on-screen. There was the chanting of incantations and the visual of bulldozers in the background.

We will step back centuries to conquer the twenty-first century. We will restore the health and purity of Delhi. She will become the ideal city-mother who will generate dreams for the rest of the country. She is special for us because our God Poornaramin appeared in her lap. He arose like a lotus from her filth and squalor.

There was sandstone dust in the air as the central monument of shame — the canopy of King George at India Gate — collapsed. The saffron of the robes of the Sadhoos mingled with the pale dust. The triumphant incantations became deafening. It was like dawn.

There was a surge of hope in the country. How do I remember hope? As the rustle of the early morning breeze and the wails of an infant. I had given birth to my third son that very year. The stickiness of fecundity — the oozing. I had felt like a laden fruit tree, so I bent in deference to the breeze. The same breeze played with the bright red borders of my silk sari and pulled at the flame of the sacred havan-fire when my son and the country were being named.

Ram-Ram Ramin-Raminland.

Raminland, the country, after Poornaramin, the God who descended to save this land; and Ram, an icon, who was recast in the glory of the old-new Poornaramin. His name remained, because thousands born in the year of Poornaramin were called Ram. My son was named Ram too, because Poornaramin is not a name that you give to fallible infants. It brings bad luck.

In the new Constitution society was divided according to generational karma, in accordance with the international standards of environmental viability, and with deep compassion into three segments: Ramins, or those who serve the state of Poornaramin; Dasas, or those who help and assist the Ramins; and Drohis, or those who rebelled but have been pardoned by Poornaramin.

Even more red was spilt in formulating these definitions than had gone into making the government of the Sadhoos. Heavy concessions and privileges made over to Dasa dons to ensure that they accept Dasahood for their community, at last settled the issue. It became a very white country — very pure but pale and anaemic.

The Woman-writer at the Mushairah

Giving concessions to the Dasas did not prove to be a popular measure for the Sadhoos, as far as the press was concerned. The government began to be blamed for being weak and ineffectual. How is this regime better than the preceding ones? journalists began to ask. The saffron needed to be rejuvenated; the government needed to woo the articulate classes once again.

Six months before the sixteenth general elections the Chief Sadhoo decreed a temple at Nizamuddin — the birth-place of Poornaramin. 'The idol of Poornaramin will be established at the very same spot where He descended', he declared forcefully. He did not add that the holy spot was just inches away from the grave of the Auliya in the Dargah.

The Secularists, led by Omar Onkar, rose to the bait. 'That spot is holy', they screeched, 'especially to the Muslims.'

The Sadhoos explained their position very patiently. 'The construction of the temple dedicated to the patron deity of the country is certainly not intended as an insult to religion. The Dargah and the Mosque will not be disturbed; the graves will also remain. The temple, like the Ramin religion, will embrace the faith of the minorities. A few unimportant structures like Ghalib's grave, though, might have to be demolished for considerations of space.'

'How can the Sadhoos even suggest the destruction of the grave of a great poet? Is the construction of a temple so important?'

'What is more important — religion or poetry?' shot back

the Sadhoos. 'Have these westernized Secularists forgotten what religion means to the average citizen of Raminland?'

As the Secularists became more high-pitched in their protest and Nizamuddin, Ghalib and Omar Onkar hit the headlines, the publisher who had been dilly-dallying for four long years over my manuscript brought out *Rajni* in hardback, changing the subtitle to *The True Story of the Secularists*. True story! I was aghast; I denied it vehemently. Though, of course, I had taken off from reality; doesn't every writer deal with reality in creation? I was a member of the secular movement and a political activist at the time; so was Omar. But I had soared so far from facts in my book that Riaz's resemblance to Omar and Rajni's to me had not even been in my mind when I submitted the manuscript for publication. Riaz Ratnakar had assumed a life of his own. Omar didn't teach Urdu, knew next to nothing about Ghalib and was unmarried. There were in fact several movements and Omar and I didn't even belong to the same group. Unlike Rajni, I had a job. I had sons, not daughters. Oh, I could go on — I had gone on, but to no avail. I did not sound convincing. The horizon for a writer is where reality ends and imagination begins, and I was achingly aware that *Rajni* was written when all boundaries blur, by the light of the stars, as far as my feelings for Omar were concerned.

Besides, the publicity for the book was magnificent. The sexual proclivities of Omar, his permissive lifestyle, were discussed in every gossip column. My photographs in some papers were even captioned 'Rajni'. My denials that were tucked away in 'Letters to the Editor' and 'Rejoinder' columns were easily overlooked.

Delighted by the controversy, the Ministry of Culture awarded the newly instituted honour of 'the best instructive fiction of the year' to *Rajni*. The citation said, 'Heartrending and poignant, this courageous novella depicts the destructive potential of feminine passion imperfectly confined by domesticity. Set in PrePoornaramin Raminland in the turbulent 1990s, it also exposes, through the sensibility of the misled woman, confusions generated in a society with a layered, multi-cultural past, when it is confronted by the simplistic agenda of secularism.'

There was an uproar from the Secularists. Former friends cut me dead. The award was official confirmation of their feeling that I had betrayed the movement.

I tried to explain my political position in various ways. I even sent the book to Omar hoping he would write something to justify my stand that Rajni is not an apology for religion and tradition. He returned the book to me and said nothing in print.

There was more. Just when the controversy was getting out of hand, my huband died. The last drops of colour were expunged from my life. I had to keep away my red-bordered saris, my sindoor, my rubies. From an Ardhangini-wife I was relegated to being a widow clad in white. I felt inertia in my bones, like the weariness that follows after giving birth, when the baby is taken away by the nurse.

In legend there is a tapasvi who sat in penance for so long that he began to look like an anthill and his embarrassingly tortured body couldn't be seen by anybody. My family consecrated me soon after as that anthill of a tapasvi, so that my book could be treated like encrustations of earth on a dead-still body. From my study I could hear them, 'She is a tapasvini, writing selflessly in penance', they said. It was in the fitness of things that the widow who had written about adultery and become known for it, be invisible.

I made a last desperate foray into the world of the visible. Despite all objections I went for the fateful meeting of the Secularists at Nizamuddin. The meeting proved to be the last nail in the coffin in more ways than one. It was also the end — of my love-story. I could only see Omar from a distance. I tried to go nearer but a cloud descended and sucked him in. When he emerged much later it was in my memory — as the blue-haired Riaz for the Rajni of sighs and longings.

The whole of Nizamuddin had been purified. All the little houses and shops that formed the 'basti' had been razed to the ground. It was now the turn of Ghalib's grave. The Secularists were going on. 'Ghalib was not only a great poet but also a nationalist', they argued. They dug out evidence from his poetry and letters to prove that Ghalib was at heart a patriot. In 1857, Bahadurshah Zafar assumed the titular leadership of the Mutineers, lending to them the legitimacy of Mughal monarchy, in what came to be known as the First War of Indian Independence. Ghalib supported him intellectually; and then later wept and mourned his deposition. There were many couplets to corroborate this. How can a patriot's resting place be disturbed? the Secularists asked.

But Ghalib is an unlikely candidate for messiahship of a revolution. He was an aristocrat — liberal and tolerant. The rough and crude ways of the Mutineers had shocked him, as much as they had his sovereign. Forced to support them, jailed and blackmailed in their own court, both of them had to turn to the more refined British. Bahadurshah apologized, begged and pleaded ultimately; Ghalib wrote the *Dastanbuy*.

He himself denied being a full Mussalman; he made fun of the clergy. He kow-towed to the British; he was disloyal to his sovereign. The Sadhoos debited from his worth, figure by figure. It was easy, because Ghalib had himself fudged accounts. He had lived in the sick body of a civilization like a parasite. The *Dastanbuy* is in portions sickeningly servile: 'Readers of this book should know that I who through the strokes of my pen scatter pearls on paper, have eaten the bread and salt of the British and, from my earliest childhood, have been fed from the table of these world conquerors.' So wrote the defeated Mughal emperor's erstwhile master of verse to save his own skin, deploying his pearl-scattering pen to heap hyperbolic praise on those who were responsible for defacing the Red Fort.

But by the time of his death in 1869, Ghalib had come to grips with the enormity of the changes that had overtaken his world. What had been for him the city of good living had disappeared behind military fortifications. The courtly splendour that poets existed in had shrunk to colourless pages between covers. The guftagu of literary criticism had drowned in the fulmination of the mullahs. He died sadder and wiser.

The charges levied against him in the twenty-first century were the same as those made in the decline of his own: anti-religion, anti-nation.

How would Ghalib have responded? Undoubtedly with the same pain and wistfulness with which he regarded his own world.

Bazeechah-e-atfal hai duniya mere aage,
hota hai shab-e-roz tamasha mere aage.

A children's playgound — such is the world before me.
This spectacle unfolds day and night before me.

It is said that when the first blow was struck on his grave such a sigh emanated from the stone that it pierced the hearts of all those who heard it, and they never could be whole again.

The Secularists protested by planning a wake at Nizamuddin. Public meetings were banned in the area, but they were trying to pass off this one as a cultural event. Surprisingly, the police remained silent while leaflets about Ghalib and the cultural heritage of the country did their rounds. The Sadhoo Mahasabha merely issued a communique in the public interest about government policy. It stated that the majority government's respect for the religious sentiments of minorities was being amply borne out by the plan of the temple at Nizamuddin. No building of any religious significance was affected by it. Those who were opposing the construction of the temple were thus enemies of all religions. Some newspapers added that time and again the Secularist leaders had proved to be out of touch with faith and tradition.

It was a full-moon night. The function was to begin at eight. The open-air space was marked out by cloth-fencing.

At one end was the strangely sumptuous stage. It was covered with rugs and white sheets. There was a backrest made of huge bolsters swathed in white. Above the stage was a canopy made entirely of mogra flowers.

People began trickling in by seven thirty. Very soon the enclosure was full. Mainly, these were the old residents of Nizamuddin who had been resettled on the outskirts of the city after the descent of Poornaramin. It was a gathering of the poor and the dispossessed though there was a sprinkling of the well-dressed middle-classes within them. The faces of the dispossessed were eager. It was as if they had come seeking for solutions.

The speakers looked woefully unfit for the task. They had settled down on the stage, gravely and silently. They were lost under the extravagant canopy of a cloying sweet odour. Many poets and singers had been invited but only two turned up.

A little girl wearing a calf-length skirt with orange flowers in her hair came to the stage and joined her hands in greeting to the audience. She picked up the incense dish from the corner of the stage and placed it in front of the first speaker: an elderly man with a flowing white beard. There was a roar of applause from the audience.

The bearded man spoke slowly, 'We are gathered here to remember Ghalib and mourn the sacrilege that his memory is being subjected to.'

He went on to talk about the life of the poet in some detail.

There was a demand from the audience for his own poetry.

'My own poor verse today is about a friend who is lost — perhaps forever', the poet said and began to recite:

> In search of yourself
> You have now reached the shore
> From where no one had returned;
> No one ever returns, my friend.
> Now you too are lost forever:
> There remains but one condition of memory
> that whenever wherever

A riot occurs —
I shall remember you.

There was complete silence. Faces became sombre, eyes filled up with tears. They all understood loss. After Poornaramin, in the violent resettlement of their destinies, much had been left out. They listened, became one with the poet, with each other.

When the poem ended, the poet joined his hands and bowed his head. At first there was silence, then some people stood up and began to clap. The volume kept increasing until the whole assembly joined in. After the applause, a few hands were raised. Some questions were asked. The bearded man answered them softly. Passions seemed to be getting inflamed when the girl brought the incense dish to the second poet.

The rotund man threw up his hands dramatically and seemed to be beseeching the house, 'Why am I being sacrificed? After such poetry who would want to listen to my tuneless voice?' The mood changed. There was release — a roar of laughter, several facetious suggestions and then an expectant silence.

A Humble Question

Where a sword is, there is blood,
Where a king is, there are the ruled,
Where triumph is, someone is vanquished.

In your legend a great king,
Poornaramin from Raminland
fights many battles and wins.

A question to brother Ramins
from this podium —
tell us who lost to Poornaramin?
Who lay vanquished?
Who bled in that battle?

There were shouts of excitement. People stood up and chanted, 'Sadhoo. Sadhoo'.

The poet threw up his hands again and made a sign of a

knife slashing his throat. People were loving him. There was further applause and laughter.

He took out a hand-drum and began to sing to its beat. The word Sadhoo was mentioned several times and the names of several western countries were narrated in quick succession. The stanza ended with 'international Sadhoo'. The poet put up one hand as if to bless the gathering. People hooted with glee. The second stanza was about the sneaky internationalization of the country. Though the Sadhoo manifesto had promised swadeshi, many more multi-national companies had entered the Indian market during their rule. The stanza ended with 'international refugee'. At which the poet beat his breast and then proudly struck a pose like a model to indicate his international status.

The audience went mad with delight. They wanted more and more. The poet sang one more song and then threw up his hands again and made as if to faint.

It was then that he walked up from the audience to the stage. He had gained in stature, or so it seemed. In the magic light of the moon he seemed taller and broader than all the others around him.

His hair made a blue halo around his face as he addressed the gathering. But he seemed to be talking to himself, so soft and inward did he sound:

'A leading national daily today has spoken about the death of secularism. I come here to admit the defeat of our movement', he began.

The audience went absolutely silent.

'I even admit death but not the end of our movement. Most of all, at this moment I am reminded of *The Last Mushairah of Delhi* written by Farhatullah Baig. The book is a fictional-historical account of what might have been the last conference of the great Urdu poets under the auspices of the Mughal emperor, Bahadurshah Zafar. I am reminded of this particular work because here Farhatullah Baig resurrected the whole age of courtly splendour. Today as I address you in what literally may be the last mushairah of Delhi, I want to be as sure of resurrection through words as I am of death and defeat.

'Step by step, Farhatullah Baig recreates the preparations for the Mushairah. The details are like the nostalgic retracing of an era: as though caressing a memento of glory in the evening of ones life:

' "The entire house had been whitewashed with a mixture of lime and mica which caused the walls to glimmer. The low-lying courtyard had been so filled up as to raise it to the level of the plinth of the house. The platform was then laid out with wooden planks on which were spread cotton rugs. These in turn were covered with chandni. On all four sides of the platform was a border of expensive woollen carpets and rows of long upholstered cushions for the seated guests. There was such a profusion of chandeliers, candelabra, wall lamps, hanging lamps, Chinese lanterns and other lights that the house was converted into a veritable dome of light." And:

' "In front of the chief throne-like seat (for the presiding poet) were set two silver candle-holders with camphor-scented candles and pale green shades made in the form of the lotus flower. Each candle-holder was placed in a small water basin perfumed with kewra."

'In this magic space arrive the guests: Zauq, Momin, Ghalib. They recite their ghazals. The situation is fictional, the poets and their ghazals, real. The fictional mushairah continues all night, each poet responding as he might have to his contemporaries.

'Towards daybreak the ceremonial shama is placed in front of Ghalib. I will quote again:

'The whole atmosphere had undergone a change. It was nearing daybreak. As soon as the shama came to Mirza Ghalib, he said, "Sirs, I too will run over the keynotes and modulate my voice before singing my morning ragini."

'With these words, he read his ghazal in such captivating and moving cadences that the whole assembly was frozen into silence. His voice was full and created a feeling of wistfulness. It seemed the poet, unable to find in the mahfil a patron who could acknowledge the full worth of his words, was pleading for understanding and recognition.

'But I ascribe to Ghalib not the ghazal that Farhatullah Baig put in his mouth as the last testament, but this one:

Yeh na thi hamari kismat ki visaale yaar hota,
Agar aur jeete rehte yehi intezaar hota.
Use kaun dekh sakta, ki yaganah hai woh yakta,
Jo dui ki boo bhi hoti, to kahin duchar hota.
Yeh masayile tasawwuf, yeh tera bayaan, Ghalib,
Tujhe hum wali samajhte, jo na baadkhwaar hota.

I was not fortunate enough to meet my love,
Had I lived longer, I would only have waited longer.
Who can see him, for he is unique, incomparable;
If there were even the faintest chance of duality,
I would have surely met him somewhere.
These matters of mysticism, and this exposition of them that you give, Ghalib!
You could have been considered a mystic, if you were not given to drinking so much.

'To me this ghazal is about the necessity of dying in order to achieve the beloved or the ideal. It is about the necessity of sacrifice. It is about love — but then to me, our movement has also been about love.'

There was a sound of gunshot. Somebody screeched 'Police', another voice said 'goondas'. A cloud of whitish gas began to seep into the gathering. Omar went on.

'The only way left open after the defeat of love is to cease. I know I have to cease.I am still not sure whether my life is ripe for plucking. I console myself with the thought that certain fruit do not ripen on the tree on which they grow but, like the custard-apple, are plucked when still hard and have to be buried deep into mounds of wheat-grain to achieve the sweetness that surpasses all bloom. Like Ghalib's poetry.'

But nobody was listening any more. People were coughing,

splutttering, choking. They were trying to run from the cloud as fast as their legs would take them.

Soon he too was enveloped in the cloud.

What did he think when he stood there facing a crowd of wronged people? Did he think of his own impending martyrdom, or did he think of *Rajni?*

From the second row, fifth from the left, I watched Omar recite Ghalib's ghazal from *Rajni.* I watched; dressed in widow's weeds. I sat alone. Because of *Rajni* I had become an untouchable for the Secularists.

When he was reciting the ghazal his eyes sought mine.

I know he was feeling both: the desire for life and the need to die. He was full of love when he gave himself up. We do not think when we love.

We were all arrested and taken to prison, but my family spirited me away from there that very night. It was easy because the police was not interested in me. I was politely warned to keep quiet about having erroniously strayed into the anti-religious mob.

The newspapers reported later that an armed group of anti-social elements had tried to steal the image of Poornaramin from the makeshift temple. There was a skirmish between the devotees and the anti-socials. The police had to resort to firing, in which ten people lost their lives.

Much later it was reported that Omar Onkar was one of the ten.

The Exiled Drohis: Hameeda's Story

So the story moves on from Rajni to me, to Rajni again. In the spiral of rebirths and resurrections that threw up Raminland, deaths merely start the process of recycling. Nothing ended at the Secularist Mushairah. Omar's death widened the scope because, besides me and the blue-haired martyr, there were others who were present there. They had been exiled from their homes, dispossessed and tortured. In the course of a couple of generations they would make Rajni's love-story happen again and generate other leaders. I am thinking of Ram and Shyam, Hameeda's son and grandson.

I feel a strange kind of kinship with Hameeda — a Drohi woman. Both of us gave birth to sons called Ram after Poornaramin appeared. Moreover, his coming froze both of us in fairly uncomfortable postures for many years to come — as in the game called 'Statue' that children play: the referee calls out suddenly and everybody has to freeze in mid-movement.

To tell Hameeda's story, I must recall the time even before the Mushairah, the third day of the miracle.

Hameeda got up with a start. The clamouring bells of the temple had pulled her out of her uneasy sleep again. She sighed and looked at the sleeping form of her husband. Would normal life ever resume? She tried to settle down in bed but she felt restless.

She got up and sat near the window. The morning chant had begun at the temple. It soothed her. She tried to pull herself up. Why was she feeling so tense? They had their miracles too. Hadn't a blind man regained sight at Gharib Nawaz last year?

A car hooted right under the window and she started again. Why did this miracle feel like a slap in the face?

Their lane had become a thoroughfare since the start of the miracle. Cars, buses, scooter-rickshaws would start plying even before it was daybreak. The devout wanted to secure a place in the queue at the neighbouring temple before it became impossible. In the evening the lane stank of milk and buzzed with flies.

In fact, Rashid had told her not to step out of the house unless it was absolutely necessary. He had been quite insistent that she stay indoors. He was otherwise an extremely mild man. Her heart swelled with love. How lucky she was to have him for a husband. He cared for her, he really did. He always came back with little gifts: a mogra garland, a sweet paan. Not like other men she had heard about, who only cared about asserting their conjugal rights. But Rashid had been returning home so late the past few days. The unaccustomed loneliness was getting on her nerves. It must be the same for everyone though. Ever since the miracle started, the women of the basti had not been seen outdoors very much. The children, too, were not being sent to school. Men, on the other hand, returned late and then congregated in the lanes.

Hameeda began to pace up and down the room.

'You are up very early, Hameeda.'

'I couldn't sleep. I think I will visit Rehmata today.'

'Are you out of your mind?' Rashid screamed. 'Don't dare to step out of the house.'

'But why? After all, it's only a puja. What's it to us?'

'You want to know how it affects us? This is a conspiracy to get rid of us. Otherwise how would stone idols suddenly begin to drink milk?'

'You mean it's not a miracle?'

'You're so naive, Hameeda. Elections are round the corner. Jamaal Bhai has called a meeting of all the young men today. We have to decide on a counter strategy.'

'But what do they do want us to do?'

'Nothing. They want to kill us, dispossess us. For them we are encroachers, living off their land.'

'Only very few must be like this. There was this lady who used to give us prasaad . . . '

'Nobody's listening to the likes of the kind lady any more, Hameeda. These people we are dealing with have a definite plan.'

'Let me go to Rehmata's please. I feel frightened when left alone.'

'Oh, you poor thing. Of course you must be worried. Why didn't I think of it. Let me leave you at Jamaal bhai's. He has a large family.'

'But you'll come back early this evening, won't you?'

'Inshallah I will. Don't worry, little one.'

Hameeda was reluctant to leave. She liked living in the Nizamuddin basti even though they did not belong to these parts. She had found Rashid's parental home at Rampur much too intimidating. He belonged to a family that prided itself as the upholder of a dying tradition of Hindustani classical music. The huge family haveli with its aura of decay had hung weights upon her spirit. When Rashid decided to move to Delhi and join a party of ghazal singers, she felt liberated despite the shock and dismay displayed by the family.

Of course she knew that the status of a ghazal singer was lower than that of an Ustad, even an impecunious one, that Rashid had occupied earlier. But she also knew that he was happier here than he had ever been all his life.

They led a self-contained, private life — the kind she had never known before. There were just the two of them and there was money; there was space for desire. There was even space for Rashid's occasional bouts of depression: when he strummed his tanpura and longed for the purity of his family-music. At such times she provided the solace he required, taking over from him the responsibility for his life and art: at times by blaming herself for his volte face, at other times just letting him smother his grief in her bosom.

All this came to an end with the miracle. She was again being carted off to live with a host of people who would make demands on their time together.

Thank God it would be only for a couple of days.

It was just as well that they got out when they did, because after Poornaramin appeared there was a curfew in Nizamuddin. Rashid told her it wouldn't be safe to go back — not until after Id, at least. When she heard that she broke into tears. She missed the lime-green salwaar-kameez in her almirah. She had got it stitched to wear on Id. She cried as though her heart would break.

Leading an uneasy life in Jamaal's two-room 'quarters' Hameeda learned new words: kafir, mazhabparasta. His family was extremely devout. From their slight reserve towards her, she gathered that her husband's profession posed serious religious problems for them. Often she caught one or the other of the family stressing some point of religious etiquette quite needlessly in casual conversation.

To make up she overcompensated. With Jamaal's mother, wife and sister she offered namaaz five times a day. She fasted, prayed, did penance.

For the first time in their married life, others became the focus of her attention. As she endeared herself to the community, Rashid began to withdraw from her. This pious woman was not the one he had married. He missed the carefree PrePoornaramin days when so often he had playfully chided her for her transgressions.

Their relationship too became like those of others around them: suspended all day and coming together in silent couplings at night.

Many days passed.

In the bus, Hameeda nestled near Rashid like a wounded animal. Where were they being taken? Why had they been plucked out from their homes like this? They had been told they were being resettled. But why? What had they done? For which crime were they being herded to another enclosure?

Rashid patted her shoulder. He had a new name now: Ramesh. The child in her lap also had an unfamiliar name: Ram. They had been told that they would have to live in this country like Indians. These names that sounded so foreign to her were Indian names.

In her heart she called the baby something else; Rashid, too, called him by another name while crooning him to sleep.

'What music will you teach him?' she asked suddenly. Her heart full of misgivings, she confronted her husband. 'Are you going to teach him kafir music?'

'Of course not. There is no separate music. It's all one music — ours and theirs.'

'Don't sing ever again of their gods and goddesses. Look what they are doing to us.'

'It's not the gods, it's the people. It's people who are doing all this to us, Hameeda.'

'Then don't teach him anything at all', she said, tears running down her cheeks as she held the baby even more tightly to her bosom.

'That's all I have left to give him. Would you rather have him forget the tradition of the family?'

'No, no.'

She came closer to him for comfort. She shouldn't give him more cause for worry. He had been so anxious all these days. But in her heart she resolved to teach little Ram the difference between theirs and ours. She resolved to bring him up according to the tenets of their religion. After all, that was all she had left with her.

Life was not easy in the suburb where they had been resettled. Every morning Rashid would leave for 'the city'. He returned late at night and wearily handed over some crumpled notes to her. She didn't dare ask him what he did. His hands had developed calluses. His back often ached. In the middle of the night she would often hear him moaning. She blamed herself for his state; she was miserable. Most of the time she felt very lonely.The neighbouring tenements housed people she didn't want to know. They were rough, uncultured and ugly. Their children played in dirt all day. She, the daughter-in-law of an old and respected family, could have nothing to do with them.

She would often cry through the long, empty days. She loved Ram fiercely. The only time she struck him was when she saw him playing with the tanpura.

The tanpura filled her with anxiety. It seemed sinful and wrong. From that instrument had emerged sounds dedicated to kafir gods. It was because of such apostacy that they had been reduced to this state.

She knew Rashid wouldn't allow her to throw it away. He had brought it in its coffin-like wooden case through rioting and arson. It had pride of place in their one-room tenement. Of course, he himself had no time for it any more. But little Ram was playing the anti-religious instrument.

Her voice rose like a whistle and she slapped him. The child cried in bewilderment. What had happened to the quiet and gentle creature who fed and petted him through the day? Why was she behaving like a lunatic?

It was difficult for Hameeda to control herself after that. At night in agonized whispers she begged Rashid to get rid of the tanpura. He shushed her like a baby and told her about the function that was going to be held at Nizamuddin.

'I have been invited to sing at the mehfil, Hameeda.'

'Over my dead body.'

'There are still some people in this country who feel for us.'

'No, Rashid. I won't let you go there. This must be a trick. Have you forgotten what they did to us just a year ago? This is a trick to finish you off.'

'These are not the same people, Hameeda. These people know Ghalib's poetry. Some of them are very important: they used to teach at big universities. The Sadhoos will have to listen to them.'

But Hameeda sobbed through the night. The next day she made him promise that he would turn down the invitation to sing. Then she too decided to accompany him to Nizamuddin.

She met many of her old friends there. Jamaal and family were present too. They all looked eager. Everybody seemed to be talking excitedly. The pitch would often rise in spikes of desperate hope. She heard Jamaal shriek that exploitation cannot continue for ever. Things have to come to a head sometime.

Hameeda felt a wave go through her. Even though there was desolation and destruction all around; even though the familiar Nizamuddin was lost irrevocably; even though all that was left was flat rocky ground, littered with the debris of the past. It was as though balm was being applied on a bleeding wound and the winds were abating in a choppy sea of pain.

There were similar hearts all around.

Hameeda's story gives an inkling as to why they converged at Nizamuddin that evening in such large numbers. They came full of belief. The past years seemed fictional. How could real life be so unfair? There would be redress, even revenge for what had been done to them. The people who made such wonderful speeches had to be influential enough to ensure that.

They ran pell-mell when the teargas hit them. They bled when the police rained blows on them. They fell, they broke bones and hearts. Their belief ebbed out and got lost in red.

Hameeda and Rashid escaped as they were on the outskirts even here.

Rashid should have thanked Hameeda for saving their lives. He didn't. He blamed her for Jamaal's death. He began looking upon her with hatred: she had never believed; she had known.

And Hameeda? Hameeda became calm — really calm. She produced one more child, a girl this time, and devoted all her time to her children. She ran the household with the minimum effort possible and every afternoon poured a long lesson about religion and religious etiquette down the ears of the new-born and her son. She seemed to know religion by instinct. Instinctively she knew that religion was about boundaries and every afternoon she drew the circle closer to herself. Right hand for the food, left hand for the bum; wash yourself after peeing; take three steps to the east in the morning, four to the west in the afternoon, etc. As she got more and more constricted, Rashid came loose. Every evening he taught music to his children to spite her. He taught it as he had known it in various forms: classical, religious, popular.

Ram and his sister grew up between imprisonment and a wilderness, but then, once planted, most often seeds sprout. They take what they can from the soil and modify themselves accordingly. Ram became a strikingly good looking young man with a sensitive, mobile mouth. He made immense progress in music: integrating all that his spiteful teacher taught him in parts. The girl became an extremely efficient housewife. She cooked and tended the family. She kept her mother alive and her father chuckling.

Ultimately Rashid worked himself to death. Hameeda tied herself up so effectively in religion that she couldn't move a muscle, not even to weep and mourn. After her husband's death she began to breathe sparingly: large gulps of air at long intervals. Nobody knew quite what to do with the immobile middle-aged woman with the breathing problem. So, her daughter, marrying early, installed her as the patron saint in her household and went on living her life. Ram found a job to teach music to Ramin girls in Kanpur and left.

Many years passed.

For Ram the job got boring fairly quickly in Kanpur. The

girls were training for marriage; after reaching a particular level of proficiency they would lose interest in learning more.

Ram taught them with half his heart. The other half was reserved for his own music. So, as one part of his life remained a desert with some cacti, the other became a lush, overgrown bower.

In Delhi, senility at last broke Hameeda's calm — a raving harridan emerged from the wreck of the immobile statue. Her daughter now found it difficult to handle her along with her domestic responsibilities; so one day she packed off her mother and son to her brother's bachelor-home in Kanpur. Her son Shyam, who was just four at the time, was sent to sit at the feet of his gifted Mamu to learn music.

Things improved for Ram. His music was unusual and he was being constantly invited to perform at private shows. The money was good and he had his nephew, who from the time of his birth had been the apple of his eye, now living with him. He began to groom him as the successor of his unique style. At last he had a family.

Ram took his dues from the Ramins; and gave Hameeda hers. Her ranting, however, could never allow him to forget that the patrons of his art were the traditional enemy of his people. Constant guilt gnawed at him when he performed at their shows. Was it the prostitution of his talent, the sale of his soul? As he grew in their estimation he hated them increasingly.

Only one Ramin could assuage that rage: Rajni. Rajni could *feel* the ragas. Ram watched with amazement when she responded with her gut to his teaching. In class, it was important for him to focus on short, simple compositions that could be rendered competently by the pre-Ardhanginis to select audiences. But Rajni would forget the words of simple songs. She craved for complexity — for the magical play of notations. She stayed after class and begged for more. Ram would then teach her as seriously as he taught his nephew, who was the same age.

But his heart was irrevocably divided. A bit of Hameeda

seeped through in these lessons: could the progeny of the sinner Ramins be as good as a Drohi? When Rajni failed to practice, Ustad Ram would tell her tales of his gifted nephew. Shyam is also a name that comes up often in music. It is the name of the classic lover.

But the first time Rajni heard of Shyam she was six. Ram used his favourite pupil and nephew as a stick to beat her with.

'Shyam learned the chhota khayal in fifteen days. You have already taken twice as long and you are not half as good.'

'Nobody's as good as Rajni', asserted the child.

'Oh yes. Shyam is much better.'

The child started to snivel.

Rajni learnt under Shyam's shadow. They didn't meet, but very early in life the image of the ideal assumed a name for her: Shyam.

One day Rajni got married and left Ram.

Karva Chauth

Rajni quit Kanpur and entered my life in its hundredth year. Or rather for reasons best known to her, her mother-in-law pushed her relentlessly at me. She would be sent to visit me for the flimsiest of reasons. Getting to know her was a strange experience. In the beginning I was a little wary of the unfamiliar human contact. But too soon I found myself completely under the spell of this twenty-first century woman — bored and beautiful — who could have so easily slipped into the nineteenth century but would have been an anachronism in the twentieth. She adopted me as her guardian.

On Karva Chauth I woke up from my siesta and saw Jagdamba standing at the bedroom door. How broad she was! The late afternoon sun was filtering in and she seemed enveloped in the soft light. She appeared like a goddess — no, a capacious apsara with a tea-tray. She would not enter unless I beckoned to her. She would stand there, dark skin glowing, dark eyes smouldering. I was often intimidated by Jagdamba though she was merely a Dasi and the law of the land ensured her complete subjugation to my authority. I fixed her salary; I gave her her midday meal; I fixed the time she returned to the ghetto; I could forbid her from taking holidays. I also had power over her womb. I could forbid her from having children. If she conceived, I could force her to have an abortion. Yet her transgressions were too subtle to be so easily controlled. It was as if she didn't quite comprehend the power we had over her. She existed in my thrall as though completely free — just as I had seen her in her jhuggi that day. In that small, cramped pigsty reminiscent of PrePoornaramin squalor, she had looked at me with her hot eyes. She pointed to the skinny three-year-old playing in a corner with mud: 'Bibiji, there is not enough to feed this one', she had said. The constable accompanying me at once replied, 'From where will your family eat? You look capable of finishing all their rations in a week.' To me he said, 'Madam, she looks too cheeky for you.' But I had made up my mind. My Ginis remarked that I was overplaying the role of the compassionate employer. Both her husband and child had to be treated for tuberculosis — I paid not only for the medicine but also for their food for over a year. 'You will never get the gratitude of these people', they warned me. 'Given half a chance she will collude with other Dasas and burgle your house.'

Jagdamba brought in the tea and reminded me that I had to attend the KC puja. Then suddenly she said, 'Ma, wear some jewellery today.'

'No, Jagdamba, I don't feel like it. I had very little to begin with and I have even forgotten where it is.'

Suddenly, birds twittered and a green light illumined the flat.

It was Rajni.

'Ma, I have come to fetch you for the KC story session. You aren't ready yet?'

Rajni was wearing what I thought was a green sari; as she moved it suddenly looked yellow.

'Psychedelic sari', she explained when she saw my bewildered expression.

Jagdamba piped in, 'I am telling Ma to wear some jewellery today.'

'What a lovely idea, Ma. Come, let me choose something for you. Oh, Ma, you actually have locks, and oh god, keys. I've never used a key before.'

Before I could stop her she took the keys from my startled hand, and ran to the spare room. She turned one of them with childish glee in the lock and started rummaging in the almirah-locker. She hadn't taken the basic precaution of sending Jagdamba out of the room. This, in spite of repeated police warnings that servants should not know where valuables are kept in a house. Ever since my Ardhangini possessions came into the house, Jagdamba had graduated from her habitual sullenness to a kind of silky subservience that I found quite alarming.

I caught Jagdamba looking at Rajni. The look was peculiarly masculine: assessing and penetrating.

'Jagdamba, make me some more tea', I said.

She cast contemptuous eyes at the untouched tea-tray that she had already brought in, and withdrew slowly to the kitchen.

Rajni was opening one locker after another and exclaiming over the contents.

'Ma, wear these, please. They are so beautiful.'

She handed me a pair of long and elaborate ear-rings. They had green and red enamel on them and ended in little droplets of pearls.

'No, child, I stopped wearing these long back, much before I became a widow. You wear them today. They will match your sari, at least one shade of your sari.'

She took off her own ear-rings, put on mine and smiled at me. In spite of my irritation, I felt a thrill in my bones. Rajni's face was capable of transformation. This face demanded that life look at it, respond to it. It was a very eager and vulnerable face.

'Are you happy, child?' I asked her before I could stop myself.

'No Ma. I'm not.'

She was looking at me directly and accusingly. 'I want to sing, Ma. Can you talk to my mother-in-law?'

'What does your mother-in-law have to do with your singing?'

'It has to do with my Drohi teacher. You see, Ustad Ram who taught me in Kanpur has a nephew called Shyam. Ustad sahib is too old to move, but my father-in-law can be prevailed upon to secure a Rajdhani work-permit for Shyam.'

'Child, it might be construed as interference on my part.'

'You are right, Ma. My mother-in-law is a bitch. She would probably bargain for it. She might even ask for Jagdamba in return.'

I was shocked and slightly afraid for Rajni. She spoke like Jagdamba. She had no business to. Jagdamba was a Dasa-woman, Jagdamba was free. I noticed there was colour in Rajni's usually pale cheeks. She turned defiantly to me and continued, 'She hates me and will never let my father-in-law do this for me gratis.'

'Why should she hate you, child? She thinks she is doing the best for her family by moulding you in a particular way.'

'No, Ma. I know hatred. I feel it. I can't sing when she is around.'

'Perhaps I will talk to your father-in-law.' The words were again out before I could stop them.

I found myself besieged with perfume as Rajni hugged and kissed me. 'Oh Ma, you will, won't you? I can't ask him myself. I even thought of asking my father. But he doesn't talk to me any more.'

'Why child? Is your father angry with you?'

'No, Ma. He just doesn't talk, doesn't listen, any more. He asks me about my in-laws and husband and that's it.'

'You are a part of this family now — perhaps that's why. Parents have to give up their children when they grow up.'

She was silent.

In the next room Jagdamba had put on the screen. It showed a group of women getting ready for the KC ceremony. The visual suddenly collapsed into the frozen beautiful face of Rajni's mother-in-law. 'Ma and Rajni,' it said, 'hurry up, we are waiting for you.'

I shivered with sudden fright. I hate this interactive screen. I know the image on the screen can't see me, but it is encroachment enough that someone should know exactly when to beam in suddenly.

I reached out for my sunshine-pill. I was certain that modern medicine wouldn't fail me. Sure enough, within seconds I began to hear the chattering birds from a distance. Panic subsided in ten seconds, as claimed by the makers of sunshine-pills.

Rajni walked briskly and purposefully in her whirl of psychedelic cloth. My lapis lazuli-studded walking stick clattered a bit as I tried to match her stride. She slowed down.

Why were we rushing for the puja? What would happen if we turned and went back to my flat? Would the news travel to the Sadhoo Math? Would we be tried for flouting the norms of the community?

There would be a jury all in saffron, shaven heads and tufts of hair sticking out obscenely behind them.These women have brought shame upon themselves, their families and their nation by their reprehensible actions. They are ordered to prove their chastity by entering the sacred fire. If they have not erred, like Sita they will emerge untouched by the flame, and if they have . . .

It wasn't such a fanciful thought! The Sadhoos were the self-appointed guardians of national culture. In my younger days, we who belonged to the east of the country did not even celebrate KC. It was a festival typical of the north of Raminland. After Poornaramin descended, the Sadhoos declared that they would 'elevate' religion and culture above regional differences. Festivals and fasts were nationalized. Durga Puja, Ganesh Chaturthi — so many of them — every second day in the week had to be declared a holiday. But then the first Chief Sadhoo made an amendment in the Dharmakarma directory. Most festivals were declared Ardhangini-specific and began to be managed only by the wives. The women's improvement group led by Sadhvi Sanjukta hailed it as a significant step in elevating the status of Ardhanginis.

In the early years of Raminism all this pother about fasts and festivals had sounded like so much innocuous nonsense to my ears until a group from the south of the country refused to celebrate Diwali. In the nine o'clock national news bulletin on the screen one evening, Raminland was shocked to witness the charred remains of young Dasas who had made bonfires of themselves in resisting Ramin cultural imperialism. Culture is serious stuff in Poornaramin's country. Rajdhani is now the official cultural capital. The city has the densest concentration of Ramins and the most stringent Ramin laws. We are intended to be a beacon to other states that have been forced into more and more 'pro-Dasa' legislation over the years.

The story session was at the pool-side. The chairs were arranged in a semicircle. The semicircle has increasingly become the pattern of such meetings as everything is monitored by the screen. There is a certain theatricality that has entered all social activity.

What a wonderful spectacle it made on the strategically placed monitors while the cameras recorded every movement: all the Ardhanginis of the family sitting bejewelled and resplendent. It was rather pleasant, a cool breeze was playing with exotic clothes and elaborate hairstyles. I had retained my white clothes, but for that day I had thought it fit to drape a green stole around my shoulders.

I was again seized with a sense of unreality. These women did it to me: they look too beautiful, too elaborate to be real. Perhaps if I looked carefully I would see the controls that operated them, electric cords and switches. Perhaps the breeze would lift their saris and I would see wooden stilts instead of legs, perhaps their lovely arms would slit open and I would see the cottonwool stuffing.

The KC ceremony began: Rajni's mother-in-law, seated elegantly on the chair facing the semicircle, was telling the cautionary tale of the violation of the KC fast by a young girl and the subsequent death of her husband. She was using a prompter. Her eyes rested disapprovingly a couple of times on Rajni.

Compared to the other women, Rajni did look a bit unkempt. Her eyeshadow didn't quite match her sari, and a few tendrils of hair, unschooled and uncurled, rested limply on her shoulder. In fact, the women behind her were sniggering about her hairstyle.

The incident of the deception of the young woman due to the misplaced love of the brothers was being narrated. The KC fast is observed by the wife for the longevity of the husband. The brothers, unable to bear the sight of their ailing and hungry sister, hold up a lantern behind a tree. Thinking she has sighted the moon the girl drinks water to signify the completion of her fast. Her husband dies as a result.

I imagined the brothers' tearful eyes resting compassionately on their beautiful sister. What a temptation it must have been to make her break the vow. Their lovely sister was not made for such ordeals. But that love proved sinful. How easily love spoils in these legends, as milk left outside the refrigerator overnight curdles by the morning.

Rajni's mother-in-law was looking daggers at her. Rajni was sitting with a faraway look on her face. Her mouth was half open. Was she humming to herself?

At night the Ardhanginis would go up to the terrace and look for the moon; after that they would eat, concluding their fasts.

The three judges who had been unobtrusively tabling the points to crown Mrs KC — the most beautiful and accomplished Ardhangini for the evening — were squabbling over the result. The prize, this time being given by my second son, was two premier-class tickets around the world. I saw Rajni's mother-in-law stalking her.

'Let's hear our Gini sing', I said, rather loudly. 'Rajni has been trained in music by a maestro who performed in Paris last year.'

I could feel many eyes on me. Nobody expected me to come up with such specific suggestions. I was a relic from the past, to be gazed and wondered at. I was not supposed to intrude so much into things; least of all, into a recalcitrant Gini's life.

The women obediently fell into a semicircle again. Rajni looked around defiantly and began to sing.

Her voice was strong and youthful. She was singing an old, old composition: *Kaun gali gaye Shyam* — tell me, O friend, where has Shyam gone? A thumri so full of longing for the 'eternally vanishing' Shyam that, even among the plenitude of the twenty-first century it took my breath away. It was a poem of uninhibited adulterous longing that I thought would explode through this group of dutiful wives; yet Rajni sang on and the ceremony for the KC fast continued as usual.

First Love

A few days after the KC puja I was writing at my desk when the incoming-call signal flashed suddenly. Who could want to speak to me at this hour? I wondered. Must be one of my Ginis making a duty-call in-between films. I moodily pressed the 'engaged' button; she should continue watching whichever film she was watching. Ardhanginis and pre-Ardhanginis, these days, are the fodder and consumers of the image-making industry.

I continued to write. The signal flashed again. Such persistence! I picked up the receiver, pressing the viewer-button as well. The screen came alive with Rajni dressed in gold and pink.

'Hello, Gini-Rajni', I said.

'Please call me Rajni. Ma, can I see you?'

'Yes, of course, child', I said, fumbling just a little to find the requisite button that would relay my image to her.

'Is this a designer dress or is it from a film?' I asked.

'From *Choli ke Rahasya*. Ma, it's so generous of you to spare time for me.'

'You are my Gini, child, not a stranger. I always have time for you. Your mother-in-law, in fact, told me that she has no objection to your learning music.'

Experience had taught me to initiate conversation with my Ginis; otherwise they could take long, precious minutes presenting their best 'angles' for the screen.

'She couldn't have said that', was the sharp retort. But then she tried to cover up hastily. 'I mean, Ma, I'm aware that my education has been incomplete, I have a lot to learn. I want to thank you for . . . '

She thanked me for securing Shyam for her, in words that overuse has made meaningless.

'Your father seems to be an exceptional person. Why didn't he remarry?' I asked to make her change track.

'I don't know Ma. He says he didn't really see the point of it. He had a family — my brother and I — and he didn't require anything else.'

She spoke almost in one breath. 'I never felt the lack of a mother, you know. He was always there for me. And I grew up knowing so much more than my friends. We didn't bother much about the house. We used to go for long drives on Sundays. He would keep Sunday for me. I would wait for that day all week. Papa told me the names of all the trees and birds we saw on the way. I would forget the names but I could always mimic the cries of the birds. He used to call me his little synthesizer.'

'What does he call you now?'

'How does it matter now, Ma?'

'I know a lot of other things become important after marriage. In course of time one gets used to the new life, as though the old one had never existed. But tell me more about your childhood.'

'You really want to know, Ma?' There was some hesitation. 'Oh, I was very happy. I sang like a bird all day. Papa loved to hear me sing. When he came back from work he would often wake me up and ask me to sing for him.'

'Then why didn't you go on to become a singer, Rajni?'

'I wanted marriage and children, Ma. I didn't relish the dull life of a Sadhvi', she replied, shrugging her shoulders.

Aberrations like Rajni had not been taken into account in the New Education Policy that divided higher education into two streams for women (to keep them abreast with men in this age of specializations).

'What did Ustad Ram have to say about your decision?'

'He was heartbroken. But then, ever since he returned from Paris he just hasn't been the same. No, Ma. I didn't want to be a Sadhvi.'

I clearly visualized the child she must have been. I could almost see the doting father with his little doll — Rajni must have the best in life: new clothes, lots of toys, lots of love — pure love, not the lumpy, odorous, curdled milk of the KC legend.

'And what did my little baby do while I was away? Did she have a good day?'

The twelve-year-old put her arms around her father.

'Yes, I did, Papa. Have you got me the yachting set we saw on the screen yesterday?'

'I hadn't promised that for today, had I?'

'Oh Papa, you said — you said you would get it before the weekend.'

'That still leaves us with two more days.'

The arms around his neck slackened and fell and he felt the dread of being abandoned. Her little mouth was drooping at the corners. He tried to pick her up but she was too big, too unwieldy. Besides, she had stiffened and become remote.

'Rajni, come here my little one.'

She walked away from him.

'I have work to do', she announced.

In that averted face, in the way her hair fell on her shoulders, he saw the woman he had married and lost. He felt weak.

'Rajni, come here, my baby. The store remains open till ten at least.'

She came to him and smiled.

'I won't, Papa. I won't.'

'Would you have done this had your mother been alive?'

'She would have understood. She wouldn't have pushed me into something I hate.'

'Rajni, my doll, you decided to be an Ardhangini. This is the lot of girls who make that choice.'

She again averted her face from him. He saw the uneven fall of hair on her shoulders, he was adamant.

'Rajni, go in', he said.

Rajni got up from the sofa as though there were weights around her feet. Slowly, very slowly she entered the beauty clinic and closed the door behind her.

'Where is the bride?' Rosie asked. Rosie had a formidable track record as a hair stylist. Beneath her nimble fingers all kinds of hair — long, short, stringy, oily, dry, normal — could sway, wave, curl or flick; a pretty girl would become exotic, a closed face would suddenly become impish. Rosie's life was one of unending creation.

In the last ten years, she had made Kanpur her home. She did not belong to this place. Born in the US as a beautiful boy, she had recreated herself into an adolescent girl of considerable charm. The return of her parents to their native Raminland had plunged her into some confusion. Trying to settle down in a metropolis, she found herself dealing endlessly with appeals from like-minded and like-bodied people to participate in underground movements. She was bored by the debates about androgyne-rights. So she came to this small town and set up herself as a woman who was openly not a woman. Nobody could challenge her here and no institution could claim her.

As a rule she didn't do bridal hair; that kind of work was for the lowest in her profession. For her hair-styling was a life-long affair, not a one-night fling. But then Rajni's father was one of the most influential men of Kanpur.

Here, said somebody, and Rajni was pushed into a chair in front of the mirror. All the lights came on simultaneously, focusing pitilessly on her.

Rosie's eyebrows shot up. Split-ends — in the eventful thirty years of her professional life she hadn't seen such a bad case. As a rule she wasn't very curious about the lives of the young women who passed through her hands, being aware that their confidences uttered at the crucial moment of their image-transformation could have nothing to do with her own concerns. She avoided any comment that could be construed as interest in their personal lives. But that day, despite herself she gasped, 'My dear, how could you allow this to happen!'

Rajni looked sullenly at her own reflection and said nothing. Rosie shrugged and then started work, expertly singeing the ends of the hair. What a sullen bride this one would make!

All the Ramin girls were pretty. The only problem was that they tended to look like each other. This one had let herself go a little. But the damage was far from irreversible.

'How long will all this take?' asked the face now framed by the rich lather of the anti-split-end shampoo.

'It will take at least a year to be as I want it, my dear', said Rosie. 'You haven't come a day earlier than you should have.'

'I'm not going to sit here for a year', the face barked.

'Tch, we'll let you get married tomorrow, don't worry, then we will bring you back here', Rosie said smiling to herself. What a bad-tempered girl! The face crumpled and began to cry.

'Really, this is a bad attack of bridal nerves, calm down please.'

Rolls of tissue-paper later, after putting the rollers in her hair, Rosie felt justified in asking, 'What's up, sweetheart? Are you afraid? You're going to look fine.'

'No, no. It isn't that.'

"Is he so ugly?"

'Oh no, he's all right. I just don't like beauty saloons.'

'You're a good-looking girl. Don't you want to look beautiful for him?'

'It takes so long,' Rajni complained, 'please hurry.'

'But don't you want to be a beautiful woman?' Rosie persisted.

'No, I don't think so', Rajni replied with a momentary insight that surprised Rosie. But then, refusing to deal with it, she wailed at once, 'Please-please hurry.'

Rosie philosophically switched on the dryer and yawned. Professional work meant dealing with all kinds and even artists like her had to eat. The girl was probably inadequately educated; the father had spoiled her. There would be ripples of some disturbance after her marriage but Ramin institutions would be able to pull her back in line quite easily.

It was what he had suspected: bilious-looking and grey. He poked at it a little. There could be no mistake. He looked at his wife. She was eating happily, shovelling heaped spoonfuls into her mouth. He looked with amazement at her plate. Should she eat so much?

He investigated it yet again with the spoon. 'Rajni, there are blobs of fat in the meat.'

'What?' she asked, looking up distractedly.

'I said there are blobs of fat in this thing.'

'Oh!' she said.

He waited for her to start the process of enquiry. The structure of the household had always fascinated him. The Ardhangini ornate and beautiful at the top of things, efficiently running the complex bit of machinery. It was all like a jewel-watch.

Rajni continued to eat.

'Aren't you going to do something about it?'

'About what?' she asked.

'About the meat.'

'Oh, yes. Don't eat it. There's some salad in the fridge.' She rang the bell.

He realized with amazement that she wasn't going to investigate. What meat was it? Who had bought it? Why hadn't it been cleaned properly? Why hadn't the cook complained? She wasn't going to apportion blame; nobody was going to be reprimanded. In fact, she had even taken a second helping of the poisonous stuff.

He looked at her reclining on the sofa. A wave of irritation ran through him. Why couldn't she sit up?

'Rajni, I'm leaving for office.'

'Bye, honey!'

She sank further into the sofa and held out her hand, 'Come and say bye-bye properly.'

The proverbial child-woman who had to be appeased incessantly, he thought. When he made love to her, it was like giving her chocolates. Loving was only self-gratification for her.

'It is nine; I have to leave', he said impatiently..

'Oh, you poor thing!' she said.

He saw that she was just half awake.

'Next weekend we have to arrange for the farm-house party.'

'Oh, no!' she groaned flinging an arm across her face. Home work! He couldn't see her eyes any more. She would make a bad job of the party. Too much food, too many fried snacks, loud music; and she would forget everybody's names. He scowled in exasperation.

He went out to his car and the pall lifted. He loved driving on Rajdhani roads.

The needle touched 120-130-160. He felt the exhilaration of speed. There would be more of that at office. He often said at staff-motivation meetings, 'Success is speed. I want to feel myself moving as soon as I enter the office.' He was moving rapidly — the receipts had doubled this year, but they had to treble very soon because the expenses had moved up as well. Suresh had joined Educating Women Ltd as Manager (Marketing) last year. He had introduced three new courses. Two had been runaway successes. 'I need one more spectacular success this year to get an edge', he said to himself.

But Rajni, didn't she smell of languor — of mustily perfumed bed-clothes every morning? She carried the night on her long after it had passed. He hated slowness. Why couldn't she move in the mornings. She was always so untidy — messing up his home, spilling all over his space. Had she been the right choice for him?

180. It wasn't like him to feel doubtful. Doubt could chew up life's work, it was important for him to be in charge. 160. No, she was all right. He liked the way she curled up to him in deep sleep — almost like a kitten.

120-130. But she would have to learn to be his wife. No, he couldn't afford a mess in his life. Dammit, why should he?

He would look up his mother in the evening. He thought with affection of the tall, beautiful woman who had borne him. He would tell her about the project he was planning to start next week: it was expensive, but one couldn't be parsimonious if one wanted to succeed in this day and age.

In his mother's fastidious blue room he found himself craving for something crisp and buttery. He usually ate very little, obsessively calculating the calories of every mouthful, like most Ramins of his age and profession. But in this blue room he felt his muscles relaxing.

'D'you want some toast with your tea?' she asked.

'Mama, how on earth . . . yes!'

Almost immediately, she handed him a plate. The toast had a golden layer on it.

'Margarine', she said reassuringly. 'If you are still following diet no. 8, you can have two portions. Only salad for dinner, of course.'

He was grateful.

'What is it?' she asked, not being one to waste words or time.

He found himself talking about Rajni. Midway, without his realizing it, she put another toast on his plate and refilled his cup.

'H'm,' she said, 'it's worse than I thought. I think it will be a good idea to let her continue with her music. The old woman asked if she could resume it.'

It was over tea and toast between mother and son that the sub-plot was conceived and Shyam's image came up on the screen.

Shyam

Shyam hummed to himself as he brushed his hair. The mirror was chipped, the sink below it had cracked, the tap dripped. He stood at a distance to avoid the dripping water. As he peered into the mirror, he made a seventy-five degree angle.

He didn't understand the words but enunciated them perfectly:

Harr qaum rast rahe din wa qiblagahe,
Man qibla rast kardam bar sim-e-kajkulahe

Every people has its right path, its faith and its focus of worship.
But I focus my worship on the tilted cap of my Beloved.

Things were beginning to look up for him. The previous year he had been sent by the Ramin government to Europe for a music festival. His rendition of Ram bhajans in London had endeared him to the NRR (Non-Resident Ramin) community so much that he was promised three sponsorships for the coming year. He had also put in an application for Ramin status here at home. The interview call could come any time. He had moved to Rajdhani recently, hoping to expedite matters.

Ustad Ram, his maternal uncle, had even secured a job for him. He would be tutoring a Ramin Ardhangini. Before this he had only tutored little girls in Kanpur. Rajdhani was a revelation. The Ramin areas in Kanpur were nothing like this. The opulence of the buildings seemed unbelievable to him.

The whole city was made of shimmering glass and steel. Of course, the meanness of the Drohi areas remained a constant, but that didn't seem too bad. For the first time since he could remember there would be some money in the house.

'Ammi', he called.

There was a vague answer from the kitchen.

'Ammi, do you know this song?' He belted it out, throatily.

His mother emerged from the kitchen, touching her ears to indicate that it was yet another sacred song that he was profaning. 'It is Farsi', she said reproachfully. Anything Farsi elicited the same response from her.

'What does it mean?'

'I don't know. Ask Mamu . . .'

'Ammi, I'm going to start work today.'

'Hoon', she said, observing his clothes closely. He wore a light-green embroidered kurta. She had spent a month making the complex pattern of flowers, leaves and netting on it. She could have sold it in the Ramin colonies; there was a ready market for such embroidery. But that was when Shyam was about to go abroad and she knew that their passport to freedom was tied to his ability to sell himself there.

'While you are in the Ramin area, try to see Ustad Brijbasan. He was a friend of your Mamu but of course after he got Ramin-status he has not bothered to keep in touch with us.'

'Ammi, this is not Kanpur. Brijbasan lives in East Rajdhani. The pass I have is valid only for Kalka-South. It will take the whole day to get to the East. There are just two buses that go there. But tell me, aren't you well today, Ammi?'

He was asking her why she hadn't smiled at him as she had always done for the past twenty-one years, even through the tears that had mourned for his father's death.

She looked at his carefully combed hair, a lock had been schooled to fall on to the forehead. She smelt the fragrance of roses that emanated from him. She looked at the trousers he wore, a bit shiny at the seams, carefully washed and ironed by her; and her heart cried out to him to stop, not to go into the Ramin areas in this big and dazzling city.

But where were the options? Where were the jobs? All the respectable jobs were with the Ramins. There was the alternative of working with a Drohi-don, earning a lot and then being found with a little hole in one's body, in a ditch.

But it was one thing to teach music to girls in a school and another thing to penetrate a Ramin-household. The Ramin-buildings, large like temples, arose in front of her eyes. Who knew what went on behind those silent, guarded walls where tall, fair-skinned Ramins lived like gods? Did they breathe, eat, shit like other human beings? Or did they suck blood off young heifers after slaughtering them on their altars?

She knew she shouldn't express her irrational fears to her son. She shook off her misgivings and smoothed back the lock of hair from his forehead.

'I want you to go very far in life, son. You must get Ramin-status or apply for migration.'

'Aha, you want to live in Paris in your old age. You want to be a memsahib', he teased.

'Yes, of course,' she said, 'I want my son to be a sahib.'

On reaching Kalka-South Shyam parked his cycle at the stand. He fished out the pass from his pocket and walked to the guard napping at the entrance.

'Music-master?' the guard enquired superciliously.

'Yes.'

The guard dialled a number and spoke into the receiver. A green light came on at once on the board behind him.

'Go up to the tenth floor and press the button at the door marked 108. Music-master, eh?'

'Yes', Shyam replied again, wondering why the man was winking at him.

'Five thousand rupees an hour, not bad. Be sure to satisfy', said the guard, guffawing. 'Saale Drohi!'

Shyam felt his skin bristle with anger. However, there was no change of expression on his good-looking face.

He pressed the call-bell. The door swung open. He walked into a blue and gold room. There was nobody there.

'Salaam, Ustad Sahib', said a disembodied voice. 'Turn to your left.'

He entered another room, this time pink. Something pink, gold and cream gleamed in the centre of the room. As he entered, she sat up on the fluffy pink carpet and repeated, 'Salaam waalekum, Ustad Sahib.'

'Waalekum salaam, madam', he replied, lowering his eyes to her feet that looked like soft doves poised for flight. She was reclining on the carpet, yet the muscles were tense.

'Ustad Ram used to speak a lot about his gifted nephew who started singing even before he could talk', she said. She spoke Raminlingo like a foreigner, stressing the wrong syllables.

He heard himself reply in English, 'Madam is very kind. But my uncle is too indulgent. I can see he has been much too indulgent with you.'

Of course it had happened before. Shyam had the feeling of having lived through all this, many times. He, too, had grown up on a diet of images.

The film of the year was a controversial one. It had been a major hit in the ghettos. Flash back! Twenty-one years ago, in a hospital for Dasa-Drohis, there had been an emergency case. A Ramin woman driving past the Drohi colony had suddenly gone into labour. In the primitive conditions that prevailed there, huffing and puffing, she had miraculously delivered a baby boy. Of course, they had been unable to save her after the trauma. In the confusion that followed her death, the Ramin boy was lifted by a Drohi nurse and placed at the side of a fellow Drohi who had just lost her baby.

That boy grows up as a Drohi. But blood will always tell: fairer, taller, prouder than any other Drohi, he catches the fancy of a lovely Ramin girl.

After an hour of incredibly action-packed footage, which includes the slow extraction of the toe-nail of a Drohi, the big screen is inundated with the tears of the false Drohi-mother, begging the hero's forgiveness. 'Go, live the life that is your due, which selfishly I kept from you. Go, Annadata, go . . . I can never call you "son" again.'

'You speak English?'

'Yes, madam. I learnt the rudiments in school. After that, I taught myself. I want to emigrate.'

'Oh', she said. 'But you haven't heard me sing.'

'I wasn't talking about that madam.' In accordance with the script, he looked at her fearlessly in the face. 'Every art,' he said lapsing into Raminlingo, 'has its code of behaviour. You call me "Ustad", so you must be my shagird.'

'Yes', she said.

'Yet you don't get up to greet me.'

A shadow of recognition fell across her face. She knew the script too. Who didn't in this magic land, where such myths were dispersed every minute through celluloid? To be Ramin, to be discovered to be Ramin, to discover a Ramin among Dasas and Drohis, was the stuff fairy-tales and fantasies were made of.

Her eyelashes were like spikes, he noticed. They stood stiffly around the swimming space of her eyes which were taking in his embroidered kurta and the lock of hair schooled to stray. Just below her left eye was a faint, bluish mark. Smudged eyeshadow? The break in perfection bothered him. He began to blush with stage fright.

'I'm sorry', she said. She stood up a little awkwardly and brought out her tanpura from a coffin-like case. Then, remembering something else, she placed it gently on the carpet and took out the tablas from their case. She placed them on the carpet,

'Please sit.'

She sat down with the tanpura only after he had taken his place.

Her voice rode down with him in the elevator, hummed at him as he steered his cycle through the bicycle lanes. Would it go home with him? He decided to wander around a bit in the shopping complex. After all, there was an hour left which he could legitimately spend in the Kalka-South Ramin area. Although, if he overstayed, the guard at the gate would flash a message to the other posts in the area. The guard at the parking lot of the building where his pupil lived would respond by saying that the Drohi music-master was no longer in the building. The colony-guard would corroborate. It wouldn't take long for the area-security men to find him and rough him up. They could hand him to the police on charges of trespassing into private property.

He looked at the Ramin property around him. The shopping complex was a huge, three-storeyed structure with underground parking. Again, he felt he knew it. He knew the escalators and the shopping-cars, the vending machines that sold everything from coffee to caviar, the rosy Ramin children who shopped compulsively, and the school drop-outs, terribly good looking, who could whip out guns at the least provocation. Yet he had never tasted caviar, or stepped onto an escalator.

But he had played out these fantasies so often with his Drohi peers. In dark alleys they had marked out their areas scrupulously, using a piece of coal to draw the boundaries. My swimming pool, my casino; don't step into my car which cost me a hundred million 'dollars'.

He had sometimes played an eccentric millionaire who buys up half of Raminland and insists that only people who can walk on one foot be allowed to enter. So many of his friends had agreed to hop on one foot for the pleasure of sharing his part of the garbage.

But Ram Mamu had been quick to pull him up, 'Shyam, have you become a Ramin that you play such games?'

'Yes Mamu,' he had replied, 'when I grow up, I will become a Ramin.'

'May God forgive you because you are still small. Do you want to burn in hell-fire forever?'

'Will all Ramins go to hell, Mamu?'

'I don't know. But you will, if you change your religion. Ramins are worshippers of idols.'

'I won't change my religion, Mamu. I will just pretend I have changed it. Nobody will know except God.'

Shyam knew now that one couldn't become a millionaire simply by accepting Poornaramin. Even if he was ready to sell it, his soul had no buyer. Something else was also required. Something that was more marketable. He wondered whether he had it.

There were Drohis who were much better off than he was. There were Drohis who were rich. They lived in Drohi areas, never travelled to western countries, never shopped in these malls. They couldn't even speak English. They led underground lives and sometimes migrated to other Islamic countries. There were others who were employed by filthy-rich Dasa-dons; they were rich too, but lived dangerously. Nothing in their lives could approximate the ease he saw all around.

He remembered his mother's suggestion that he should visit Brijbasan.

There wasn't a way of getting in touch with Brijbasan beforehand. Shyam did not have his phone number. To find it he would have had to reveal his identity. Like other Drohis, he was reluctant to divulge his name and address to disembodied foreign-sounding voices on the phone. Though the long and tortuous journey could be fruitless, it was preferable.

The bus, an antediluvian creature, dragged on its patched and peeling tin body, spewing out and sucking in grimy, sweaty people at regular intervals. A woman carrying a child in her arms came and sat almost on Shyam's lap. He squirmed; he was wary of the Dasas. The woman noticed his shudder and responded by spitting near his feet.

'Ram-Ram,' she said, 'I will have to bathe as soon as I get home.'

'Might do you good, Amma', said a lad from the next seat, grinning at Shyam.

They had realized he was a Drohi. No Dasa would be caught dead in an embroidered kurta, though the Ramins paid a fortune to buy 'ethnic' stuff. Of course, no Ramin would ever travel in a bus.

The woman again intoned Ram-Ram and closed her eyes. The baby stuck out a foot that went straight into Shyam's pocket. The woman saw that from the corner of her eye. Shyam gently took out the foot from his pocket and placed it on her lap. The woman made a great pretence of wiping it. The baby began to squeal.

'Ram-Ram', said the woman.

Why was Ram Mamu called that? 'Ram' belonged to the others — to the Ramins and their Dasas, but then so did 'Shyam'. What had happened to their original but now forgotten names — Ahmad, Ruab, Javed? Brijbasan was Habibullah. For a long time he had called himself H. Brijbasan.

Shyam pulled himself up. He wasn't going to be like Ram Mamu. Just when Ram's family had thought things were beginning to change for the better for them, he gave up the fight. They had not bargained for the pain with which he had returned from his spectacularly successful foreign trip. People had sat at his feet there but Ram returned not with the readiness to fill in visa forms, and discuss sponsorships but with the reluctance to talk at all. It was from his accompanists that they got an inkling of the reason for this. People there had wanted to know about him: how he lived, what he ate, what time he got up, the exact number of hours spent in riyaaz. They had wanted to know about his father and his father's father. Was his family kalawant — did he come from generations of maestros? They wanted to know.

Ram didn't know, none of them remembered that history. They knew that somehow they had survived a bloodbath in the the early twenty-first century. Then they had been plucked out from their homes and 'resettled'. The luckier ones, the ones with resources, had fled the country. All that Ram remembered was the music lessons his father had given him and the religion his mother had taught him.

He began to mourn his lost name.

Shyam had been taught in school that it was because of such illiteracy and lack of reason that Drohis had refused progress and change through the ages. They had focused only on the outmoded values of their religion and culture and not kept in step with their Ramin brethren . . .

It was a long walk from the bus-stop to the East-Rajdhani Ramin-colony where Brijbasan lived. The heat got unbearable and Shyam wet his handkerchief and tied it around his head.

The guard at the colony gate scrutinized him and then his Identity Card.

'Music-master?'

'Yes.'

'Why do you want to meet Brijbasan?'

'Some personal work.'

'Why didn't you get a pass made?'

'I couldn't get in touch with him earlier.'

'Are you related to him?'

'Yes', said Shyam, uneasily.

'People who live in such palaces don't honour the ties of blood', said the guard, waving his hand towards the building.

Shyam kept quiet.

'Do you want water?'

'Yes, thank you Bhai', said Shyam, taken aback by such kindness.

'You don't look as though you're from these parts.'

'I am from Kanpur.'

'My family is there, too. People like you and me don't have the fortune of living with our families. Here!' he said, 'for one hour, not a minute extra.'

Shyam extended his hand for the pass.

'What!' exclaimed the guard, 'Empty-handed? Have you forgotten the tehzeeb of Kanpur?'

Shyam wanted to hit him. He took out a hundred-rupee note.

'What! This will not buy me even peanuts, whereas your relative will ply you with sweets.'

Shyam took out two more notes.

'May God bless you. Life is hard for people like you and me.'

The guard at the building was too sleepy to extract money from Shyam. He grudgingly fed the information about the visitor into the register. Simultaneously, it was faxed to Brijbasan.

It took a while for the green light to appear on the board.

Brijbasan's sitting room was almost bare. In fact it did not seem like a room at all. One wall was painted like a calendar. It showed mythological scenes from the legend of Poornaramin. In one panel a six-armed figure dressed in gold and saffron, brandishing a sword, a lance, a shield, a lotus, a pitcher of water and gold coins was emerging from a turquoise-blue sea. In another, Poornaramin quelling an army of bearded soldiers, had only two arms but three eyes, one like the flame of a candle on his forehead.

Shyam couldn't have known that there was a great deal of overlap between Poornaramin and the other gods. However, nobody painted deities other than Poornaramin and Ram any more and they could be distinguished by complexion: Poornaramin was always peaches and cream, Ram was blue.

In yet another panel, Poornaramin looked on benignly as Ram killed Ravana. As official legend would have it, Poornaramin was chronologically the first God before he split into the trinity of Brahma, Vishnu, Mahesh. He belonged to the beginning of time. He had appeared again in the twenty-first century to show the way to his people.

Shyam almost didn't recognize the new Ramin. Brijbasan was dressed only in a saffron loincloth. His head was shaved except for the sacred tuft that stuck out behind him. Shyam wanted to laugh. Brijbasan had outdone even the Sadhoos in his attire.

'Oh, son Shyam, how are you.'

'I'm well, Mamu Jaan — Annadata.'

Brijbasan did not contradict that form of address.

'You have come at an auspicious time. I'm holding a saaz-puja in the house.'

Shyam looked at him blankly.

'The musical instruments will be anointed. Sadhoo Shri Shrinivasanji is coming. You know, Shri Shrinivasanji who has the Housing and Sanitation portfolio in the government.'

'Oh', said Shyam unenthusiastically.

'How is Ram?' Brijbasan asked, not meeting his eye, embarrassed at having adopted Ramin customs.

'Quite unwell. He refused to move to Rajdhani with us. He's still in Kanpur.'

'He didn't even come for the first stage of Ramin-status interviews.'

It was not a question. The silence between them grew oppressive. Shyam said, 'They took away his work permit after that.'

'Then how does he . . .?'

'I send him money. In fact, I've applied for Ramin-status. I wanted to ask you if you could . . .'

But Brijbasan had turned away.

'Look, who's come, Rukhsana! Shyam.'

Brijbasan's wife came in. Shyam remembered her as a fragile, delicate woman. She weighed at least 100 kgs now. Her arms, neck and ears shone with gold jewellery.

She embraced Shyam, almost stifling him in great mounds of flesh. Shyam saw that her eyes were full of tears. Brijbasan had gone out of the room.

She was pressing money into Shyam's palms. Her pudgy fingers were encircled with gold bands. The rings were digging into her flesh, perhaps even restricting blood-circulation. The nails were colourless.

'Mamijaan, I can't accept this.'

She couldn't speak because of the tears.

'For Ram', she whispered. 'Go, now, son.'

When he came out of the flat, Shyam realized that he was thirsty again. He looked at the money in his hands. She had given him fifty thousand rupees.

The elevator door opened. He felt an arm on his shoulder.

'You left this behind', said Brijbasan waving an envelope in his face.

'It's not mine.'

'I might be selected for the RACUF (Ramin Cultural Festival). It will be a very prestigious nomination. All the Sadhoos will be there.'

He thrust the envelop into his hands and disappeared. It contained a note of twenty thousand rupees.

'*Ab na bolo mosey Sham*, Madam, if you can remember the notations of ragas, then why is this poor thumri forgotten every time?'

'I'm sorry', Rajni said, raising a tired face and looking vaguely at the ivory-and-gold drapery rod.

'*Na bolo Sham, jhooti preet ki batiyaan, O Sham.*'

'That's your name, isn't it?' she said, suddenly. 'Shyam Sham?

'My grandmother named me Rashid Ahmad, Madam', he heard himself say. 'Shyam is just a disguise my mother makes me wear. But will you please concentrate on the thumri? I don't travel for an hour a day to discuss nomenclature.'

'Then please go', she said, haughtily. 'I only want to discuss names, today.'

'As you like, madam. Here's my resignation.'

'You can't resign like this.'

'I can madam. I am not a Dasa.'

'Please. Ustad Ram used to allow me to use the tape-prompter.'

'Over my dead body, madam, classical music is not learnt with gadgetry.'

'I can't remember words. I don't know what they mean.'

'You don't understand Raminlingo?'

'Not this kind of Raminlingo. I mean these words, *ratiyaan*, *batiyaan*, etc.'

'Do you want me to teach you music or not?'

'Yes yes.'

'Then you forget about the gadgets. Sham is Krishna. Krishna is the embodiment of romantic love in classical music. His beloved is expressing her feelings of jealous love for him. The words are those of rejection, but the mood is love — *shringar*. She tells him not to beguile her with words any more but to go wherever he spent all those nights away from her', explained Sham, exasperatedly.

'Will he go away, then?'

'Madam, this is poetry.'

'But if she tells him to go away, he will and then . . . she doesn't really want him to go, does she?'

'Madam, don't we often say the opposite of what we mean? Like . . . like a few minutes ago, when you told me to go away.'

There was silence for a while. Shyam was suddenly embarrassed.

'But then, you were leaving.'

'Well, madam, Krishna would probably plead with his angry mistress. That is what she wants. Should we begin again?'

'That is what I wanted, too', said Rajni, looking at him naughtily. '*Ab na bolo mosey Shyam*.'

Flushing beetroot red, Shyam pretended to study his fingers as they danced on the tabla.

'Salaam, Ustad Sahib', she said coquettishly.

He knew the stages of seduction. She would first be an obedient pupil, then a wily courtesan.

'Salaam', he said.

'Ustad Sahib, I practised all night. You can't be angry with me today.'

'What did you practice?'

' "*Nindiya na aye, Sham, daras bina, Nindiya na aye*." And I know it means I can't sleep, Sham, unless I see you.'

Her arms had a sheen on them. Like pearls. She was wearing pearls in her ears.

Once in his arms, she would be what he wanted her to be, pliant and demanding at the same time.

What was he doing? He could be killed for this. Yet hadn't he known, hadn't Ustad Ram known what would come to pass if he started teaching her? Did he have a chance? He had never known such wealth. She seemed to be the embodiment of poetry, of every love song he had known.

'Ustad Sahib is feeling out of sorts today.'

'One who risks his life does at times fear the consequences.'

'And don't I risk anything?' she asked, her lips trembling. That was a trick that undid him completely. Did she know that? With superhuman effort he kept his distance.

'What do you risk, Madam?'

'Why, Ustad Sahib, this unfortunate creature has a heart, a heart that she cannot control.'

'And what does your heart say?' he asked smiling, in spite of himself.

'Oh, it wickedly keeps repeating a name.'

'And what name is it, madam?'

'What will you give me if I tell you?'

'What can I give you madam? I have nothing.'

'Which is to say, you don't want to give anything.'

'And do you think that allegation is true?'

'As true as your heart.'

'I wish I could reveal it.'

'What stops you?' she asked inching closer. 'O Sham.'

An Affair in the Twenty-first Century

Rajni did not bother to hide her affair from me. With the casual possessiveness of the privileged, she had marked me out as hers. Besides, as I found out later, deceit had far transcended the verbal in the twenty-first century.

I asked myself whether she was fulfilled at last. But where was the hunger in Rajni in the first place? Where was the desperation of desire? Rajni's life had always been crammed and over-flowing. Shyam was a new flavour that had been sold to her.

And Shyam? On the one hand there was his desert in the Drohi-ghetto, on the other, the cornucopia of Rajni. Three months of tasting morsels only whetted his appetite for more.

After three months of love-making Shyam's stray lock of hair went back to the flock. He seemed to have lost his panache. When he started his career it was with the belief that there was a possibility of getting himself declared Ramin, leave the Drohi ghetto, move to the centre of the city, or migrate and settle abroad. But none of these options, he realized with a sinking heart, led to Rajni.

Now he was beginning to understand Ram Mamu's insistence on continuing to live in the ghetto. He was beginning to understand the pain in Ustad Sahib's voice when he discussed the rate of mortality in the Drohi colonies. He was in fact beginning to despair.

Yet he still came up to the gates of the caste-colony regularly and had a pass made for two hours.

He would come wearing the same cloying perfume of roses.

It would rise up in the musical elevator with him to her flat on the tenth floor. He would press a bell and a robot inside would dutifully go from room to room announcing the arrival of a 'male', age — young adult; height — five feet nine inches . . .

The robot would still be making its rounds when Rajni pressed the remote to open the door. He would enter, diffident at first, aware of the fact that he was being watched on the screen.

That day, sick with a heart that wouldn't stop aching, Shyam sent a message saying he was unwell and would be unable to 'teach' madam.

Is it the law of love that there is a lover and a beloved, a worshipper and an image? Why do romantic twosomes on my screen keep slipping into this familiar sacerdotal position?

Perhaps love is essentially unfair. Perhaps it is one of those confounding, confused things I will never understand. Some must love; others must be loved. I can say on oath I was not interested in Shyam until he appeared on-screen almost of his own volition. He loves so well, so completely. He has such a wounded heart, so much pain that I can't do without him.

And Rajni? After receiving Shyam's message that day, Rajni went into the bathroom and stepped into the alabaster tub. The tub was foaming with extracts from herbs. She sat in the tub and rang the bell for her maid. The maid came at once and took down jars of unguents from a little shelf. She slowly began to rub Rajni's shoulders and back with it, slowly making circular motions with her finger tips and palms. She kneaded the soft flesh and Rajni sank deeper and deeper into the sweet-smelling water. She kept rubbing till only Rajni's head was out of the water. The jacuzzi jets teased various contours of her body, whetting the blood corpuscles beneath the delicate skin. Just above her left thigh was a small scar.

From here a tube had been inserted under the skin the previous year to suck out excess fat. Rajni's husband had objected to her thick thighs. The right thigh had healed but the left had got rather complicated. Rajni was now supposed to go in for plastic surgery to remove that scar and another operation to reconstruct her thigh and butt. She had held out for six weeks, refusing any more tampering with her body. She had had her fill of hospital procedures. Her nose job had taken three years of her life. Yes, it was painless. But soon she knew she would be called upon to bear a child. That was painless too. But she was tired of intrusions into her body.

Were her knuckles white with the disappointment of not meeting Shyam? Were her hands clenched into fists with anger? He could have at least come in or called. I cannot see because the green of the water has obstructed my sight. But I know that after she steps out of the bath, she will stand below a dryer that will pick up the surplus moisture from every pore of her body. She will spray herself with perfume with a diamond studded, gold dispenser. Then the maid will come again to help her dress. And thus bathed, perfumed and dressed, she will wait for her husband and the evening revelry.

Nothing obstructs my sight when I want to see Shyam.Perhaps it is because of the vacuum in which he lives. In the tiny hovel, it surrounds him like a halo.

Shyam's mother huffs up the stairs with a bucket of water. For the past week the Drohi colony has been without electricity and water. She is cooking the evening meal by candle light. Thanks to the Unmentioned-God there is money to buy candles. Shyam is making headway with his music. Her gamble has paid off. His father, bless his soul, had wanted him to train as a chauffeur. But she had seen where true mobility lay. She had presented the four-year-old to her older brother Ustad Ram to be trained in vocal music and now, thanks be to the Unmentioned, they had money. They would continue to get much more, she hoped, but the discontent that sat attractively on the twisted corners of Shyam's handsome mouth was beginning to fill her with misgivings. Something had happened to him recently. Was it Ram's influence that was showing up only now? Along with instilling poetry, had her brother also ignited a spark in Shyam's soul?

She could blame only her own side of the family for this. Their mother had turned into a raving fanatic in her last days. Throughout her life, she had never raised her voice, never struck her children and yet her religious teachings had always been incendiary stuff. She herself remembered hiding to avoid the lessons and then being dragged out to listen to the mad calm voice of Hameeda. But Ram had always listened spellbound. Now in the evening of his life, he had begun echoing their mother.

She sighed and wiped the perspiration from her face. She herself had been too busy to bother about religion. There had always been other pressing concerns. It was difficult enough to manage the solar cooking apparatus. It was made locally and was full of faults. Often the battery would run down when the rice was half cooked. Shyam's foreign trip should secure for them something better. She wasn't quite sure what would work in the primitive conditions in which they lived. The neighbours burnt the garbage they collected from Ramin colonies. Really, if Shyam could do a bit of this; if he would only pick up some things from their bins! Who knows why he went there if not for some scraps of their privileges. She raised her lined face and saw Shyam looking at her intently.

'Ammi, it's not being fair to you but . . .'

She wondered whether she should mention the cooking apparatus.

'Ammi, you look so, so old.'

'I am old son. I have such a grown-up son.'

'But Ammi the women I see there are quite different. Their hundred-year-old women look like you.'

'Oh, Unmentioned God, I don't want to live that long. Son, we are not Ramins.'

'You know, we could be if I try hard enough.'

'Have you received the papers?'

'No.'

'Then, son, I know it cannot be accomplished in my lifetime. I only wish you could try for some more Ramin state-privileges. Though of course it might be much better to concentrate on the procedure for migration. But all this will be for you, I won't be around that long.'

'Ammi, why d'you keep on saying this?'

'Because I want you to pay attention to the future. You have your life in front of you. Ram and I will not be here forever.'

'Ammi, do you know how they live, these Ramins?'

'I don't want to know, son. I don't want to know about the differences between heaven and hell. But I do want to tell you that for a Drohi the space between birth and death measures an inch. You can progress that much and no more.'

'I will change that before I die, Ammi.'

'Son, dreams that beguile the night should not invade our day.'

'The night has lasted for years because we have forgotten how to wait for the day', replied Shyam, quick as a flash.

'Perhaps the sun has forsaken us.'

'If we call out loudly to him, he will respond.'

They looked at each other and smiled. The warmth suddenly bound them, as did poetry.

Ammi hummed to herself as she bent towards the cooker. Lights came on and the room lost its mysterious quality. The paint on the wall was peeling off and in the top right corner was a large damp patch where rain water had seeped in. In the left corner, standing straight like a ramrod, was the tanpura.

Shyam was making towards it when Ammi said, 'How's your pupil doing?'

'Fine, Ammi.'

'Shyam,' she said suddenly, 'Ramin women are poisonous.'

'What do you mean?'

'I should have told you before. Ramin women have poison between their legs.'

'Have you become senile?'

'Some can destroy just with their touch. That's why they look like this', she continued.

'What about Ramin men?'

'Ramin men are born of poison.'

'You mean they are poisonous, too?'

'No, they are neutral, they are nothing. It is only the women.'

'Ammi, this kind of talk is crazy.'

'Son, I should have told you this before.'

'Ramin women are kept in chains.'

'And rightly, son. Imagine what they would do if they were set free.'

'Why, they would spread their wings and fly like birds.'

'Like locusts they would destroy everything that comes in their way.'

'Who would come in their way?'

'Men who love.'

'Ammi, you hate them.'

'On the contrary, they are fascinating, son. I can keep looking at them for hours.'

Shyam went up in the elevator, a gnawing in his heart. What was he doing? A predictable affair with a Ramin woman. That was all, wasn't it? He was wasting his youth, his energy, his emotion on something that approximated to a cold unfeeling idol.

Khwahish ko ahmqon ne prastish diya qarar,
Kya pujta hun us but-e-bedaadgar ko main.

The undiscriminating confound desire with devotion,
But why do I worship this cold, unfeeling idol.

He was confounding desire with devotion. But his feelings for Rajni went beyond desire. Something else in him besides desire was stirring vague misgivings about Rajni's health, for instance. She looked so breakable. What if she was really ill; what if she was dying slowly, her shapely limbs atrophying one after the other? Perhaps one day when he rang the bell, the servant would come out and say, 'She's not in . . . she's not in the world anymore.'

He was being silly. She wouldn't die. More likely, she would one day turn her face away haughtily and say, 'Ustad Sahib, no more. It's no fun, any more.'

And he would be the one who would lie vanquished.

Even if she didn't do that, was there anything in the affair that would last? Something in him rebelled against the transience inherent in the nature of their relationship.

He didn't wait for the traditional greeting.

'Janab, I have got something for you today.'

'Ustad Sahib, no greetings for this poor soul?'

'I thought I would first amaze you with the gift.'

'You amaze me with your looks today. Uncombed hair and an unshaven chin!'

'Do I offend?'

'You will have to try harder to do that.'

'Then let me offend fully.'

'Ustad Sahib, I am relieved. You smell the same.'

'Can I now give you my gift?'

'Umm. Give it gently.'

'It's rather big and unwieldy. Weighs sixty-six kg in fact.'

'Yes, that's rather unwieldy.'

'Should I slice myself and give you the parts one by one?'

'Oh, you give what is already mine.'

'Then I give to ask for a receipt, Madam.'

'Will a kiss do?'

'Only as a preliminary.'

'God, the extent of your desire makes me tremble.'

'Yes, it is enormous. I want to gobble you up.'

'I've been gobbled up. The time for that is over.'

'Then I am going to take you away.'

'Do so. I am all yours.'

He looked at her as she extended her arms seductively towards him and knew with pain that it was a game for her. There was no commitment in the lovely eyes that had faint lines around them today. She would only respond with alarm if he asked about those. She would whip out a magnifying mirror from somewhere and stare in it, excluding him totally.

'Sing, Madam. Durga today.'

With his heart melting in tenderness, he saw her stumble a bit as she rose to get her tanpura. Her long fingers strummed the strings and she began: *Sakhi ri . . .*

He, in turn, began on the tabla, waiting for the pain to leave his heart.

The Ramin Ardhangini

Rajni watched her husband interact. She knew that as his Ardhangini she ought to be by his side, clinking glass with glass; but after a while parties — especially ones as focused as this — started boring holes into her. There were so many people, so much to drink and so much gaiety — all directed to the business of making 'contacts'.

She knew that if she tried to interact she would feel her stuffing spill out; she would feel herself collapsing. She would become a shapeless nothing by the wall.

She saw her husband's flawless skin and clothes. Suresh was very good-looking. He also spoke and moved well. Her father had produced him with the air of gifting her the best: 'He is an intelligent boy; he will go very far in life', he had said.

Suresh definitely intended to go as far as possible. He made the best of every situation. She thought of the accessories he carried with him everywhere in his 'seamless' invisible pockets: a little mini-office and a minscule tape-prompter. The tape-prompter had hundreds of party conversations to choose from. He must have made his selection beforehand. Utterly confident, he would carry on talking with aplomb, sure of being bailed out by technology if his own wits should falter. He was one with machines.

Her heart did not leap when she saw him.

Marriage was not proving to be the joy-ride she had once thought it would be. She looked at the woman who was talking with her husband: undoubtedly, a Sadhvi. Perhaps she should have been one.

Suddenly she saw another Sadhvi she recognized —

Ms Aruna — breeze past her, 'Hi Rajni, you seem lost in thought!' she said looking elsewhere.

'I was wondering whether I should have been a Sadhvi', said Rajni.

'How weird!' Aruna muttered, uninterested.

Propping herself up with some effort Rajni realized that Ms Aruna in her supercilious way had ignored her comment.

Ms Aruna gushed, 'Oh Rajni, this is a marvellous dress!'

Rajni grit her teeth. For some reason, the compliment sounded like an insult.

'I think I should have been a Sadhvi', she repeated, her voice rising.

'Oh,' said Ms Aruna, 'yes, perhaps. But to be a wife and mother is fairly significant, you know. In the ultimate sense, one can't imagine a life without Ardhanginis, whereas we Sadhvis are dispensable creatures.'

'Really', said a male voice.

Ms Aruna turned back sharply, 'Sudhanshu, hi! I was talking with Ardhangini Rajni, Suresh Roy's wife.'

Sudhanshu joined his palms to make the traditional greeting. Rajni was taken aback. What did this excessive politeness signify? She noticed that Sudhanshu had a striking resemblance to her own husband. The impeccable clothes, the glowing skin, the straight features, were almost interchangeable. If he was a rival, her husband wouldn't leave the conversation to her. Sure enough, Suresh was soon by her side, fixing Sudhanshu with a gimlet eye.

'I hear that Educating Women has dropped the SA course', said Sudhanshu silkily.

'It was a dry-run', said Ms Aruna. Rajni noticed how clipped she was sounding now. All the gushiness, it seemed, had been reserved for her.

Sudhanshu threw back his head and roared with laughter, 'Dry-run for sexual awareness, eh? Great! It makes for a great corporate paradox.'

'Like a peaches and cream ad for a Dasa soap', said her husband at once.

'Or, as Aruna was saying Dispensable Sadhvis and Dried-out Ardhanginis', retorted Sudhanshu.

'Why dried-out?' Aruna asked aggressively.

'Haven't you seen the latest census report? The Ramin population has gone down by another two per cent. Obviously your Ardhanginis aren't producing much.'

'And why is that our responsibility?'

'You guys have a monopoly on motherhood courses. You claim to be the biggest.'

'It's for competitors to come up with alternatives', said Aruna. 'What do you think Rajni?'

Rajni started to ebb out through the holes their conversation had made in her mind. The three of them were sparring with relish. There was colour in Aruna's cheeks.

As Rajni felt increasingly diminished she knew with a sinking heart that she ought to have known what all this was about. In fact, a couple of times she caught Aruna's speculative eyes upon her. Was she wondering what a dumb woman Suresh had married? Rajni felt like passing quietly through the mock-parquet floor into the bosom of the earth — like Sita, who had been called upon to prove herself.

That night she flinched when he touched her. Surprise leapt to his face. He started to say something but then, restraining himself, turned over to the other side. A deep breath, almost a sigh, emanated from him as he switched off the lights.

In the darkness Rajni asked, 'Has it been a big loss?'

There was silence. 'No, not too big'. After a while Suresh said, 'Rajni, it's time you shifted to Rosalind.'

Rajni's heart sank. Rosalind was much too élitist and impossibly expensive. It was meant for the wives of spectacularly successful managers and industrialists. People like her normally did not aspire so high.

'Can we afford it?'

'It seems to have become a necessity.'

Rajni did not ask why.

'It's very difficult to get admission in the first place', she said in a low voice.

'I know. But I have an idea about that. I plan to use the hundred-year-old crone.'

'Ma?'

'Yes.'

'What can she do?'

'She is a hundred years old and quite a matriarch. She's also written some books. Our family profile is quite spectacular, you know. There are hardly any daughters, for one. My company should be able to use all this exotic material for an Ardhangini course.'

'How would that help me?'

'I'll make your admission a condition for the college we choose to introduce the course in. But she'll have to be sold first.'

'She's too old; what can she do?'

'Teach, or something.'

'She'll never agree.'

'You ask her. You seem to have a hold on her.'

There was silence again between them.

'Suresh, do you wish you were living with someone else?'

'Someone else?'

'Someone like Ms Aruna.'

He shrugged. 'I wanted a home and children. I love you Rajni.'

He turned to her and she saw that he was smiling slightly. He looked wistful in the dark. She moved closer and they kissed. After a while, removing his mouth from hers he said, 'Rajni, we might have to think about another operation for your thighs.'

She did not move away again. But after making love she felt so weary that she couldn't keep her eyes open a second longer.

She got up with a headache the next morning. After Suresh left for his office, she sat at the window with her cup of coffee — more chocolate than coffee — and stared out. She saw toy cars gliding out for work. She saw little bicycles with their Dasa riders wheeling into the Ramin area. She began to feel chilly so she rang the bell for her Dasi and asked her to turn down the air-conditioning. She would refuse the operation, she decided.

The sun was strong outside — the Dasas must be sweating it out on their cycles. Shyam, too, must be perspiring like them. She thought with slight distaste of his crumpled kurta-pyjama.

Shyam too had a flawless skin. Would she have got into the affair had he been mottled and pimpled? She knew of the rigorous medical check-up that all outsiders had to undergo before being allowed into Ramin households. But what if she were to contract an undetected virus from Shyam? What would Suresh do to her then?

Her heart began to hammer against her ribs in fear. Of course he would turn her out — politely, firmly, quietly. It would be an excellent excuse to get rid of her. Suresh never raised his voice. He didn't need to. She would have to go back to her father — disgraced — to the delight of her mother-in-law.

She would have to live in Kanpur again. Would she like that? Would she like her father's company, not arranging any more parties — not drinking any more? Would her father let her drink?

Rajni rang the bell for her Dasi again. This time she asked for fresh orange juice.

Pouring a liberal dose of vodka in it, she went back to the window. As she sipped, she calmed down gradually. What an idiot she was being! Of course Shyam had no undetected virus; he was clean. She began to think with pleasure of the perfume he wore. In the beginning she had found it too strong. Then later, when Shyam told her about how it was made — out of real roses — she had started liking it. He had even got her those roses once: bright pink, droopy-petalled, unlike any others she had ever seen.

Shyam was late that evening. He walked in rather uncouthly, she thought, and asked her to begin with the sargam. She started shakily and then stopped when she saw his frown.

'Rajni, this is ridiculous.'

'What's ridiculous, Ustad Sahib?'

'You are singing off-key — absolutely off, in fact.'

'I'll try again.'

'It's quite clear that you haven't practised in the last three days.'

'I was getting the bathrooms redone, Ustad Sahib. In fact, I'm so tired that I can hardly speak today.'

'In that case, perhaps I should go. After redoing the bathrooms, you can start with the kitchen.'

'Shyam, I have to do all this — you know I have to!'

'I don't. Why must you do all this continuously? How does it matter whether the pots are blue or green?'

'That's my work — I mean, I'm an Ardhangini.'

'The only thing you do which has any use whatsoever is your music, Rajni. And you spend weeks and days choosing pots.'

'Who's going to do all this then — Suresh?'

'I don't know. I just know that teaching you is breaking my heart. Just when I feel I've reached somewhere, you collapse and disintegrate.'

'Shyam, does it matter? I mean, how does it matter whether or not I sing well?'

'Then stop learning. Stop insulting the art. I didn't imagine you would play games with music. Let me resign immediately.'

He was screaming. Rajni saw that there were tears in his eyes. A muscle was quivering on his neck. He looked very young. She felt old suddenly. She reached out her hand to pat his shoulder, 'You know I don't play games with music. You know that. Please, please . . . I promise I will practise this evening.'

But in the evening Rajni did not practise her music. She lay stretched lifeless on her ornate bed. She looked rigid, both hands clenched tightly, arms and legs ramrod straight. She was imagining herself in the operating theatre. She transcended her body and watched it from a distance. The instruments around her looked menacing as they seemed to glare down at her white face and body. It was her face that looked more naked, shorn as it was of all embellishments, a vulnerable statement of terror.

The lash of the switch, the bite of wild dogs and the distant crowd of alien, masked faces.

She was being sliced into small and yet smaller pieces: the eye, the ear, the arm, the thigh, the breast. Why did it feel like being mauled and lashed? There was no punitive wildness here except in the terror of her own heart. Here was a methodical restructuring of the body. The process would be explained gently and firmly. 'Madam, you are beautiful — waist upwards. But look at these heavy thighs and the shapeless butt. Imagine yourself in a bathing costume. Tch, this won't do at all, Madam. Now, what I will do is move the fat around a bit. You will be asleep Madam, like Snow-white. When you get up you will be transformed into a beauty. You are lucky, Madam, to have such a caring husband.'

Rajni jumped up and tried to call her father. Nobody could force her to have an operation she didn't want, she told herself. A machine-voice told her that his number had changed. The fact that he had not bothered to give her the new number felt like a slap in the face.

She left a tearful message on the machine. She waited for his call, pacing up and down restlessly. She began to think of what she would say to him. There was nothing that would make sense, she realized with a shock. They had not talked to each other since her marriage.

Why didn't he return her call? She used to be able to get him immediately. Was she no longer the first — the first woman — in his life? Her throat dried up with misery.

Suresh wouldn't push her into something she didn't want, would he? He was a considerate man. She dialled Suresh's number and got his secretary instead. The secretary's bright and intelligent voice pierced through her head: yes, he would start for home shortly. No, he was at a meeting and couldn't be disturbed. What? Yes ma'am, of course she could tell her who were at the meeting: Ms Aruna, Ms Kanta, Ranjan Chowdhary, Von Schmidt.

Rajni poured herself a stiff whiskey and soda. After half an hour she made another drink — the same but bigger. After another fifteen minutes, yet another, and bigger. Interrupting incremental repetitions, the phone rang; the display showed her father. After two hours he was at last ready to receive the frantic call from his daughter.

'Papa,' she heard herself screech, 'Suresh wants me to have an operation again.'

'What operation Rajni? What are you talking about.'

'Papa, don't you remember? I have barely recovered from the thigh SAL.'

'Come on, sweetie. That was such minor surgery. You're a big girl now.'

'Papa, I don't want to have it.'

'Sweetie, how will it look if I intercede on your behalf every time? By the way, have you been drinking again?'

'Yes, no, yes. You don't love me any more.'

She banged the phone down and took a big gulp of the drink. He appeared again on the display but she pressed 'engaged'.

She didn't know when she fell off to sleep that evening. At half past twelve, when Suresh returned, he found her sprawled on the sofa. He covered her with a light blanket before turning in himself. Rajni's father had called him at his office.

Part Three

The Image

And time slipped out from her agonized hands . . .

Mother of Sons

It was a heartless war, as it often is in triangular love stories. Rajni's husband wanted her body, her lover wanted her soul. I got implicated in this one like never before in life. I got divided too.

It was Rajni's mother-in-law who won from me the favour of my image for her son.

'Ma, I have come to beg at your feet', she said. 'My son told me that his company has approached Rosalind College with a proposal for a new course. He would like you to introduce the course and take a few lectures — on an honorary basis, of course.'

'Oh, but who would want to listen to me?' I replied coyly.

'His company will see to all that. Ma, we will be eternally grateful if you could accept the offer because that will give us a launching pad for Rajni's admission there.'

Rosalind was the best Ardhangini college in Rajdhani.

'But Gini, I haven't taught for ages', I continued in the same mode.

'Oh, Ma, it's well within Ardhanginilaw for a widow to practice as a Sadhvi after the children are above eighteen. I checked that, of course. Besides, its for your family that you will be teaching.'

That wasn't what I had meant, so I shook my head vigorously indicating extreme embarrassment at the honour that was being thrust on me.

She flashed her trump card, 'Ma, Rajni needs to do something with those shapeless thighs of hers. Rosalind has the best gym in the country. She can try shedding the kilos there, otherwise it will have to be the much costlier operation, for which her father has agreed to pay only half.'

I shifted uncomfortably. As the mother-in-law spoke I began to sense the horror of hospitals on Rajni's behalf. I realized I had again made myself over. In return for their story I had already given my heart to Rajni and Shyam. The mother-in-law's faultless eyes rested quizzically on my face as I nodded my agreement. She folded her hands and bowed in mock gratitude.

As I got ready to address the Ardhanginis of the twenty-first century, fiction after fiction was constructed about me. I was on-screen almost every day. 'Pristine Past: pearls of wisdom strung by the hundred-year-old Ardhangini Shrimati Roy. Nothing will stand between you and the teacher: no monitor, no visuals: only unadulterated words.' Rosalind College in the background alternated with the sepia-toned visuals of a toothless old woman sitting on a string-bed, surrounded by young women, one of them pressing the grinning hag's legs. 'Mother of Sons imparts a hundred-year-old tradition of natural motherhood: Rosalind College where tradition blends with modernity.' 'The magic of words! Hear her talk continuously for half an hour without tape-prompters: Ardhangini Roy, the tapasvini, brought to your Ardhanginis by Educating Women Ltd at Rosalind.' Sadhvi Aruna endorsed me tirelessly: one visual showed her at my feet, gazing adoringly at my face. It was withdrawn rather hastily — to show a Sadhvi at an Ardhangini's feet could lead to controversy.

Questions were asked about my married life. Answers in large print would reach me an hour before the live interview. I told the demure city of Rajdhani about marital duties and responsibilities. 'My husband,' I said, every wrinkle glistening with glycerine and fond memory, 'used to be a sports-addict. He applied a number of times for membership to the Cricket Federation. The President would take no notice of the request until I got into the act. (Stress *I* please, Retake!) I invited him for dinner and he was bowled over. The second time he came he brought the nomination letter along with the flowers — not because I was a great cook but because I had taken the trouble to find out about him. Being a bachelor and a natural-food enthusiast, the man usually starved at parties. When I served him peas and carrots cooked in the way his mother used to, he felt he had attained heaven. Let me tell you that coveted nomination was referred to as the Roast Cabbage Nomination for years afterwards in my family.' (Cut, Retake.)

The course-content seemed equally incredible when it reached me. It was for love that I grit my teeth and became a mouthpiece for the producers of ideal Ardhanginis.

The first day at the college I saw twenty-five pairs of glittering eyes focused on me. Traditional kajal, kohl, or eyeliner cannot accomplish this; must be the new range of Incredible Fascinations from Seduction Cosmetics, I thought. Immediately I slipped into the role of a disapproving mother-in-law: shouldn't they use their Seduction sparingly; why wear it to college?

'Ladies, all of you are probably aware of the fact that this new course called "Natural Motherhood: Tradition and Practice" is being introduced on an experimental basis in the Ardhangini syllabus. The proprietors of Educating Women Ltd, after initiating the debate in various national fora last year, reached the conclusion that such a course definitely merits a trial. Out of forty odd colleges, they have selected Rosalind as the testing ground. Your college already enjoys the distinction of introducing in Raminland the new line of psychedelic eyeshadows and the hugely successful Corner-Clean detergent.

'The need for this course arose from two interrelated factors. First of all the fertility index of Ramins is showing an all-time low. There are simply too many cases of sexless marriages among Ramins. Secondly the Dasa population is burgeoning and their incursion into Ramin society foretells the spawning of a new race of Ramin-Dasas. It is not a secret that the concept of sexual purity, which is more or less being preserved for the world by Raminism, is being undermined even in this land these days. The incidents in the ghettos', I paused here, 'as all of you are aware, are showing a dramatic increase. Too many Ramin men are having liaisons with Dasa women. In fact, some Ramin men have gone so far as to adopt their children through Dasa women and make them legitimate heirs.'

Was this really a trend? I wondered. There had been a much publicized case last year, but to my knowledge that was the only one.

'This course, through lessons in natural sex to Ardhanginis, aims to reinstate the pristine and populous Ramin household.

'To be scrupulously fair to all concerned, let me begin with a quick outline of the debate that took place last year in the Sadhoo-Mahasabha concerning the feasibility of such a course. I am giving you both the pros and cons so that you have enough time to withdraw if you should so decide.

'The idealistic Sadhoos felt that a course on natural motherhood would lead to a dilution of the role of the Ardhangini prescribed by the ancient Lawgivers, as it involves lessons in sexual intercourse. A wife isn't and shouldn't be an object of lust. Men and women come together not merely to copulate but to live their lives according to dharma. The wife need not be seductive. If she fulfils her duty of lending her egg for producing sons, she should be cherished. An advanced course in sex, it was said, could create unreasonable expectations from a wife. Also, some expressed the opinion that detailed information on sex has been traditionally intended for the ears of courtesans and men, and would only work to destroy the captivating innocence of the Ramin Ardhanginis.'

There was a twitter in the class and two young women in the second row dissolved in helpless laughter. I watched their faces crumple. How unattractive they looked, with their pink gums exposed and their mouths wide open.

'Ladies,' I admonished them, 'have I strayed into a preliminary catering class for unmarried girls, or am I addressing young women who have had the good fortune of becoming Ardhanginis?'

There was instant silence. But the miasma — exhalations of perfume, deodorants, talcum powder etc. — arising out of the exotic group was enveloping my mind, threatening to snuff it out like a candle. I continued, suddenly on slippery ground.

'As I was saying, the question of propriety was raised most strongly by the idealistic Sadhoos. On the other hand, the pragmatist Sadhoos, stressing the fact that the age of innocence and truth has passed, also garnered support for their arguments from ancient texts. They argued that the law for an Ardhangini as described in most texts enjoins her to be attractive to her husband. For example, an Ardhangini gets permission to chastise her body only after the husband's death. This, the pragmatists pointed out, is an indication of the fact that the ancient Lawgivers understood the need for a wife to be sexually aware. However, the main thrust of their argument was expediency.'

'What does expediency mean, Ma?' asked a girl with purple hair, who was sitting next to Rajni. I noticed that Rajni's recorder was taking in practically every word I uttered. I answered the question, imagining the recorder gobbling up and then spewing out my words at her will, lengthening out syllables, creating arbitrary pauses.

'The pragmatists expressed the opinion that the whole purpose of the institution of marriage is to maintain purity, which is the essence of Raminland. And as that concept is being threatened today, radical measures would have to be undertaken to reconstruct the social fabric.

'We certainly do not want legitimization of other-wives, do we? We do not want to lose our privileged position by letting the distinction between child-of-wife and child-of-other-wives lapse, do we? We want to preserve the purity of race and caste; and Ladies, it is to this end that our course is being directed.'

Would my tongue shrivel and fall off? I wondered. Is there retribution for mouthing other people's lies? Nevertheless, I ploughed on

'I think most of you will be surprised to learn that Ramin women of my generation and even the succeeding generation gave birth very much like Dasa women: sometimes going to the doctor only after having carried the foetus in the womb for nine months. Very few needed fertility experts or in-vitro fertilization devices. In fact, so many needed to be on the pill to prevent conception.

'I am not going so far back as to privilege the regressive Dasa-process of biological births over laboratory births. I only propose that conception should as far as possible be during sexual intercourse. This would be a poetic moment that would imprint itself on the man's mind. He would realize that it isn't only the egg but his Ardhangini herself who is the instrument of his rebirth. He will feel united with you for ever. Also, it will be several times cheaper than ART (Assisted Reproductive Techniques).'

There, it was over, I comforted myself. Soon, I can escape.

'As you probably realize, at my age it would be impossible for me to conduct classes on a regular basis. And really, I have also forgotten the finer points of lovemaking, it was so long back.'

The class giggled tentatively.

'So the lectures will alternate with visual material. In the bygone glorious age of religion, which preceded the Pre-Poornaramin period, the science and the art of the erotic were highly developed. We have obtained slides and pictures of centuries-old temple sculpture which we will display in due course.

'I would like to know whether you have any questions and as we have not been introduced I would be grateful if you tell me your names.'

There was a long gap before a girl in the third row got to her feet.

'Ma', she said. No doubt it was my age that made them

address me as Ma. 'I am Sushmita, Ardhangini-wife of Dr Ranjan Gupta, MD, FRCS. My husband feels that this course will not be complete . . . will be . . . incomplete unless a survey is undertaken to find out what exactly Ramin men like. I mean . . . '

'You mean a course built on a purely theoretical basis is not likely to accomplish very much', I said, taking over in desperation. 'This is a good idea. As I have already said, a great deal of research has gone into devising this course. We could also incorporate counselling sessions. Of course the expense, in that case, is likely to go up.'

'Ma,' said another voice, 'I am Rakshita Jain, Ardhangini-wife of Akshay Jain, Proprietor Magic Years-Childcraft. I want to know why, if sex and conception are natural processes, we need to learn about them.'

'My dear child,' I said — I was prepared for this question — 'your argument, that is, pitting the instinctive against what is learnt behaviour, reminds me of the propaganda that has been on for the last three years, which is intended to destroy the very foundation of Educating Women Ltd. I need not name the progenitors of this fallacious point of view. There are commercial interests at stake, and Educating Women Ltd is a fast expanding concern. The rating of Womened Culture, for instance, has dipped considerably ever since EW started ten more courses last year. Womened Culture has been insinuating that women who emerge from EW courses are too mechanical in their approach to domesticity. I ask you ladies, what should be taught in Ardhangini courses, if not a pragmatic and dynamic approach to the household? Why have the courses at all if everything is instinctive?'

'I am Ranjita, Ardhangini-wife of Kamal Kakkar, Middleman for Lerouche. Ma, I want to tell you how much I enjoyed listening to you. It has been a wonderful experience.'

My throat was parched after my performance.

'Thank you, I will now take my leave. I hope there will be more questions next time, after you have pondered on today's lecture for a while.'

I saw them leave, one by one. Rajni was taller than the average Ramin woman. Otherwise there was little to mark her off from the others: a pale, vacuous face framed by waves tinted auburn, and glittering jewels. But the mascara was smudged even today, giving her eyes the same bruised look that I had noticed the first time we met. She was wearing a shimmering dress, black and navy blue. It had a little train. She had to hold it up when she walked. In the land of Poornaramin women are dreams.

The Last Lover of Raminland

That night I was almost asleep when the videophone started buzzing insistently. This late! I picked up the receiver.

'Sorry to trouble you so late at night, Ma. It's me — Shyam.'

I was surprised.

'You must be taken aback', he continued. I got up with slight difficulty and pressed both the view-buttons. Shyam appeared on-screen, looking quite bewildered himself, probably at the sudden coming on of the screen at his end also.

'Shyam! Are you Rajni's music teacher?'

'Yes', he said, as though surprised that I should ask.

'Where are you calling from?'

'Ma, I cannot tell you. Can I come and talk to you tomorrow?'

'Yes', I said.

'I will come at . . . ' There was a slight disturbance and he went off the screen. The connection was broken.

His eyes were close together. That squint made him look rather unfinished, perhaps even younger than he was. Shyam must be spending long hours in front of the mirror. He probably took time deciding what to wear, meticulously arranging his charms like a peacock — yes — that is what he was. A peacock with his plumage on display. Why was he strutting for me?

The next day I waited for the bell to ring all morning. Shyam came at four in the afternoon.

'Ma, I made bold to see you, today.'

'Yes', I said, inadvertently sounding Ramin and forbidding. It was one thing hearing tales of love from my Ardhangini, another to admit the adulterer into my house.

'Ma, I am a poor Drohi.'

'Nobody is poor in Raminland', I reminded him.

'I mean, I'm a nobody and it is presumptuous of me to address you directly.'

'Yes', I said. The words were seductive and I was at once on my guard.

There was a long silence. What had he expected? That I would lay the red carpet for him?

He twitched nervously on the sofa.

'I have my tea at four-thirty', I told him. It was a quarter past four.

'Ma, I have come to see you for something very important.'

'I am waiting for you to begin telling me about it.'

He continued as if he hadn't heard me. 'Ma, I want to talk to you about Raj . . . about my pupil.'

I was suddenly curious. This was Shyam the lover — the bold, foolhardy lover.

Perhaps he sensed the change in my mood. He relaxed a bit and continued, 'Ma, I am risking my life. Yesterday, I made a call from an acquaintance's house in his absence. I had to cut off because he came in suddenly. In fact, he saw me putting the receiver down.'

'Yes?'

'Rajni isn't well. I mean, I want to tell you that something is wrong with her.'

He seemed to be suffering.

'There's something wrong with her. It seems as if she's under some tension. Have you noticed her eyes? I mean, it's as though she swings from crying to laughing to crying again. And she grips things so tightly, her knuckles are always white and her hands always clenched into fists.'

'Why are you telling me all this, Shyam. I think there's precious little I can do.'

'Ma, if anybody can do anything in this case, it's you. I know you love her as she loves you.'

I felt as though somebody had slapped me across the face. He had no right to talk to me about that illicit word, 'love'.

'Ma, I've been teaching her for more than six months now. Let me tell you she has the potential to be a great artist. Often, I feel humble before her. At times she surpasses everything that I have taught her. But these days, I've begun despairing of her. Ma, the world of music will lose if she doesn't give herself to it.'

'What do you want me to do?'

'Help her, Ma.'

'What do you mean? She is a Ramin woman, not a Dasa. She can do what she wants. What do you mean?'

'I don't know. Please don't take offence at what I've said. I'm just a Drohi. So often I don't know what I'm talking about. My soul said I must come here and talk to you.'

He was young and earnest; his eyes dreamed.

'I'm not angry. Go now. I'll think about what you have said.'

After many years that day I smelt the odour of a world that I had locked out. Shyam was male, impoverished, and yes, he smelt of roses and perspiration. He brought into my living room the bus-journey he had made to the Ramin colony and the inadequate lunch he had grabbed that afternoon. But nothing in the conversation had prepared me for what happened the next day.

I spent the morning writing, and then at about eleven I went into the kitchen. I opened the fridge for a glass of water and found Jagdamba sitting there. She was scrawling on the inside. She pulled me in and shut the door.

My refrigeration system is a veritable walk-in cupboard with inner compartments of varying temperatures. The outermost portion, where Jagdamba sat, was maintained at a slightly lower temperature than the rest of the flat; the idea being that before a party chilled foodstuff could be meticulously arranged on serving trays without the danger of its melting. So much is geared for parties in Raminland.

'Go to ghetto 99 at once. Meet Shyam. The driver knows', said the graffiti in a large and neat hand. I was surprised that Jagdamba could write at all. They are not doing a bad job of educating the Dasas in Raminlingo. It was stupid of Jagdamba to fall into this great secrecy act. She probably thought that my family had installed a spy device in the house. Surely my family wouldn't stoop to . . .

Jagdamba was watching; there was trepidation in the large dark eyes. She was risking her life. I could run her in for complicity with the Drohis. Nobody would challenge my word as a Ramin and employer. I saw that she was gripping a rod with one hand . . . did she . . . could she? Did she think she could kill me and get away with it?

'The life of a Dasa is of no account whatsoever. We live and die for Maya', she hissed dramatically.

Who in Poornaramin's name was this Maya?

'Jagdamba, there is a strange smell inside.' I said, 'Clean the fridge properly', I continued, while stepping out with the uncomfortable feeling of facing a camera.

Ghetto 99 was not in our sector. We drove through the élite twice-born colony; huge family houses nestled here in glowing green lawns and turf. We reached the flyover beside the Great Poornaramin temple where giant steel screens reflected the sleek silver body of my car. Beyond the shining metal I could see the rounded domes sticking out like outsize breasts. Yes, that seemed to be the analogy for the building: the obscenity of contrast between the clean angles of flawless steel and the old curvaceous stone monument of a bygone era struck me with new force.

The construction of the temple used a technique called wrapping, which is centuries old — dating back to the Vaastu shastras, which in turn are about the science of magic in architecture, we had been told. The wrapper around the pre-existing Dargah and mosque is in the form of giant inverted cones leaning outward. The idol of Poornaramin, who is also the patron deity of Raminland, is installed in one of the cones.

At some distance from the temple there are other domed relics: an austere imperial tomb, an octagonal prayer-hall. They all had long complex names and histories. They are now pretty curiosities in the gardens that surround the temple. There is a silence that is appropriate for worship all around, as it is an exclusive Ramin area.

As soon as I saw the temple, I began to sense the squall of the former Nizamuddin basti and the makeshift bazaar: shops selling embroidered caps and cheap plasticware, the muezzin's call to prayer, the smell of kebabs cooking on skewers. I could almost hear the beat of the Qawwali as it used to be sung at the Dargah there: the Sufi Qawwali of love, shocking in the directness of its erotic imagery.

I asked the chauffeur to pull up and got out of the car. For a while, I stared at the temple. This was where the high-pitched call used to come from: a call for devotion and prayer different from ours, an alien call as though from another country. There stood the Ghalib Academy once. Hadn't I gone through all this before: some sixty years ago when I heard the Qawwali at the very same spot and a story started about a woman called Rajni?

There was no need to go on. But somehow the discovery of the future had become incumbent to — to cessation. Was this where I was going? To discover the end in ghetto no. 99? Surely this was the end of the road, the last adventure, the last book.

Suddenly the bells began to clamour in the temple and the electronic sound-system took over the environment, 'The evening hymn to Poornaramin sponsored by PVT Japanese Bathroom Fixtures and Fittings.'

The soft Poornaramin chant seemed to wipe out even the vestiges of memory.

I straightened myself. My chauffeur, who had come out of the car and was supporting me, looked uncomprehendingly at my face. We walked back to the car.

I noticed that as we progressed toward their outskirts the colonies became poorer. Where they touched the Ramin colonies, the Dasa colonies had rows of neat identical houses often sporting the name of their patrons in neon lights. Towards the other edge, houses were made of junk, plastic sheets and old hoardings. The effect was bizarre. We would unexpectedly come across the picture of a table laid with diamond-studded cutlery but a dog would be lifting a leg to pee on it.

The houses showed that there was a caste system strictly based on the economics of employment operating here. Jagdamba would be a Ramin-dasa — the way she fleeces me at every opportunity, I thought.

I put the window down and the blighted landscape blew into the car. I felt buried in sand. The driver gesticulated wildly to me. I ignored him.

Ghetto 99 seemed to house the lowest of the low, even among the Dasa-Drohis. Heaps of rubbish lay everywhere. Stray dogs with huge, staring eyes were rummaging in them. The driver parked the car and started following me at a respectful distance.

'Sit in the car. It's not safe to leave it like this.'

He bowed his head in acquiescence and handed me the phone.

'Ma, I have dialled security. Just enter the call if necessary.'

I was amazed at his initiative.

'Who asked you to do this?'

'Annadata.'

He meant my oldest son.

'How does he know about this?'

'I am supposed to file in your programme every day.'

The family hadn't called me to remonstrate against my

going alone. That would surely have been the natural thing to do. I took the phone from him as though it were a living thing with teeth. Holding it gingerly, I began to make my way to the ghetto. They could have inserted a listening-in device or even a watching-device in the phone. But these things are expensive; would they bother?

I decided I couldn't really risk it. As I stumbled and almost fell over a pile of stones, I deliberately flung the instrument viciously on the ground.

'Careful Ma', said Shyam coming out of the hut. With all the rubbish for a backdrop, how clean and handsome he looked. 'It's broken', he said, picking up the phone.

'Go and give it to the driver. Perhaps I can get it repaired.'

I wasn't going to let the mask of a thrifty old woman drop. I saw Shyam walk to the car. He had a swagger too. I saw him slap the driver's back in greeting and suddenly felt alienated. I was among people of a different class and caste. What was I doing here?

'Ma, come in. That was an excellent idea', Shyam said. He looked confident in a way he hadn't before.

'Why have you called me here?' I sounded angry, even to myself.

'Ma, Rajni your Gini, told me that . . .'

'What did she say?'

'Ma, I love Rajni. I want to marry her.'

'Have you asked her?'

'Not yet.'

He looked obstinate and beautiful. I said nothing. He seemed to disintegrate with the poignancy of what he had said.

'Rajni told me that it is only because of you that she could start her music again. Then, Mohanty Bhai said it might be a good idea to tell you about ourselves. We need your help.'

'Who is Mohanty?'

'Mohanty Bhai?' He thrust a paper into my hands. 'Ma, Mohanty Bhai has written about Maya here.'

Jagdamba had mentioned Maya too. 'Who is Maya? What does she have to do with Rajni and you?' I asked.

He said it would take him very long to explain. He insisted that I read the paper first.

It looked like a broadsheet. 'From the Margins of Raminland' it proclaimed in embellished letters. The paper was rough to the touch but I liked its feel. 'What is it?' I asked him.

'Mohanty Bhai said it's a draft of the information-file he intends to start about us.'

Shyam held it out to me as though it were the holy Gita. Having studied in a Dasa-Drohi school, he still had the reverence for the printed word that screen-taught Ramins had lost completely.

This is what the paper said:

Sixty years after the appearance of Poornaramin, a new deity is stalking the heavily guarded boundaries of Raminland. It is doubtful whether her presence can be spotted accurately even by the most sophisticated radars in the world because she is reborn with every infant in the Dasa-Drohi colonies. The Dasas who sing hymns in her praise and the Drohis who bow to her reverentially, do not know when exactly the original Maya presented herself as an alternative to Raminism. Only one statement can be made with some degree of certainty: Maya does not offend the multifarious streams of religious sects that were driven underground by the victory of Poornaramin. In fact, the concept of Maya is non-combative enough to have Islamic Drohi recruits in her fast expanding cadres.

Maya is an ancient philosophical concept that in literal translation means illusion. Maya can be good or bad, creative or destructive. Traditionally, the material world has been called Maya, but the Almighty has also been revered as Mayavi or the mesmeriser. Besides this, in common parlance the word Maya has the connotations of 'engagement' and 'involvement' from which release can come only in the form of ascetic renunciation or death. 'We live and die for Maya', is the refrain of the devotees who call themselves Mayans.

There should definitely be some political agenda associated with a group that professes a readiness to 'die'; but the Mayans put forward no alternative scheme for the political or economic reorganization of Raminland. All that they have is a ritual: the creation of Maya, which is to be performed all night by every Mayan, after a birth in the community. Their definition of Maya defeats argument: Maya is 'what isn't'; and Maya is created by live music, poetry recitals, and by making articles that cannot be duplicated. All this is dedicated to the new-born to equip it for life as a non-Ramin. Increasingly, these meetings are getting more volatile: more explicitly anti-Ramin than they ever were before.

My contention, which may appear far-fetched, is that by this ritual the Mayans are setting out to provide an alternative to the Ramin social structure. The display of group creativity by Mayans is a challenge to the sophisticated stratification of society effected by Raminism. They are more significant than other protest groups because their focus seems to be social regeneration. Mayans are using the dormant strains of religion (with all its obscurantism) to harness fertility and creativity against the values that give Ramin society its hierarchical shape.

Biswajeet Mohanty, the writer of this piece, was doing an ethnomusicological study of the Rampur gharana of Hindustani classical music, Shyam told me. He had come to the Dasa-Drohi ghetto like any other Ramin, armed with vaccines and a working knowledge of Raminlingo. His university had given him three years off and very little money. He had been lucky to get some funding from publishers of travelogues.

He knew what he had to do to keep body and soul together. For the travelogue, he had to capture the mystique, the sheer magic of Hindustani classical music: show it emerging like a lotus out of the muck of the Drohi ghettos; he had to produce in six months an exotic documentary called 'The Lost Generations of Music: A Discovery'. For his thesis, that very few were interested in, he would explore the changing codes in performances, relating them to the Sadhoo's policy of selective patronage of classical musicians. Writing the latter would take many years. Like most academics, Biswajeet had made his peace with market forces.

He had discovered Shyam accidentally. Scouting around for a music-teacher, he was introduced to the young lad and was at once struck by his earnestness.

'I will teach you only if you do riyaaz regularly, Mohanty Bhai. People at your age take much longer to learn.'

Biswajeet could see that here was a vocalist who would in time be devoured by the international market. He had the right admixture of conceit, good-looks, ambition and talent.

'Who is your own Ustad?'

'Ustad Ram Kanpurwaale. He is my uncle.'

Mohanty knew that Ram had been unofficially blacklisted by the Department of Culture. During his last foreign trip he had spoken too much about the Drohi ghettos and too little about Raminism.

'Ustad Ram! Really! I met him last month. He is very ill.'

A shadow of pain passed over the youthful face.

'The Ramins have finished him off.'

Mohanty was excited, 'Do you hate the Ramins?'

Shyam was silent.

'Do you think — do you think they have destroyed the rich and diverse heritage of this country?'

'I don't know, Mohanty Bhai.'

'You are a Drohi. Don't all Drohis hate Ramins?'

'I am a worshipper of Maya.'

'You mean you are not a Drohi?'

'I was born in a Drohi household, Mohanty Bhai, but it was Maya who taught me who I am.'

Maya

Shyam told me the story of Maya.

Maya was born in the furthest ring of the Dasa-Drohi ghetto. This community of the urban-dispossessed had been housed at the brink of the city by the government. The flotsam that they were, it was hoped that they would wash ashore into villages. When the Sadhoos reorganized Rajdhani their pavement dwellings in the city were wrecked — so was their livelihood. They used to provide shoe-shine boys, coolies, paani-wallahs, chai-wallahs as well as pimps and prostitutes to Delhi.

Soon, they became associated with other petty offences: pilfering, foraging, etc. Or they worked as the servants of servants, petitioning other dispossessed people to make two ends meet. They were not docile enough to be absorbed in Ramin households and not lethal enough to make inroads into them. They continued to live on the outskirts of the city even though they were irredeemable exiles from the pure heart of Rajdhani.

The community continued to dwindle rapidly. Unlike some Dasas they were not able to work out any survival strategies. It was as if a collective death wish had replaced their life force in the upheaval during the transition from PrePoornaramin to Poornaramin days.

What did Maya's father do? Anything and nothing! Maya didn't know how he earned the meagre amounts he sometimes brought home. She had never talked to him. Ever since she could remember he would return home drunk, beat her mother and then there would be another kind of scuffle in the dark corner of the hutment.

Every two years her mother's belly would begin to swell. She would start looking like a doll improvised with matchsticks and a balloon. And one day she would pop and out would come a sister to increase Maya's problems.

Maya had had to be a nurse since her childhood. Someone was always ill in the house. The usual childhood ailments were compounded by the mother's ill-health. Maya was so used to looking after the ailing that as a rare treat when she was once taken to visit an aunt, she rushed to the corner where the bed lay and peered under the bed-clothes. 'Where is she?' she demanded. When asked who she meant, Maya replied, 'The one who is ill, of course.'

When she was not nursing the ill, Maya spent her time picking up fights with family and friends. There was continuous biting, scratching, screaming, kicking. It was as though there was a volcano bubbling inside her which needed frequent minor eruptions so as not to explode through the thin body.

After witnessing three pregnancies and births, Maya told her mother to stop. Her mother mumbled that there was no boy in the house. This was when Maya uttered her first wise saw: 'Saali, are you trying to be Ramin? Are you going to fry the boys and eat them to fill your tummy?'

At that time Maya was eight. She had never met a Ramin. She had attended the Dasa-Drohi school for a couple of years and then dropped out. She was of course aware of the existence of Ramins. Along with other children, she too used to walk miles to watch films: she was aware of the difference between Ramins and others and it had got her gut. Perhaps this was the first indication of the contrariness Maya was going to show through the rest of her life.

It was her mother's seventh delivery that launched Maya on to her public career.

Nobody expected Ramvati to survive the seventh. Pale and emaciated, she dragged her overworked body around the house. If it hadn't been for Maya she would have dropped dead in her fifth month. The sixteen-year-old cooked, cleaned, fed her sisters and her inebriated father. She was Ramvati's pole of strength. Wiry of build and sour of expression, she lashed out at everyone. Even the drunkard did not dare lay his hands on his wife before Maya's angry eyes.

Ramvati went into labour at three in the morning and Maya ran to call the neighbours. None of the neighbours was home. A Dasa-don had organized an all-night film show to celebrate his son's birthday. In fact, Maya's father was there too.

By the time Maya returned, the labour was well advanced. The baby's head was showing. Barking at her mother to stop squealing like a pig being slaughtered, Maya set to work.

It was a miracle. How did the young, inexperienced girl know what to do? Young and inexperienced? But that's what Ramvati said.

Ramvati told the people of the ghetto how a halo of light had surrounded her daughter as she resuscitated the still-born male child. Maya simply commanded the baby to live and the blue puckered body began to breathe, she said.

Soon after, in fact just a week later, there was another complicated delivery case in the neighbourhood. Maya heard the screams and decided to assist in the delivery that was being conducted by an aged midwife. She rubbed the belly of the labouring woman with oil and a healthy boy was born.

Two boys in a week and one of them born to a woman who had had six fruitless pregnancies! The community began to invite Maya to assist at deliveries.

It is said that in the beginning of her career as the divinely inspired midwife, Maya brought forth a string of strong babies.

I am aware that a rational explanation exists for Maya's successes. Rationalists, for instance, might want to counter the miracle of resuscitation by saying that Maya must have pumped the placenta to help the baby breathe or she could have thumped him hard, the way traditional midwives do.

Shyam himself said that the second delivery case was not complicated at all: the expectant mother, being too young, was screaming her guts out in sheer fright; and it wasn't the oil massage as much as the tongue-lashing that Maya gave to the husband that calmed the woman down and made the birth possible. But Shyam gave me this information without perceiving the contradiction. For him Maya was miraculous *because* she was always so rational. I agree. Rationality is miraculous in the state of Poornaramin.

Shrivelled like an old woman at twenty-one, Maya exercised all the privileges associated with old age. She cursed and abused the family members of pregnant women for neglecting them; she threatened the husbands with castration. Besides, she refused to marry. I have seen it all, she would say. This would be followed by a sneering comment on the limited usefulness of men's private parts and the trouble they created for women.

The legend of Maya through the process of osmosis began to seep into the upper Dasa-Drohi ghettos. There is a woman who looks like a churail but who is actually a divine being caged in an ugly body. She is the messiah of women and children, the preserver of the wordly Moh-Maya. She has been sent on earth for the rejuvenation of the downtrodden. The upper crust among the 'downtrodden' still preferred the hospital for deliveries but Maya began to be called to nurture the womb for boys and to cure ailments that Ramin doctors gave up on.

Shyam told me about one such incident with great relish.

The Dasa-don from whose house Maya was catapulted to the heights of fame, lived in a fifty-room mansion. The problem was the daughter-in-law who wouldn't conceive. One after the other, four women had entered the life of the moustachioed, muscular young man who was the heir to the ill-gotten fortune of the Don, and then been kicked out for not extending the patrilinear. The son was being rather mulish about sending off this one. She had large eyes and long hair, but then what use was all this to the Don and his millions?

Maya was called as a desperate last bid because the private Ramin doctors, after extracting their unmentionable fees, had pronounced the girl healthy and capable of bearing offsprings.

Maya disappeared indoors with the girl.

'Do you like him?' she asked.

The girl blushed and nodded.

'How many times do you do it?'

'All the time', answered the girl with a giggle.

'Do you want to stay with him.'

'Oh yes', the girl cooed.

'Then why . . .?'

'Perhaps God doesn't want it.'

'Are you trying to be Ramin or what, you simpering raand?' scolded Maya at once.

'What can I do if I don't have children?'

'This bloody house has fifty rooms, you daughter of a mindless churail; so many male relatives crawling all over the place', said Maya. 'If you don't produce something to show for your nocturnal activities, you will be out on your bum very soon.'

'He will never leave me; he loves me', said the girl.

'Forget it', said Maya. She pointed to the screen, the music system, the silver furniture in the room, 'Do you think he will leave all this for you? If you want all this, produce something — any way you can.'

It is said that eleven months after Maya began visiting the girl, the Don's family was blessed with a daughter. The Don tolerantly said that as the skies had opened up with so much difficulty, a downpour couldn't be expected immediately. It is also said that when he first heard of the pregnancy, he took off the gold chain he used to wear around his neck and gave it to Maya.

After this, as the people of her community say, Maya's hut began to fill up with strange and priceless things: many gold and silver ornaments, four dinner sets, six tea sets, twenty make-up kits, one rusted pedicure kit, one tool kit, one antediluvian black and white television, one vacuum cleaner which only exhaled. Maya's had become a name to swear by in the ghettos.

There are some ugly incidents associated with this period: incidents of raised voices and squabbles, incidents of curses flung at the new-born when the gifts were inadequate.

But later on she realized her mistake for giving in to the lure of things, Shyam said.

Money is not an unmixed blessing. It can entrap you for life. You have to be divinely inspired to be able to renounce the things it can buy — or hellishly condemned.

Maya's family developed gargantuan appetites. Her father would drink, her sisters and brothers-in-law would watch movies, Ramvati would exchange one piece of jewellery for another at the local goldsmith's — all day.

Spartan and disapproving, Maya watched all this with her beady eyes. Her wants perforce had remained few and limited. Her shrivelled body rejected all lushness and her sourness did not allow sumptuousness.

It is said that at twenty-five, when all her hair had turned grey, Maya started slipping into long spells of catatonic stupor. She was often in pain. At times, especially at night, she felt she was being de-boned with a sharp knife. She would treat herself with a combination of herbs and pain-killers bought from Ramin shops, but resolutely refused to see a doctor.

One day, returning home late from a delivery she found her family glued to the screen. Maya was tired and hungry. No food had been kept aside for her. She cursed but nobody heard. The heroine was being molested by six men. Too tired to shout any louder Maya fell off to sleep.

That night she ascended to a higher plane of existence. From the next day, she would accept only a very small amount as token money. She refused presents altogether. People were surprised and then delighted. Many more sighted the halo around her head. They gave her no rest: she was out from morning till night. She treated the slightly ill, the terminally ill, the dying, the old, the young and the very young.

'We are not Ramins', she would retort sharply when asked why she was refusing the gifts. 'Why should we waste our days and nights collecting things we do not need? I have no time for all these gadgets.'

Her sisters cursed silently. Maya was acting true to form: mean and selfish. But they knew they were defeated. Brothers-in-law had to be sent out to look for work. Ramvati returned grumbling to the kitchen. The drunkard could start drinking only at midday.

But nobody could say a word to Maya. She was too well entrenched as the tyrant in the house and as the messiah outside. Besides, if she left they would be deprived of the plum position in the community that brought in the bread if no longer the butter of the household.

Shyam said that during this period Maya learned to want nothing more from this world. She became truly divine. I disagree. It was a springcleaning of sorts. In this period Maya got rid of the inessentials and began to wait for something much more precious.

The state of affairs where Maya doctored for free did not last very long. Very soon things started going wrong. She appeared to be fumbling. A couple of boys she delivered were still born. Then a labouring woman died, spewing blood even as Maya massaged.

People trembled with fright. Were the gods forsaking them? Was the miracle going to end? Maya's refusal to accept presents was undoubtedly the manifestation of divine wrath. People in the ghetto knew that favours — whether divine or otherwise — are always on a pay-back basis.

Maya would have to be propitiated, mollified, tricked, brought back into line; a web of maya would have to be spun for Maya.

The next family she went to was that of embroiderers who

had fallen on hard days because the motifs they made were no longer fashionable. They presented her with a shawl. It had been made by the women of the house for the Ramin market. The family, misinterpreting the sparkle in her eye, pleaded with her to accept it. It has cost us nothing to make and it is nothing, they begged.

The shawl was beautiful: flowers and leaves in complex stitches and bright colours lay on a cream background.

Maya had never seen anything like this before. She ran her hand over the pattern; it felt exquisite. Maya was transported to the fairy tales that she had never heard in her childhood — but which are an integral part of a child's mind. The shawl felt like a full belly and the warmth of her mother's body. She rubbed it against her cheek. It felt like sunshine; there was something extravagant about it.

Maya asked the family suspiciously what it was worth. Nothing, they reiterated, nothing. They were right. In the Dasa-Drohi ghetto nobody could buy it — and the Ramins wouldn't buy anything outmoded.

Maya came home and spread the shawl on her bed. The lonely shrivelled up body found a strange solace in beauty. She slept well, caressing it.

After each delivery it became the practice to present Maya with things whose worth was denied. This was the high point in her career as one around whom the Dasa-Drohis would later organize their belief. Over months her hutment filled up with other nothings: paper lanterns, cardboard boxes, gaudily painted clay birds, exquisite wood carvings, blocky stone sculptures: a medley of the priceless and the worthless. These were from folk artists whose craft had not found buyers, from tribes who had forgotten their skills. Maya was making them remember. Each pregnancy — and pregnancies there were many — stirred chords of memory, rejuvenated half-smudged patterns, rekindled hope. The moneyed Dasa-Drohis of course, would employ others to create for them, but those who had nothing at all offered their music, songs or poetry at Maya's shrine. They had to give of themselves.

So they were forced to find themselves, extend themselves, reach out to a future that with the descent of Poornaramin had been snatched away from them.

Such is the law of life. I who have brought forth three lives, know that the swelling of the womb can challenge the deepest death wish and make the deadest heart beat with hope. I believe in the miracle of Maya.

Maya was attached by a thousand threads of love to her newly found wealth. She would come home and smile at the colours and motifs around her. At music-vigils she would close her eyes and drink the rhythm in.

In contrast with the gadgetry she had brought home earlier, the knick-knacks that she now collected seemed a heap of rubbish to her sisters, brothers-in-law and brother. They stopped encircling her like vultures. For the first time in her life, Maya knew a kind of peace. She still treated everybody — women, children and men. But her stupors were getting longer; her tongue was softening and not lashing out as much as it had once. Maya was not tense and restless any more. She was unwinding into eternity.

She was thirty when she died.

Maya and Shyam

'How did you get embroiled with Maya?' I asked Shyam.

It was an improbable coupling. They were moving in different directions — Shyam towards the stratosphere on wings of love and hope; Maya on the ground reality of sweat and blood.

It was just by chance that he found out about Maya, Shyam told me. One day when he returned early from the Ramin colony he saw his mother toiling over a piece of complex embroidery.

'Ammi, I'm not going to wear this strange pink colour', he said.

'It's not for you.'

'Nobody will buy it.'

'I am not going to sell it.'

'Who is it for, then?'

'Arvind's wife is going to have a baby very soon.'

'Is it for her?'

'No, it's for Maya.'

'Who is Maya, Ammi? A Dasa-woman?'

Ammi nodded, 'She died many years ago.'

'Then how can this be for her?'

'Whenever there is a birth, Shyam, we pray to her. She protects both mother and child.'

'We? Who are the we, Ammi?'

'All of us — all who live in the ghetto.'

'Drohis and Dasas?'

'Yes.'

'Ammi, how can you go to a meeting where there are Dasas?'

'Maya was a Dasa-woman and had it not been for her, son, you would not have been here either.'

Once, in the middle of the night Maya was called to the Drohi ghetto — Hameeda's daughter is in labour, she was told.

She was struck by the peace that seemed to radiate from the face of the labouring woman.

'Hey, you,' she said roughly, 'why have I been called if you aren't even screaming yet? I don't have the time to sit and stare for hours at your beautiful face.'

The young woman flinched as if in fear and whispered softly, 'Aapa, the pain has been coming for six hours. It is almost continuous now.'

Maya felt a wave of love engulf her. This was a frequent irritant: the sight of a pregnant woman would often reduce her insides to swirling water. Shrugging off the feeling, she subjected the woman to her experienced scrutiny and concluded that it wouldn't take long.

'How's it that you aren't screaming your guts out? It's your first, isn't it?'

The older woman by the labouring one's side, who had been a part of the decor up till now said, 'You belong to these parts, still you ask. Pain is the condition of our being. My daughter doesn't waste her breath needlessly.' Saying this, she went back to being a statue. Her face immobile, she sat rigidly at the bedside as if any movement would make something precious spill over.

As if to prove her mother wrong, the younger woman began to make a kind of crooning noise. Maya realized that she was singing. Often she would gasp in-between, but then continue. Bemused, Maya went about her work.

Only at the penultimate state of labour did the young woman give herself up to soft cries of pain. Maya stroked her back, making soothing sounds all the time.

The baby was born choking within the loop of the umbilical cord. Maya extricated the little head, thumped the body to make it breathe easily and looked up to see the older woman at her knees thumping her own head on the ground.

'Oh, to be reduced to this', she was crying. 'I can't even take my little girl to a proper hospital for her first delivery. Oh, to be reduced to this, O Unmentioned-God.'

It seemed that she had lost her head completely. Her voice had risen to a hysterical pitch and she was trembling violently.

'You selfish hag', screeched Maya at once. 'Your daughter has just given birth to a bouncing son and you split the heavens with your shrieks.'

The older woman collapsed sobbing on the floor.

'Let her be Aapa', said the soft weak voice from the bed. 'My father passed away two years ago and she has never been the same since. See how my Shyam is suckling at my breast.'

The sobbing woman reared up from the floor like a snake: 'You are giving him a kafir-name. You want to go to hell?'

'Bhaijaan said I was to call him Shyam. He said he went to Auliya's tomb and took the blessing from the mazaar for this name. Shyam, your Ram Mamu said I was to call you Shyam.'

On her way back to her own hut Maya found the song of the woman playing in her ears. No, it was definitely not film-music: it was strange, slow and meandering. It sounded easy. She tried to sing like that and found her voice tripping and falling in the most ungainly fashion.

Try as she might she could not get rid of the haunting music. Maya was longing for the sound of the younger woman's voice, for the sight of her lovely face that radiated compassion: Aapa, she had said, but on her own tongue the word sounded ugly and abrupt.

On the fifteenth day after that birth, Maya found herself making towards the Drohi ghetto once again.

There was another person in the house that day. Maya regarded the young man with a jealous frown. He was sitting very close to the young woman and running his fingers through her hair. The woman was singing.

'Bhaijaan, this is the lady I told you about.'

Lady! The word was unfamiliar, but Maya knew it connoted worthiness and respect and Bhaijaan meant brother. She was mollified. She noticed the resemblance between the two, but the brother seemed more elongated and fragile. The expression he wore was also much sadder. Now that he had removed his hands from his sister's hair, he seemed particularly vulnerable.

He folded his hands and spoke in a magnificent voice.

'We owe you everything, lady. Even the next seven generations will not be able to repay this debt. My sister is my life; if anything had happened to her or Shyam, I would have killed myself.'

'Why weren't you here then?' asked Maya, at once wary of male protestations of loyalty.

'Lady, you destroy me with this question. Of course I should have been here. But this unfortunate being along with my brother-in-law had gone to Kanpur to look for some decent employment. I wanted to welcome the baby with some good news.'

'Bhaijaan has got a job in a big school in Kanpur', said the woman happily. 'He will teach singing to Ramin girls.'

Maya spat in disgust: 'Ramin girls — Ram, Ram!'

The woman laughed, 'Yes, that's his name Ram — Ustad Ram. Ustad Ram Kanpurwaale. But Aapa, you are like my mother. Every time the Ramins are mentioned, bile rises to her mouth.'

'And rightly, child', said the young man looking sad and worn out. 'I went to the Poornaramin temple today and . . . '

'That was Nizamuddin', screeched the older woman suddenly. She had been very quiet till now. 'That was Nizamuddin. Your father used to sing there before these dogs . . . these dogs . . .' She was trembling.

'Ammi, enough, that's enough', said the young woman.

'These Ramins drowned everything in their milk. They broke Ghalib's grave,' lamented Hameeda, 'they destroyed everything. Your father cried so much when they killed Jamaal. How could they . . . how could they!'

Maya put her arms around her shoulders, 'Saale vandals. Were they relations of yours: Ghalib and Jamaal?'

'Aapa, Ghalib was a poet. My father used to sing his ghazals', said the woman.

Maya looked nonplussed.

'The song I was singing today when you came — that was Ghalib's.'

Maya sat watching the three interact. Ram and the woman shushed their mother, massaging her forehead and legs. The older woman was soon controlled and put to bed.

'Aapa, eat with us today', said the woman with relief.

'No, no. I should be on my way.'

'Please Aapa, it will just take a few minutes. The meal is ready. Let me feed Shyam and then I'll serve it.'

She began to hum again while nursing the baby. Maya watched greedily.

'Is this Ghalib-baba's song?' she asked.

'Oh no, should I sing Ghalib's ghazal? '

'Anything.'

'I'll sing his sad-sad ghazal', she laughed and sang for Maya: the kind of extravagant offering that only child-bearers and nurturers are capable of.

Midway in the song, while she laid out the meal, Ram joined in. If the woman's voice had been attractive, the brother's voice captured the soul. Strange and beautiful words flew out at Maya from the duo's rendering. Ram broke off a couple of times to scold the woman for her pronunciation. Maya caught on that Ghalib was not to be treated lightly.

From that day, Maya's fulminations against the Ramins included one more theme, 'the murder of Baba Ghalib.'

Twenty years later Shyam went with his mother to a birth vigil dedicated to Maya.

It was a full-moon night. Arvind Dasa had prepared the shamiana as though for a wedding. The mother with her new-born baby sat on a rug in the centre of the shamiana.

Shyam looked around: the men were dark and sweaty, the women fat and ungainly. Everybody was talking in loud, excited voices. But very soon people settled down. The women formed a ring around the mother. The men dispersed all around the shamiana, a part of the birth ceremony, yet they were careful to keep their distance from womanly functions. First of all, an old woman prayed over the baby asking Maya to protect it from the evil eye. Then one of the younger women began to play the dholak. It was a simple beat — ta tin tin ta. Another woman began to sing.

It was a song that all of them seemed to know well. All the women joined in. Shyam saw his mother close her eyes and incline her head as she did when praying. The song was about the perfection of the new-born child. It went on enumerating different parts of the child's body. The feet like lotus: they are worth much more than big shiny cars. The eyes like those of a gazelle: what are diamonds and rubies worth in comparison to these? This baby is not produced in a factory, the women sang, so its worth cannot be determined. Nothing, oh nothing in the world can buy this baby from us.

The imagery was rough and stark, the voices unschooled. Shyam shifted uncomfortably. But the words interested him: they challenged the privileged to try and take this wealth away from them.

Other such songs continued — the burden was the same. The baby was worth much more than anything else in the world because it was the only one of its kind. During the song many people rose to give gifts to the mother and child. Shyam saw his own mother place her embroidery reverentially on the heap.

It was getting late. Soon the mother and child went indoors, followed by most of the women.

The men continued to chat. The talk shifted to the Ramins almost naturally. It was as though, after the foolhardy challenge flung at the privileged by the women, the men were taking stock of the real situation. Ramu the driver began to narrate his tale of woe, 'What is the life of a Dasa, tell me! I just got this cough and Madam had me examined at the hospital. She threw me out after that without an explanation. No letter of recommendation, nothing. How will I get another job? Madam says I have got the Dasa disease — tuberculosis. She said they will employ me again after I've been cured. Now, who will feed my family until then?'

The others clucked their tongues in sympathy. They all had similar tales to tell. Ramin employers could be kind and generous but they could also be whimsical. The conversation focused on the complaints; unreasonable working hours, indifference, pettiness. Most of those employed earned enough to feed and clothe their families; it was something else that was bothering them. Perhaps it was the disconcerting knowledge that, if their own employers decided to throw them out, they would plummet down to the starving brigade. Or perhaps it was the proximity to Ramins that reduced their own lives: what they had, seemed like so much tin and pastiche compared with the luxury they saw every day. Shyam recognized his own pain in their disgruntled observations.

'They think they own us', said a man spitting paan juice. 'What they don't understand is that only love, not money, can buy people.'

'Let's stop talking of these demons. We have to deal with them every day, anyway.'

Some men began to play cards.

Shyam asked tentatively, 'Then what is the way out?'

'Way out of what?'

'Way out of their control. After all, it's a fact that they can do what they like with our lives.'

'Only if we let them', said the paan-juice man.

'What do you mean — if we let them; as if we have a choice', said the second man.

'I would destroy the whole lot of them if I could', said the third.

'We must all get together and wipe out that lot', said yet another.

'We must go away from all this and start a new life',

interjected the paan-juice man again. 'We can grow our own food, make our own clothes. Then what control can they exercise on us?'

Some laughed and called him the great sanyasi. The paan-juice man suddenly turned to Shyam and said, 'You teach singing to the Ramins, don't you? These women have assaulted our ear-drums for so long with voices like split flutes being played by asthmatics. Now we deserve something better. Why don't you sing a song for us?'

'My songs are of a different kind', protested Shyam.

'Songs are songs. They don't belong only to the Ramins. We can understand them too. Maya used to like Ghalib baba's song. He was a great Drohi baba, wasn't he?'

Shyam's first visit to Maya's shrine ended with poetry. He sang Ghalib's ghazals for them. In the beginning they asked for the meaning of every word. After a while they gave up trying to understand and just drank in the music. Shyam went on — it wasn't often that he got an uncritical audience like this.

His mother came out, to go home with him. When she heard Shyam singing, she went in proudly and got the other women out. She knew she could show him off here without danger of the evil eye falling on him.

Shyam sang till it was almost morning and then he talked. He was unable to stop. He told them the story of demolitions, the murder of memories, the crucifixion of history. The tale of injustice and lies came pouring out, engulfing with love the images he carried in his heart: his raving grandmother, his saddened uncle Ram, his mother's face — innocent and prematurely lined; and above all the picture-perfect Rajni with a smudge on her cheek. The Ramins — Ramin men, Rajni's husband — were no ordinary villains; they were diabolical. Their might extended beyond discernible time and space. As Shyam spoke, his own future began to crystallize in front of his eyes. How could he have ever wanted to join their ranks? They were the enemy of every single dream and hope he had. His future clearly lay in their defeat and extermination.

The people had grouped around him to listen. They looked with awe at him and sipped their morning glasses of tea. In appearance he was like the Ramins: tall and fair. But he was on their side. He could be their avenging angel. They came up closer, to look at him in the light of the rising sun.

I asked Shyam whether he was the leader of the Mayans.

He told me that he was sure he was the chosen one to carry on the work Maya had started. 'That evening in the Dasa ghetto I had felt special, Ma. It was as though I was inspired by an unknown power. I don't know where the feeling came from.'

But I do. Love is a miracle. It changes dross into gold, profane into divine, people into images. Nothing would ever be the same for Shyam again.

'What do you have in common with Maya?' I asked, prodding him further.

'Ma, I sing. I create music. That's what Maya is about — creation. It's taken me a lifetime's labour to learn this much. Ustad Ram used to make me do eight hours of riyaaz every day. Rajni can be a Mayan too.'

'How?'

'When she sings, I can feel her soul soar. She's very special too. She belongs here, with me.'

His eyes, beseeching and proud in turn, followed me as I got ready to leave the ghetto. What he wanted was not mine to give. Would the Creator feel helpless, too, watching the created scale precarious heights to pluck the moon from the sky? I wondered.

Faith

Back in my lavish flat, the image of Shyam's eager face lingered in my mind's eye. His expression was the same as I had often seen on the faces of people queuing up to offer prayers at temples. The image of the beloved is the ultimate illusion, the deepest involvement — the strongest maya. It can extract the biggest sacrifice from human beings. Shyam was hell-bent on slitting his throat on the altar of love. But then, I consoled myself, only images can save their lovers. Didn't the idol of Shiva come to life in a temple to stay the tapasvi's hand as it rose ominously to commit self-sacrifice?

At last routine pulled me back, but in my world I realized with a shock that Shyam's love-story could lead to disaster. My family would definitely press charges against Rajni. They had spent a lot fashioning her, and adultery is a punishable act under Ardhanginilaw. It could be used to shoot down Rajni if she came unstuck from her pedestal: 'If a woman made insolent by the rank of her family or by her own parts, proves false to her husband, the Sadhoos should have her devoured by dogs in some much frequented place.'

Shyam himself would fare even worse: 'If the woman is a Ramin and the paramour a Dasa or Drohi, he will be deprived of his member and of all his property if she be not guarded, and of all his property and his life if she be guarded.'

I trembled for myself. I had dared to lend a sympathetic ear to what could lead to the annihilation of their lives. I would be equally responsible if anything happened.

Shyam's faith and the reality of Raminland clashed, crumbled and spilled over into the stream of my life — muddying it further, retarding its flow.

But to my surprise I saw that there was no case-law attached to the section on adultery in Ardhanginilaw. No wife had ever transgressed it in the state of Poornaramin.

It was not a good time for fulfilling other obligations.

I was feeling out of sorts when I addressed my class of Ardhanginis at Rosalind that week. I began shakily: 'Ladies, natural motherhood is not only a matter of the body; it is also a matter of the mind. I would like to refer to a report by one of the most famous fertility experts of Raminland. Dr Rajan suggests that it is not only the infrequency of intercourse but also the kind of relationship between men and women that affects the conception of babies.'

Dr Rajan had spoken mainly about the fall in sperm-count because of tension, anxiety and the fast-paced life which was the norm among Ramins. The brief sent by my great-grandson's company had focused on the power of the mind on the body. Of course, it was Ardhangini-power that was discussed. Ardhanginis could make the husbands relax and feel powerful and potent. With love and a transparent faith in the husbands' performance they could achieve anything they wanted, the brief concluded.

There was a reference in the brief to a film released the previous year. The film, *Devi,* is about a woman who falls in love with an explorer called Arvind. As she travels all over the world looking for him, she is raped several times by secret tribes and robots who trick and betray her. I had puked. Every rape had been shown and the image of Arvind hid the censored bits every time. The heroine later kills herself. In spite of public opposition, Arvind installs her mummified body in a temple. The child she had conceived grows in a tube and Arvind adopts him after his 'birth'. Eighteen years later, the boy develops into a miraculous Arvind clone and his dead mother begins to be worshipped as a Devi.

I hadn't figured out how to talk about this vulgar metaphor for the triumph of love over all man-made hurdles to the infallible women who sat listening to me. In a strange way they looked too asexual to give any love at all.

'I realize I have been growing old in a little island quite untouched by the sea-change around me,' I continued fumblingly, 'it may be even right to say that I don't know you at all. I would therefore like to talk to you, instead of lecturing . . .'

'This is not fair', exploded Mahima in the second row.

'I don't understand', I said, a little uncertainly.

'Ma, we are paying through our noses for this course. And we are not much wiser than we were before.'

'Only one of us has conceived.'

I was struck dumb. I was not only supposed to package knowledge and deliver it, but also to get results. These glossy women were asserting their rights as consumers.

'I realize that this course is extremely expensive but, my dear, the creation of a baby is, as I said, not a skill that I can teach. I can deal with your minds only when I know them. Also, I am not teaching this course for the money. I can increase its duration and deliver a few lectures for free, if you feel it necessary.'

A murmur of affirmation in the room convinced me I had struck the right note.

'Ma, we would like the potion for free as well', said a voice.

'Potion?'

'Yes, the conception-potion.'

'I am not a magician; I don't know about any such potion.'

'But the course-content promised traditional methods. It's not fair to charge extra for the potion.'

It seemed they were demanding a medicine from me. My head began to ache.

'Ladies, I don't know what you're talking about. Don't you know that there are no magical potions that can form babies?'

There was an uneasy silence.

'Ma, I hope you are aware of the fact that Richa has

conceived after buying the Roy conception-potion being marketed by the college', a girl called Rati said in clipped tones.

I was shocked; I had not been informed of any such scheme. 'If Richa has conceived it must be because of the natural biological process. There can be no other reason', I replied.

'Richa's husband has been abroad for the last two months and she didn't go to a fertility clinic', Mahima said looking straight into my eyes.

'Ladies, I'm sorry. I cannot endorse a product I know nothing about. I can't imagine why it's been given my name. I can only say once again that no potion can lead to conception without there being sexual intercourse between a man and a woman.'

'Kunti in the Mahabharat is supposed to have conceived from the Gods.' 'Lord Shiva's semen is supposed to have floated down on a lotus leaf to six women who bore his child.' 'What do you think Assisted Reproductive Techniques are?' 'What are you teaching us then?' Questions came at me in a deluge, threatening to drown commonsense. They spoke of myths and medicines in one breath; fiction and reality clashed in a single sentence. Coloured lips set like rubies on pale faces made short shrift of human processes and claimed magic as a way of life.

'Ladies, I will register a protest to the college as well as Educating Women Ltd. They have no right to play this confidence trick on you. I hope all of you will support me in this.'

There was silence. They looked at me suspiciously.

'We have no problems in registering our protest as long as they give us a complete refund', said Mahima at last, a bit uncertainly.

I nodded, wondering how to ensure that.

A whisper ran buzzing around the room several times.

Rati stood up and began to speak, 'Ladies, let us not forget that the Roy conception-potion has already led to one success which has been reported in the journal *Nari*. Richa describes the potency of the potion in some detail. She says in the interview that when she drank it a ray of light seemed to go through her body like a wave. She found out about the baby soon after. It seems to me that Ma is denying her own success to put her price up further. This should be resisted at all cost.'

'My dear Rati,' I countered exasperatedly, 'surely you know that conception cannot be immaculate. If Richa has conceived it is because of sexual intercourse.'

'What are you suggesting?' asked Rati coldly. There was complete silence in the room. The beautiful faces in front of me suddenly began to look dangerous.

'I am not suggesting anything that isn't self-evident', I said.

'What is self-evident? If her husband was away how could she have had sexual intercourse?'

'You should ask her this question.'

The hiss in the room was one of incredulity.

'I hope you know that we can report your aspersion on the fair name of Ardhangini Richa to the Purity Party', said Mahima.

The Purity Party had stoned a Sadhvi teacher last year for saying that the institution of Ardhanginis was one of the biggest mistakes of the Sadhoo regime.

'Ladies, this is unethical and unbelievable. I refuse to be party to such a discussion any more. I have nothing more to teach you.'

As I came out of the room, my lapis lazuli-studded walking stick clattered a bit against the silence that was rising behind me like a wall.

The Ramin Ardhangini is a work of art. She could be divine or demonic; she could never be human. The country was being flooded with perfect images: stamped and guaranteed to last a lifetime. As long as there are images, there would be believers.

But too soon, my family intervened once again between me and higher education.

The Ramin Man

The twitter of the doorbell next morning took me unawares. I looked at my great grandson with something approaching awe. He had not bothered to fix an appointment. Everything about him had the gloss of perfect finish. His clean-cut patrician features were set in an expression of quiet dignity. The mouth was luscious but too well-controlled to dissolve into emotion. He had got his degree in business management two years ago from the States at twenty-three. Last year, at twenty-four he had married Rajni.

'Ma, I've come to thank you for all you've done for my wife.'

This was a masterstroke: begin damnation with gratitude.

'There's no need Ma, to carry on.'

'I had no intention of continuing with the Natural Motherhood course — if this is what you mean.'

He whipped out a little machine, placed it on the table and spoke in it. 'Yes, fax me the resignation, please. Yes, resignation to be signed by Shrimati Roy.'

The machine beeped obediently and smoothly unravelled a plastic sheet.

I signed it equally obediently.

'We are also withdrawing the Roy conception potion.'

'I am glad.'

'Our family has gained a lot from the sacrifices of the older generation.'

'Yes', I said blankly.

'Your lectures could have meant a net profit of one thousand crore for Educating Women Ltd, after paying for the space in the press.'

'I cannot condone lies.'

'The potion was a kind of mind-medicine being marketed to "encourage reproduction". We hadn't made any promises.'

'Why have you withdrawn it then?'

'Because of their loss of faith in you as a teacher. Perhaps I should have spoken to you earlier and explained our strategy in detail. I thought the project would take off on its own momentum. The mistake was probably staking all on one individual.'

'Where did I go wrong?' I asked and my voice sounded tight even to me.

'You went wrong when you fumbled and they responded by asking for discounts. There have been twenty applications for refund, since then. People — and women particularly — always have to be made to feel that they are getting much more than their money's worth. You practically told them there was no need for such a course. But Ma, I haven't come here to blame you. You can now rest your old bones. I know you tried your best for all of us.'

'What will you do now?'

'Regarding this project? Well, first of all, we'll try and restore your credibility as the mother of sons.'

I opened my mouth to protest, but he carried on.

'One option could be to project your resignation as moral outrage against the youth. I have other ideas — perhaps a medical scare, something to do with fertility. The fertility rate has already caught the imagination of the people. There is anxiety that the Ramin people are facing extinction.'

'Are they really?'

'Oh, I don't know,' he said, shrugging his shoulders, 'there seem to be enough men and women queuing up for everything.'

I remained silent but he pressed on.

'We could use fertility tips instead of natural motherhood', he said.

'What is the difference', I couldn't resist asking.

'The difference is always one of perspective, Ma. Natural

Motherhood was a woman to woman — Ardhangini to Ardhangini — course. Fertility tips would comprise tips from experts. Only thing is that the overheads are extremely high when doctors are involved. These medical practitioners have become sharks. The number of times they botch up simple things is to be seen to be believed. Rajni's SAL, for instance,' — as if being patient with a child he broke off to explain, 'SAL is suction aided lipolysis: the procedure is simple and has been in use for the last hundred years. Rajni was in pain for almost three months after her SAL and the scar has still to heal. To top it all, she regained her fat almost immediately. I had not gone in for the more sophisticated "restructuring" where the fat would have been pushed up to fill out her hips a little, thinking that the simplest surgery is the best. I was planning to take her for a bathing holiday to Nice but as she hasn't lost any of the fat in Rosalind either, restructuring will have to be done.'

'It all sounds terrible. No wonder she looks so strained', I said.

'Oh, she's all right in spite of what this Shyam creature has been telling you.'

I balked. Was there anything this boy did not know?

'As you probably know she has been conducting an X-rated romance with Shyam. It's interesting but I think she's a bit undiscriminating. I won't tolerate a Dasa', he said and frowned a bit.

'Don't you mind?' I stammered, stunned.

'I'm a liberal man and this is the twenty-first century. Ardhanginis do make a lot of mistakes, don't they? I wish she wouldn't be so pig-headed about this cosmetic surgery, though. No Ardhangini gads about with thighs like hers. Didn't you know about Shyam?'

I didn't reply.

'It's a bit of a lottery this way, isn't it? When one marries one doesn't quite know what one is being landed with: a frigid woman, an oversexed woman, an extravagant woman. I'll take your leave now.'

Was there a hint of grief there, some emotion, some wringing of the heart? There seemed to be only a swagger of accomplishment in his walk. I looked at his retreating back. He was holding his head high, impatient to speed away in his accident-proof car. Speeding was a way of life in Raminland. Whoever could afford it, imported accident-proof radar cars. Accidents, thus, usually claimed dispensable lives: Dasas who walked, and sometimes Ardhanginis who had not been provided an adequate expense account.

I wanted to crack him to take a look inside.

I wanted to find something glittering in the sun, by the roadside. I wanted to take it in my hands, caress it and then throw it vehemently at the proud retreating back of my great grandson. I wanted blood to pour in streams down his pearl-sheen shirt.

The End of the Affair

After my great-grandson left, the blood started to sing in my ears. I felt like a crusader. I emptied the contents of my lockers — my jewellery — into a sack and asked the driver to take me to Shyam.

Shyam gripped my hands tightly in gratitude. 'Ma, thanks for your support.'

'My blessings will always be with you, Shyam. Take my car and run away with Rajni.'

He was quiet for a while and then he said, 'We only live once, Ma. Don't you think it would be foolhardy to throw away the only life one has on the Rajdhani roads? I have work to do here. Ustad Ram died yesterday. The permission to shift him to the Ramin area did not come through till the end. We could have collected lakhs in his name but we couldn't even get adequate medical help for him. He died of asthma in the general ward of a Dasa-Drohi hospital. The ICU there had run out of oxygen.'

'How old was he?'

'Sixty.'

'I'm sorry, Shyam.'

'We are going to organize condolence meetings all over the country, Ma. We are going to tell people the whole story.'

'How?'

'I'm going to get in touch with his students. There are thousands of them. So many are Ramins, and then Mohanty Bhai has promised help from his colleagues at the university.'

'But what about Rajni?'

'I sent in my resignation this morning. It might be too dangerous to continue.'

'You mean you won't see her again.'

'Not in that house. No.'

'Did it mean so little to you?'

'I'm doing all this for her.'

'How?'

'Love isn't only union with the beloved, is it?'

'Then what is love?'

'It is carrying the image of the beloved in ones heart always', he said ardently.

'Does she love you, Shyam?'

'Yes she does. But she doesn't know it herself.

'How will you meet her again?'

'I will wait for her Ma. I will wait for her all my life', he said.

At a propitious time in life the beloved image has to be recast in its most miniature form and placed in an auspicious amulet. Wearing that amulet one can plunge into battle. What could I say? I was feeling light-headed.

'Ma, you aren't well? You aren't looking all right.'

"I'm old, Shyam. Its been years since I spent so much time in a natural environment. Has Delhi always been this hot?"

'You say Delhi?'

'Yes. I have gone back many years today.'

'You should be resting, Ma.'

He put his arm around my shoulder and told me about his last meeting with Rajni.

Shyam held the lovely face in his hands and his mind worked furiously. He had often wondered about the possibility of his love affair being avidly watched by Rajni's husband. Being watched was a danger Drohis grew up with in Raminland. But that day he could not risk it. He decided to take her out of this house. He was going to declare his intentions.

'I feel mad, Madam.'

'Isn't that your normal state of mind?'

'When I come to see you, yes certainly. Otherwise I am a reasonably wise man. But today, I'm madder than usual.'

'So should I sing an insane raga?'

'No Madam. Today I want to sit beside you in a fast-moving vehicle and you must sing, you must reach the *sama* at every speed-breaker.'

She laughed, 'I have sent off the chauffeur.'

'Madam, this low-down fellow has a license.'

'Whatever for?' she asked, with the insensitivity of the rich.

'I learnt driving to earn a livelihood and then chose music to lose it. But surely you drive yourself?'

'I do', she said simply. And, of course, he understood that she didn't want to be seen driving him.

After some hesitation she settled in the seat beside him. That was perhaps more acceptable than driving a Drohi.

Shyam drove carefully for a while and she sang the raga Yaman in a low, measured voice.

'Madam the car's stalling. I'll have to check. He bounded out before Rajni could turn on the auto check and signalled furiously to her to stay put. After a momentary fumbling she continued to sing. Shyam fiddled around with the insides, disconnecting the batteries.

'We will have to call a taxi, madam. The batteries have to be recharged.' Rajni dialled her phone obediently.

Within minutes they were in a solar-operated taxi — not as fast or smooth as the electric car and certainly not as elegant. Shyam knew that his exertions could still have been in vain if they were being followed professionally. His only hope was his own marginality. With the screen drawn between them and the driver, he sat back with relief.

Shyam leaned towards Rajni, their shoulders touched. Both bodies trembled and Shyam felt something change suddenly in his pupil; she became malleable. She laid her head on his shoulder and he began to stroke her smooth rounded arm. She nestled closer, as if seeking his warmth. In their relationship he had always been the seeker. She was the monsoon cloud, whimsical, yet overwhelming on his horizon. Her sudden vulnerability almost hurt with its unexpectedness.

'Dearest Rajni, are you all right?'

'Yes, Ustad Sahib.'

'I'm not well at all of course.'

'Really!'

'Yes, a certain illness has made me forget everything. How is it that you don't catch that illness? You come close enough.'

'What do you want me to forget?'

'Forget that you are you — a Ramin woman.'

'All right. I've forgotten.'

'Good. Now I will tell you who you are. You are a beautiful singer — a Mayan.'

'What is a Mayan?'

'A Mayan is somebody who can create beautiful music.'

'So are both of us Mayans?'

'Yes. You are a beautiful, wonderful singer.'

'Okay.'

'So unenthusiastic about your new self? I take "beautiful" back.'

'I won't give it', she said smiling at last. 'But perhaps it's not mine to give.'

'Of course it is. It's yours. Don't give it to anybody, not even to me.'

'What are you teaching me, Ustad Sahib?'

'I am teaching you to live. No, I'm teaching you to love, which is the same thing.'

'I don't understand.'

'All right. I'm going to tell you a story about two lovers and you will have to write the ending.'

'Okay,' she said, 'what happens to the two lovers?'

'People hate them for loving and try punishing them.'

'And then?'

'And then they are left with nothing except each other. I have a problem in this story. The woman is Ramin.'

'What is the problem?'

'Do you think I can ask her to leave everything and live in a Drohi house?'

'Can she do it?'

'There is a law against it. She can be fed to wild dogs for being adulterous.'

'She may not want that.'

'Yes. But this is just a threat from those who don't love.'

'And anyway, this is only a story, isn't it?'

'Oh no, it's real.'

'If it is real, it's a terrifying prospect.'

'The terror is in equal measure for both of us.'

'What will happen if we succeed?'

'We will live together, we will sing together, we will travel a lot.'

'That sounds strange.'

'What sounds strange?'

'This being together so much. But where shall we be together?'

'I don't know, love. We will have to create that space. It doesn't exist yet.'

'Everybody will say I've gone mad.'

'Perhaps you have gone mad. Isn't it better to be mad?'

'I feel mad — totally mad — and there's no therapist to drag me back.'

'That's a poem, my moon.'

'I can't write poems.'

'In a story you can do anything.'

'What will people say?'

'They will talk about you and me.'

'What's special about you and me?'

'That stories like ours are possible.'

I wanted to believe Shyam. This ending had everything I had always striven for — roundness, continuity, completeness.

Art-of-the-State

On the way back from the ghetto after handing over my worldly wealth to Shyam, I paid a visit to the Chief Police Officer of Rajdhani. I declared in writing that I had made over my Ardhangini-wealth in favour of a Dasa woman called Maya, willingly and in full possession of my senses.

In my lonely flat, I waited for a word from my family.

There was deathly silence. Nobody came to visit me, nobody remonstrated against my unprecedented gift to outsiders. I had won, I thought. My books had at last percolated down to my family. Shyam would organize his protest; Rajni might even join him there. I had opened the door for her to walk out.

But then on my hundred and first birthday I was told I would be given yet another state-award.

The cameras dwelt lovingly on what would provide the backdrop for the function: the Great Poornaramin Temple.

As I sat in the studio, watching the temple on the monitor and patiently waiting for the gaze of the cameras to mark me out for media attention, I remember feeling home-sick for the squalor of the forgotten Nizamuddin basti.

My function was going to be relayed with a pure Ramin ambience. The Director had told me that they were going to do a traditional-outdoor-public-function format for it: a hundred-and-one-year-old-writer being felicitated by the Chief Sadhoo, overlooked by the great Poornaramin, softly cheered by fellow Ramins.

My entire family sat to the left. There seemed to be hundreds of them. I was nervous about the function: afraid that my voice would quiver too much as I addressed the city of Rajdhani. No longer was I a mouthpiece for Educating Women Ltd. I would be speaking in my own voice about the power of a writer's life-work.

When I saw the Chief Sadhoo, I was a bit taken aback. I was so used to his screen image that he seemed terribly shrunken and older in real life. They probably use image-correctors. I too, I realized, would appear years younger than my age.

The performance took only a few seconds. 'Sequence II', said a voice. As the recorders chanted Hey Poornaramin and the cameras started to roll, the Director asked me to bend lower to the Chief Sadhoo. The Chief Sadhoo lightly brushed the top of my head with his hand, making me start. He gave me a packet and folded his hands. He did not ask me to speak. And then as miraculously as he had come, he disappeared. The faint hum of the hovercraft faded into the distance in no time. After that, the cameras lost interest in me. I was confused; what kind of felicitation was this?

I told one of my grandsons that I wanted to watch the rest of the programme being shot. He took me into a much smaller enclosure where several monitors were catching the image of my family from several angles and the Director sat on a stool barking instructions into a mike. I settled down behind him, facing the screen that was right opposite him.

Sadhvi Kalpana soon came stalking to the rostrum with a firm and heavy tread. I had heard that she was slowly gaining power and influence among the Sadhoos; she was gaining a lot of weight as well. She seemed almost like a saffron barrel with her too-broad shoulders and broad waist. She was in with the latest androgynous fashion but I couldn't help wondering why she must wear the fact of being a political-Sadhvi on her person: so much saffron!

The Director gave her the signal to start. 'Sequence I', he said into the mike. To show her ease before the camera, Kalpana cleared her throat loudly and flicked back her shoulder-length, dyed-saffron hair. 'Remember the night of the descent', she said. The familiar Poornaramin-story tumbled out from her mouth while her eyes sought the imagined audience. 'Hey Poornaramin', said the recorder. 'Cut', said the Director. All the monitors went blank except the one I was looking at. A man rushed up to Kalpana and fussed a bit with her hair.

The cameras started to roll again. She continued from where she had left off.

'Today is very special in the annals of not only Rajdhani but also Raminland. Today Ramins spread far and wide, all over Raminland and abroad should honour the earth from which blooms forth our national identity. Where would we be or would we at all be if glorious women like Shrimati Roy did not inhabit our country? From her womb emerged three sons, spitting images of their father. From her sons' loins sprung several sons, and from her grandsons still many sons emerge. In the present time when the Ramin population shows a decrease every year, her family appears nothing short of miraculous.'

One of the monitors was showing my family. Really! Were there that many of us or had 'extras' been commissioned for this programme? And why was she going on about my sons? 'Shrimati Roy has turned one-hundred-and-one-years old today. On her birthday she is taking a vow to do for the entire country what she has always done unobtrusively for her own family: she is going to become a vehicle for the perpetuation of dharma for the Ramin race.'

She bent towards the left and beamed. 'Cut', screamed the Director. 'I want that mole on your cheek, sweetie. Make-up, highlight mole.'

'Shrimati Roy has lived through Godless times, the descent of Poornaramin and the reinstating of dharma in this country. Last year, when she turned a hundred the state revoked her widowhood and she stepped out once again into society after sixty years. To her horror, within the course of the lessons in dharma that she was imparting to young Ardhanginis, she found that in spite of the efforts of the Sadhvis and Sadhoos, the high ideals of Raminism are being eroded. She was shocked by the lack of morality among some young Ardhanginis. She tried to explain their folly to them — the folly that is leading to the gradual but sure decimation of the Ramin race — but her efforts were in vain. Thus, she has decided to do go into *samadhi*: do severe penance on their behalf, asking God Poornaramin to grant the boon of motherhood to every young Ardhangini and thereby perpetuate Raminism for centuries to come.'

My hands moved of their own volition to wrap my pallu around me. I felt panic gnawing at the bottom of my stomach.

Sadhvi Kalpana continued: 'I would like to say something about the importance of such an act. Ever since the Sadhoos won the freedom of our women by splitting education into two streams — Ardhangini courses for Ardhanginis and Professional courses for Sadhvis — and recognized Ardhangini-work as compensatory, our society has undergone a transformation. Professionalism has increased by leaps and bounds and Sadhvis as doctors, engineers, executives etc. are second to none in the world. But, perhaps in this euphoria women forgot that the backbone of the society are our Ardhanginis. Our tradition accords the highest place to Ardhanginis. It is only through his wife that a man gets the opportunity of ascending to heaven. As is said in Ardhangini-law: "Offspring, the due performance of religious duty, obedience and the most profound voluptuous joy are dependent upon the wife; so also the attainment of heaven for the husband's ancestors and for himself." '

This is ridiculous, I said to myself. Why am I letting this bombast affect me like this? It's been there like tinnitus in my ear ever since Poornaramin appeared.

Sadhvi Kalpana was going on, 'Being an Ardhangini is not an escape from the rigours of life, it is the assumption of the highest responsibility. The culture of this land is vested in the Ardhanginis, in their generosity and their self-sacrifice. Mothers, this holy land needs selflessness; you have to water it with tears of sacrifice. Let all my mothers and sisters who are at this very minute sitting glued to their screens watching this function learn from Shrimati Roy's life. It is no accident of genes that so many generations have been begotten in the Roy family. It is because of a unique combination of the active and reflective aspects of life: on the one hand Shrimati Roy's karma, her action of dedicating her womb to her race and on the other her dharma or the tapasya of writing instructive books for other Ardhanginis. I repeat, her tapasya, for by keeping her soul on the strictest path and not letting her feminine mind stray from the path of duty she has already achieved the status of a tapasvini.'

Desperation hit me like a deluge. I had gone along too far with them. There were no U-turns left.

Sadhvi Kalpana sounded very distant. 'I will quote two more clauses from Ardhangini-law which are specially relevant to the life of this ideal Ardhangini: "Women are not guarded by being confined at home by men however cleverly they attempt it. Those women who guard themselves through themselves are alone well guarded." And "When women are found blest because of offspring, worthy of honour, true lamps in the house, then there is not the slightest distinction in the homes of men between them and Happiness."

'Shrimati Roy has requested total solitude. She will gradually become one with the bosom of mother earth. Her family — that has more than once proved itself to be the custodian of the traditions of this ancient land — has pledged to oversee the details of her samadhi.

'The Sadhoo Mahasabha in appreciation of Shrimati Roy's service to Raminland is according her the title "Mother of Sons".

'I ask the Chief Sadhoo Shri Shri Nityanand to present Shrimati Roy with the Order of The Mother of Sons. He will also make the first offering to her: Rs one lakh one thousand and one only.'

Hymns to Poornaramin began to emanate from the recorder.

'Cut!' screeched the Director and bounded out of the room.

I saw on the screen that he had rushed to Sadhvi Kalpana and was kissing her on both cheeks. As the camera and the sound system relayed reality to me without recording it for posterity, I heard him say to her 'What a performance, baby! You're going to get all the Sadhvi votes. What a sterling performance!'

'It's the hard hitting script', Kalpana said modestly, 'Sheebu is very good with all this traditional Ardhangini stuff.'

Throughout the last bit, I had knotted and untied the edge of my sari. Not a single tear had fallen from my eyes but I felt as though a lifetime was washed away. I had receded and an image had taken my place — in the continuing fiction of my life.

Epilogue

While I was writing all this, Rajni was granted special permission to see me. I lead a protected, guarded life now. Since my hundred and first birthday I have become a valuable asset for my family. She was going for a bathing holiday to Nice, she told me. She had come to seek my blessings for a baby.

I asked her what had happened to her music.

'Oh, Ma, there's no time for all that now.'

'You don't sing any more?'

'I do. But with Suresh's promotion it is becoming increasingly difficult to find time.'

'Rajni, I'm sorry to hear this', I gasped.

She looked directly at me and said, 'I'm no longer the child I used to be. As you said to me once, other things become important after marriage. I have got my degree from Rosalind as well.'

'What about Shyam, Rajni? How is he?'

'Oh, Shyam. You still remember him, Ma? He went quite mad, you know.'

She told me that a warrant had been issued for Shyam's arrest on the charge of attempted kidnapping of a Ramin woman. She had agreed to testify. It was rumoured that he had fled the country to join an international gang of terrorists.

I asked her what really happened the day Shyam came to tell her about the Mayans. Rajni told me rather reluctantly.

Shyam turned to Rajni in the solar-operated taxi, 'Rajni, I have to talk to you.'

'Yes', she said raising a made-up, tired face to him. She feared that her mascara had stained her cheek. She didn't want to be out in the harsh light.

'Do you know what I'm going to say to you?'

'No.'

She wanted to move away as far as possible from him.

'Won't you give me your hand?'

She extended it slowly towards him. It was like touching him for the first time. It felt real for the first time. How easy it had been indoors.

'Rajni, I love you to distraction.'

'Yes', she said.

'Do you know what that means?'

'I know, we are involved.'

'I have reached the stage where it is impossible for me to live without you.'

'Will you die then?' she said, wondering where the conversation was going.

'I will die, a part of me will die if I don't get you.'

'This is very filmy', she said firmly.

'No, it isn't. Tell me what you feel when you see me.'

'I'm pleased to see you.'

'Is that all?'

'I don't know what you mean.'

'I mean, when I'm not there do you want to see me?'

'If you are not there how can I want to see you?'

'You may just want . . . '

She laughed a little. But it was an artificial laugh — tight and sharp. It grated a little. 'Oh, Shyam, is this what you wanted to say?'

'No, I wanted to talk about your operation', he replied, sounding angry.

It was none of his business. She felt angry too. 'Who told you about it?'

'Have you forgotten? You yourself did.'

'What do you know about it?'

'Rajni, you don't have to agree to it.'

'I know I'm a Ramin woman; I'm free to make choices. But my thighs are ugly. In the clinic they had these mirrors and I saw myself from all sides. There was also a wax-model there — of Miss Raminland.'

'But you're not a beauty queen.'

'You don't think I'm beautiful?'

'I think you are very beautiful, the most beautiful woman in the world.'

'You are a Drohi.'

'So, don't Drohis have eyes?'

'Ramins are different', she said turning away, wishing he would disappear.

'Rajni, isn't it enough for you that I should find you beautiful?'

'Enough for what?'

'To be satisfied.'

'I am satisfied. This isn't what I want. This is what my husband wants.'

'Do you love him?'

'Love happens in films.'

'Then why has it happened to me?'

She didn't want to answer any more. 'You are film-like, that's why. You say things that you see in films.'

'Does a Drohi man love a Ramin woman in a film?'

'No, that would be strange.'

'And in real life — can a Drohi love a Ramin woman?'

'I don't know.'

'But I'm telling you I love you.'

'Yes.'

'Does it make you happy?'

'Yes.'

'Then, won't you make me happy?'

'Okay, I love you', she said without trying to disguise the flatness of her tone.

'Will you do as I tell you?'

'I might.'

'Come away with me.'

She was amused. 'Where?'

'Come and live with me.'

'Where? In the Drohi colony?'

'Why? Can't you live there?'

'No, of course not. I'm a Ramin.'

'If a Ramin woman decides to live with a Drohi what will happen?'

She lost her patience. Her next statement came cold and cutting like a knife, 'Shyam, this keeps happening, you know.'

'What?'

'It happened to Madhu too — she told me. A Dasa wanted her to live with him.'

'So you knew what I was going to ask you today?' he said, squirming with pain.

'Yes.'

'Then why did you come away with me?'

She shrugged and sighed a little. 'I thought you had more sense than this.'

The silence between them grew oppressive. At last he perceived the lack of co-ordination between her body that still curved seductively at him, and her empty eyes; and he knew that, like an image in a temple, she couldn't even see he was offering her a real life.

He asked the taxi to stop and got out on a wide, open road of Raminland.

Acknowledgements

My journey started with Ghalib's poetry and lasted several years. I asked many questions on the way. Some books replied and many friends opened their minds to let me read.

I have helped myself liberally from Pavan K. Varma's *Ghalib: The Man, The Times*; Ralph Russell and Khurshidul Islam's *Ghalib, Life and Letters*; Ghalib's *Dastanbuy* (translated by Prof. K.A. Faruqui); Farhatullah Baig's *The Last Mushairah of Delhi* (translated by Akhtar Qamber); Aijaz Ahmad's *Ghazals of Ghalib: Versions from the Urdu*; Regula Burchhardt Qureishi's *Sufi Music of India*; Arthur Coke Burnell's *The Ordinances of Manu*; Janet Chawla's *Childbearing and Culture: The Role of the Midwife as a Ritual Practitioner*; and Gyanendra Pandey's article *In Defense of the Fragment*.

My deep gratitude goes out to the following: Gyan Pandey for generous help; Khalid Alvi who has an anecdote for every monument, a *sher* for every occasion, for revealing facets of Nizamuddin and Ghalib that I could never have come to know otherwise; Partho Dutta for letting me dip into his astonishing knowledge of music, musicians, and Delhi; M.K. Raina for insights into the workings and machinations of the media; and Dr Sudha Marwah for information about cosmetic surgery and fertility clinics.

I was fortunate to find support in what was for me uncharted territory. I thank the administrative staff of Ajmer Dargah, the library staff of Zakir Husain College and the Ghalib Academy, and the people at SAHMAT for fielding naive questions so kindly; and in the same breath, Ramachandra Guha for his time.

Which is not to claim I always knew where to go next. Fairly early, I found Ravi Dayal who set the standard and unobtrusively provided the pointers. I will always be indebted.

I would also like to thank Vikram Chandra who helped with suggestions and comments at a particularly difficult bend; Rajeswari Sunder Rajan for detailed discussions on adultery; Amy Louise Kazmin, Pragati Mahapatra, and Manju Kapur for reading and responding to an earlier draft; and the other members of my writers' group — Janet, Gopika, and Sujatha — for their unstinting encouragement.

To some who are familiar landmarks I would want to say a thank you for being there as usual: my father, Mukul, and Fr Lesser.

For Manju, friend and guide, who made me bold to go back and forth as I pleased, secure in the knowledge that she would hold, I can only say once again that it would have been inconceivable without her.

Last but not the least, there were fellow travellers: Abhijit, Partho, and Dubdub. To them thanks for bearing with my delays and postponements.